Noa Jones

THE INCORRIGIBLE PATSY JAMES

Big Kid, Big Shot Summer

Illustrated by Michael LaDuca

A Very Berry Tale™
Splash of Sass, New York

ISBN: 978-0-9817205-0-0

Printed in the United States of America

Visit us on the World Wide Web!
www.TheIncorrigiblePatsyJames.com

For Kaila Olukame, my inspiration...

Aja Denae, my laughter...

Xiaoli Naira-Iman, my joy...

And Tiran Allan, my champion, whose lenient ears and quiet faith safeguarded Patsy to the light of day...

CONTENTS

PART I

....

CHAPTER 1

....

Upper Grade, Big Kid, Big Shot

Patamela or "*PATSY!*" (as she was not so affectionately called when caught in some rascally adventure) would be entering the fourth grade in September and turning nine years old just a few months later. Her life was about to change. She was leaving her days as a lowly third grader behind and was well on her way to becoming an official big kid. The sooner September rolled around the sooner her new life would begin. But first, she would have to complete her current school year. Thank heaven the last day of school was only one week away.

"One more Melbourne day meets the dust bunnies," Patsy touted, marching behind her older sister as they turned the corner to Beecham Street. She was not at all interested in keeping up with Patience and knew she was walking fast on purpose. Patsy was more interested in giving her place as an almost promoted to the fourth grade third grader serious thought.

"Hmmph, I'm already a big kid, big shot," Patsy proclaimed just as Patience turned to make sure her younger sister wasn't lagging too far behind. With each parked car the girls passed, Patsy caught glimpse of her pecan-brown complexion and two double-ribbon-tied pigtails (which looked considerably higher than they looked in the very same car windows two weeks before).

I really have grown—just like mom said, she thought. And since she was a *bigger* kid, that could only mean she was that much closer to sealing her fate as a big kid. Especially since she had stopped beating up on the neighborhood boys and ended her career as a no-holds-barred tattletale. Once she figured out she had a better chance at being accepted as a big kid if she learned how to keep her hands to herself and keep secrets like a big kid, her bully-bruising, squealing days were over.

But if you asked Prince, the eldest of the James children, and Patience, Patsy's squealing days had not missed a beat. They could not keep up with the number of secrets she constantly let out of the bag—though Patsy would say those particular secrets did not matter. To Patsy, most of the gossip (even the scoop she felt was not worthy of being classified as a secret), she kept a tight lid on. The only secrets she laid over on deserved to be told. She was a strict follower of her parents' golden rule when it came to secrets: "When the goods needed to be shared, the goods needed to be shared."

The Jameses counted on Patsy to share "the goods" too. Whenever Prince's or Patience's behavior struck them as odd, they knew it would not be long before Patsy came running with the scoop. Patsy knew her job and took it very seriously. If a grownup needed to find out about some secret going around, it was her duty to tell it. She loved overhearing Mrs. James sing the praises of her snooping skills after they helped to catch Prince or Patience in some "off limits" activity. That had to make her a big kid in her parents' eyes, she thought.

"I don't want to be a big kid in *their* eyes," Patamela whined. "Who wants to be a big kid based on telling dumb secrets? Not me!"

Patsy did not even want to be a big kid based on the number of secrets she overheard and never spilled the beans on. Deep down, Patsy felt that was not what being a real big kid was about. "Who needs tattle telling and secret keeping?" she grumbled.

"You do...Little Bit," Patience said as she swung the screen door open to ring the bell.

"I don't need it! I'm already an upper grade, big kid, big shot," Patsy defended. Mrs. James slowly opened the front door to greet the girls.

"More like an upper grade, big kid, big not!" Patience snapped. She nearly knocked Patsy over as she made her way toward the stairs. "You're not even out the baby school yet!" Patience jeered.

"Alright ladies, is the name calling necessary this afternoon?" Mrs. James asked.

"It's not me, Mommy, it's Patience. But she's supposed to be so *missy prissy pash!*" Patsy taunted, hoping to anger Patience and impress Mrs. James with her choice of word at the same time.

"The word's posh...You incorrigible youngster!" Patience exclaimed slamming their bedroom door.

"Patience, the door slamming is going to have to stop, ya hear?" Mrs. James yelled from the foot of the steps. "So, how was your day, Pattie Cakes?" she asked turning her attention back to her youngest daughter. "I guess you'll fill me in a bit later," her mom gathered, noting Patsy's disgruntlement.

Patsy was in no mood to give Melbourne Academy updates. The more she thought about secrets, secret-keeping, tattle-telling, Mr. Piccirillo, Melbourne Academy's principal, and Patience's name-calling, she fumed.

"What's wrong with being *incorrigible*?" Patsy griped. "Nothing, that's what."

Patsy's parents would tell a different story however. They wished Patsy's adventures did not call for the heap of trouble she often found herself in. They realized Patsy was brave, but sometimes her activities were downright hazardous to her safety and her parents' peace of mind. (Not to mention how disturbing her activities were to some of their not so understanding neighbors.)

If there was trouble in the air, best believe Patsy's name was stamped on it. After all the dust cleared, there Patsy would appear, clothes rumpled, guilty as charged and squirming to be released from the grips of some neighbor as they knocked on the James's door to complain about her *incorrigible* behavior.

"Mrs. James, do you know what I found this *incorrigible* child doing?" they would say.

"Yep, that's right. *Incorrigible*. That's just what she called me," Patsy would boast to her pals recounting her capture after an ill-fated adventure.

For most of her eight-year-old friends, the word *incorrigible* was way too advanced to comprehend. But not for Patsy, for this particular word was used alongside her name too many times to count. So much so, it no longer bothered her when someone used it to describe her personality.

"It simply means to *be adventurous*," she would say, assuring her buddies it was a compliment. Although every adult within earshot seemed to know it meant something closer to being *impossible to control*—and so did Patience.

"*Posh* isn't so big of a word. It's not bigger than *in-*

corrigible," Patamela quietly sassed. "And *I know* what that means."

How the entire neighborhood—and Patsy's parents—wished that one day Patsy would cut out her incorrigible ways, play respectable little girl games, remain tidy, and keep that hair of hers in place.

Patamela tugged one of her pigtail ribbons until it came down long enough to twirl around her finger as she followed her mother in the kitchen. She was never afraid to get her hair a little ruffled. I've got more important things to do than worry about a couple of frizzes, she thought. She could not be the princess of hairdos, an adventurous big kid and protect her face from the cheek-pinching frenzies she was bombarded with daily.

Patamela's cheeks were the home of three dimples—one on each cheek and one smack dab in the middle of her chin. Surely being an A-class, fence-climbing, superb rollerblading, Safari-rated action hunting, *X-chaser* of unruly neighborhood boys, pudgy-cheek protector counted for something. She did not have to keep any secrets if she did not want to in order to be a big kid. She did not have to stop chasing boys either.

"I don't ever have to go to Melbourne's stupid upper grade school!" she shouted, hoping her voice would travel upstairs to Patience's eardrums. I'll earn the right to be a big kid, big shot all by myself, by my own rules, Patamela thought. But boy had those Melbourne rules done a number on her usual high spirits.

CHAPTER 2

The Melbourne Blues

Maybe Patience *is* right, Patsy thought as she watched her mom peel and cut potatoes in preparation for dinner. The tried and true big kid, big shots lived and breathed at Melbourne's upper grade school. Yet, when school started in the fall, Patsy too would be in the schoolhouse up the street with grades four through eight. No longer would she be in the school building with the kindergarteners and first-, second-, and third-grader babies. Come September, she would be where the action took place.

Patsy knew all about the action in the other school firsthand. She heard about how Mr. Piccirillo visited the upper grade classrooms to joke around with the kids. Mr. Piccirillo was the youngest principal in the world (well, that's how her parents acted when talking about his age, but he looked old to Patsy) and he loved to play favorites. And Patamela James had his number.

Never in the history of Patamela's attendance at Melbourne Academy had Mr. Piccirillo come to her class to joke around and Patsy knew this for a fact. She'd attended Melbourne since kindergarten and had a perfect attendance record. Mr. Piccirillo, Mr. P as the older students called him, only visited her class when the boys were clowning around too much. "Ahem, a-hem," Patsy would hear as Mr. Piccirillo cleared his throat at the classroom doorway. He would arrive immediately after the teacher sent a better-behaved student to summon him from the other building or the front office.

Patamela never moved a muscle (not even a pinky) once Mr. Piccirillo entered the room—not like those silly boys. Now Patsy was tougher than most of the boys in her class, but she was no fool. She kept herself in line just enough to avoid a major run-in with Mr. Piccirillo. She would simply watch in silence as Mr. Piccirillo bent over to point his long finger in the face of some doomed class clown. Sometimes he came by to personally congratulate an honor roll student or a spelling bee winner, but that was rare enough. Usually, he stopped by her classroom to straighten someone out. And when he came, boy would he look upset! That was the Mr. Piccirillo Patsy knew, but not the Mr. P she heard about.

"What a fake," Patsy scowled.

"Who's a fake, Patsy?" her mother queried.

"Hmm? Ah, no one," Patsy answered, dodging the lecture she would have surely gotten for calling an adult anything other than their name. Yet why else would Mr. Piccirillo be so mean to the younger grades? That is exactly what she would ask him if she had to spend one more year in that school. Luckily, she did not.

Patamela was well on her way to the upper grade Melbourne school up the street. She could not wait to get all the special treatment she knew the upper grades enjoyed. Patsy had never witnessed a surprise pizza party for her and her classmates. Sure they had birthday parties. Parents brought cake and ice cream for their child's birthday celebration all the time, but a surprise pizza party?

Of all the extra gooey, cheesy, pepperoni-good-time-for-no-reason-at-all nerve, Patsy thought. Yet, that type of stuff happened all the time in the big kid building.

That was not all either. Patsy even heard the students were taken to the park on spontaneous outings. These top-secret trips did not require permission slips signed by their parents and sometimes lasted two whole class periods.

If that isn't the most unfair, downright rotten thing I've ever heard," Patsy fumed.

"Patsy, is there something you want to share?" her mom pried.

"No Mom, I'm just thinking—that's all. It's nothing," she sighed.

Yet it was something, something else how those students in the other school behaved. They never had to stay in a single file line at assembly like her class did, especially the seventh and eighth graders. Although the school dress code clearly stated the boys should wear white shirts with their navy blue pants on Assembly Wednesdays, they never did. Instead, the boys swaggered into the auditorium wearing yellow, blue, or gray shirts.

The girls, even though they wore their navy blue skirts, were no better. You could hardly see their white school blouses under their huge busy sweaters. They always wore sweaters different from the school's sweater with fancy colorful socks to match. Patsy wanted to wear fancy sweaters and socks too, but all of the girls in her school building were too afraid. They wore the same white school-handbook blouses with their white knee-highs to match every single Wednesday.

"I've had it!" Patsy exclaimed, recalling one particular

Assembly Wednesday. Taking a daring stand, she skillfully snuck her favorite orange sweater and orange-and-green-striped socks in her book bag before leaving for school with her mother. When she reached Melbourne, she changed into her secret outfit and entered her classroom. After refusing to change clothes and throwing a temper tantrum about the unfair treatment she was receiving, the Melbourne staff had had enough. Patsy, unlike the older girls, was sent to the front office until Mrs. James could pick her up.

"Your school may have an unfair policy, Patsy, but you're not to sneak clothes out of this household," her dad scolded that evening.

"If you truly believed it was okay to wear your orange sweater and striped socks, Pattie Cakes, the right thing would have been to put them on in front of your father and me, not to change at school," her mom added. "And once your teacher asked you to change clothes, you should have done so, end of discussion."

Patamela's parents were furious. And Patsy, she vowed to count the days until she was able to attend school in the big kid's building. And now, there were only seven more days (five if you did not count Saturday and Sunday) before school was out for the summer. "Seven more days, ha-ha-ha-ha-ha!" Patsy chimed. She was finally kissing the Melbourne Blues good-bye.

Patsy could almost taste the special treatment heading her way. There was no reason to pipe down the excitement. Not when she had seen some of the bigger kids' privileges with her own two eyes. And the information she collected from her sources? Forget about it. There had to be more to come.

CHAPTER 3

I've Got My Sources

Patamela was certain she did not have *all* the inside scoop about the privileges she would soon enjoy, but she believed she had a pretty good idea considering her sources. Patsy was sure their information would help her when she moved into Melbourne's infamous upper grade building. She would be in much better shape than her naïve, fourth-grade comrades because she would already know the ropes.

"I've got sources—top Melbourne experts," she ragged before biting into the snack her mom placed before her to tide her over until dinner.

One of Patsy's sources was cooperative; that is, he allowed Patamela to stick around even after he discovered she was secretly hanging onto his every word. Patsy's older sister, Patience James, was *not* the cooperative one, however.

"What an eavesdropping, troublesome spy," Patsy would overhear Patience say to one of her friends in response to Patsy's meddlesome activity. And if she was really upset, she would yell, "Patamela James, you're *incorrigible!*" Still, Patience was one of Patsy's best sources, even though she never officially signed up for the job.

Patience James was going to be a sixth grader at the Melbourne Academy in September. That was the only reason Patience had the lowdown on the other school building and Mr. Piccirillo. She thought she was hot stuff because of it too. Ever since Patience began attending the other school, she thought she was *so special,* Patsy reckoned.

Truth was, although Patsy hated to admit it, Patience was always into big girl things. She read hip teen magazines, painted her fingernails and toenails red, and talked on the phone. She went to the mall with the older girls from their church and shared boy crushes with her best friends Lizzie and Tamara. She even did her own hair.

Patience was actually very good at doing her hair and could copy any style she saw in any one of her magazines. Her hair never looked all over her head like Patsy's hair. She had a thinner build than Patsy too and was quite a bit taller. Patience had an almond brown complexion, a head full of dark brown hair, and big brown eyes like Mrs. James that came with an extra-long set of eyelashes she frequently snuck mascara to doll up.

Patsy never wanted to be as girly or prissy as Patience, but she did want to be a big girl. And that is exactly what Patience was—no question about it. No one ever called Patience a baby. Patamela would have loved to hear her name in the same sentence as Patience, especially when her parents talked about the honor roll. Problem was, Patsy had run into some minor problems with a couple of her subjects. Yet this year, Lizzie had helped her improve her penmanship, language arts, and listening skills.

"I've got it! I'll make the honor roll!" Patsy declared.

"Wonderful, Patamela! You made the honor roll this marking period? Wait until your dad finds out," her mom gushed as she placed their roast beef dinner into the oven.

"Ah, I don't know...I don't think so," Patsy sheepishly replied.

Patamela wished she hadn't made the outburst or even had the silly thought. It's too late to make it this year, she thought. "The honor roll can't be all there is to being a big girl anyway," she grumbled. "Even cry baby kindergartners make the honor roll," she said, recalling last year's honor roll ceremony. There was nothing left to do but to step up her sleuthing skills. "I'm going to eat, drink, and sleep Patience James," Patsy vowed. "I'm gonna make sure I know everything she talks about every second of the day."

Luckily, big girl conversation was Patience's specialty. Patience was always yapping. Patamela never meant to be the eavesdropping brat Patience accused her of being. She never meant to invade Patience's privacy. It was just that Patience was an easy target. They lived in the same room for goodness sakes!

Many times, Patsy would actually be busy minding her own business. She would be completing homework, practicing a new song she recently learned to sing in Spanish ("Twinkle, Twinkle, Little Star," also known as "Estrellita, Donde Estás?" was her latest victory), or she would be drawing a treasure map to pass out to her pals. But, before she knew it, she would overhear some juicy tidbits about the big kids' school. What did Patience expect her to do anyway, get earplugs?

Although Patsy never meant to master the art of eavesdropping or *ear hustling* as her father called it, she was definitely a pro. "*PATSY!*" her dad would yell after Patience pleaded for her own Pasty the snoop free room for the thousandth time. "You aren't ear hustling are you?" he would ask.

Prince, Patsy's older brother, would always come out of his room or around the corner at that exact moment to add his own comments. "Of course she is. Right, Little Bit? A *little bit* more information?" he would snicker.

Patsy hated when Prince called her Little Bit. She knew exactly what he was referring to whenever he called her by that name. On the one hand, he called her Little Bit because of her height. Even with her recent growth spurt, she was still much shorter than him and Patience. But, most of all, he called Patsy Little Bit because of her constant eavesdropping. Although Patsy hated the name and the teasing, she loved her big brother, Prince James, to pieces. He was her favorite, most cooperative source of all.

Prince was tall for his age. He was slender with a dark coffee complexion just like their dad. He shared the same eyelashes Patience and Mrs. James had with pearly white teeth like Patsy. Prince had only one dimple on his right cheek and wore his hair low like his father.

All the neighborhood and Melbourne Academy girls had a crush on him. Not one day went by without a group of girls yelling across the street, "Hey Patience, hey Lil' Patsy. Is Prince coming out today?" Or they would shout, "Does Prince have a game today?" since he was on the county's ice hockey team and the school's basketball team. He was even on the honor roll and attended a junior ministry program at the church on Saturday afternoons.

In September, Prince would be attending the eighth grade and it would be his last year at Melbourne before going to high school. Patsy was glad she'd have at least one year in the same school as him. Not only would Patsy get firsthand experience of the special Melbourne treatment, but she would get the skinny on the biggest, oldest Melbourne kids of all—the eighth graders. Patsy could not wait. Prince was not at all as testy as Patience, even with his teasing. It made getting the scoop from him as easy as one-two-three.

Prince, unlike Patience, would let Patsy sit in on his conversations with their cousins and his pals. He would only kick Patsy out of his room when they started talking about girls. Even then, Patsy would not be defeated. She would stay really close to the door so she could hear that part too.

This summer, Prince did not have to worry about Patsy being interested in any of his secrets about pranks, girls, or private handshakes. Patience did not have to worry about Patsy being an eavesdropping, spying, troublesome pain in the neck either. Well, they did, except this time it would be different. Patsy had a purpose. This time, there would be a reason for her constant prying. Every bit of big kid information Patience and Prince did not guard with their lives, Patsy would use to her advantage. She would find out just what it took to make it in Melbourne's other building and be considered an official big kid. She was not interested in entering Melbourne as Prince and Patience's little sister. She wanted to enter as a full-fledged upper grade, big kid, big shot, and she knew her sources would lead the way.

Chapter 4

I Am what I Am

Patsy scooped the last of her green peas onto her fork. "So...Little Bit, what's news?" Prince queried.

"She thinks she's a big kid—but there's nothing new about that," Patience chuckled.

"No fair, he asked me!" Patsy hissed, swallowing the leftover peas in her mouth. "And for your information, I AM A BIG KID," she declared, wishing she had used her spoon to launch her leftover peas into Patience's eye instead.

"Patsy," her father chimed as a reminder for Patsy to watch her tone.

"Aww, Little Bit, it's like this," Prince began to explain," You know how you aren't off the clock until you turn thirteen?"

"The clock, what?" their mom interrupted.

"Yeah, you know, the clock goes from one to twelve. I won't be off the clock until I turn thirteen and Patsy, until you get to Melbourne's upper grade school, well, you're still considered a ..."

"Don't you say it!" Patsy railed. "I don't have to put

one foot in that dumb old school to be a big kid, do I, Dad?"

"Uh, of course not, Pattie Cakes," her father half-heartedly assured.

"See," Patsy sassed sticking out her tongue.

"Young lady, that behavior won't be tolerated. It isn't very big kid like either. Maybe you should turn in now" her mom suggested.

"See Patsy, *that* only happens to babies," Patience stated.

"Watch it, Patience," their dad reproved.

Patsy pushed away from the dinner table and stomped up the stairs, (well she did stomp, but not hard enough to alarm her parents). Yet she had had it.

"That's it!" she stewed, "Friday, 12:00 p.m. on the dot, the very minute school lets out, I will be an upper grade, big kid, big shot no matter what anyone says! This summer, I'm going to act just like an upper grade big kid too!"

Patsy decided she would be sure to spend her summer in a way that fit her new upper grade big girl image perfectly. Any activity she was going to participate in, any camp she was going to attend, would fall right in the *performed-by-big-kids-only* category. Prince and Patience's summer activities were always big hits in that category. And their summers were always totally different from Patsy's.

In fact, Prince's and Patience's summer activities were so different from Patsy's that the James's used bigger words to describe them. Whenever her parents talked to her brother and sister about their summer plans, they used that word *re-spon-si-bi-lity*. Patsy could not spell the word to save her life, but she knew adults threw it around all the time to big kids. And not just when they were speaking of summer vacations either. *"That is your responsibility. It will help you learn how to handle responsibility. Growing up is sometimes about responsibility,"* Patsy would hear.

"I know what I've got to do!" Patsy exclaimed. This time around I'm going to shut them up for once and for all," she vowed, kicking the edge of Patience's bed.

Patsy knew she would have to level the playing field. This summer, she would have to do something that required the usual adventure and a bit of responsibility. She would have to get into something that would show her parents, siblings, and entire neighborhood she was a big kid, big shot way before entering the other Melbourne building. She would have to make huge changes to her usual summertime activity plan.

"I've got to sign up for a big kid, big girl activity that's larger than life!" she determined. Prince, Patience, and her expert spying techniques would help Patsy figure out exactly what that big kid activity needed to be. But whatever Patamela decided, one thing she knew for sure, her usual playtime buddy and neighbor, Miles Malone Davis, would have no part of it.

CHAPTER 5

....

Operation Sell-A-Stray

"I've got news for you too, Miles Malone Davis!" Patsy seethed, as she pulled her teddy bear pajamas out of her drawer. This summer, Patsy had no plans to get tangled in his hijinks or charades. Under no circumstances would she share her strategies for a big kid, big shot summer. Although Patsy and Miles had been friends, best friends, since kindergarten and they'd be starting fourth grade together in the other building, Patsy was determined to take on her summer adventure without him. Take that Miles Malone, she thought.

Patsy's mind drifted to the many adventures she'd shared with Miles. Every summer they seemed to get into a stew of brand new trouble. Just two summers ago, one of their charades nearly landed them in the doghouse. It all started with Miles's wish to build his very own tree-house fortress. Miles wanted a tree house so badly, he harassed his parents every day.

He spent days studying each tree in his backyard. It was not long before he was able to tell his father which tree would best hold up his house and why. He handed Mr. Davis ten different drawings with examples of how each tree house should look inside and out. Mr. Davis had to come around, and one afternoon he finally caved in.

"Okay, son, I'll tell you what. If you can earn a couple

of bucks for the supplies, we'll build that tree house of yours," his dad promised. Before they could seal the deal with a handshake, Miles had put his brain to work. It was not long before he revealed Operation-Sell-A-Stray.

The operation was simple. Miles and Patsy would search the neighborhood high and low for stray dogs. After cornering an unsuspecting pooch, they would clean him up, then sell him to a loving family for top dollar. Miles and Patsy planned to comb their area the moment they got up until it was time for them to go in. When Patience saw the duo chasing two scruffy mutts down Kissamaine Avenue near the 7-Eleven convenience store one day, she ran home to tell her mother.

Patience was genuinely worried about Patsy's shenanigans this time. "But, Ma, she could be bitten or catch rabies! If that munchkin brings one flea into our room..." Patience threatened.

Patience had read all about fleabag motels in the detective novels she read. The last thing she wanted was Patsy bringing fleas into the room they shared. She threw such a fit, Mrs. James had to do something—and fast.

She asked Mr. James to jump in his car and search the neighborhood for the children. Mr. James never worried about Patsy much, but he did not want his wife to fret. When he finally caught up with the children, both Miles and Patsy were covered in mud and the dogs were nowhere in sight. Mr. James lectured the ambitious dogcatchers all the way home. He forbade either of them to chase down dogs again.

Yet the next day, the hound-hunting pair was back at it. They marched back to Kissamaine Avenue where they last had one of the dogs by the tail. It was right before the dog slipped away leaving Patsy face down in the mud. But this time, they had a plan.

This time, Patsy and Miles were armed with a treat to bribe the dog into approaching them. Actually, it was a piece of Patsy's grandmother's famous lemon meringue pie. There was no way they could lose. That slice of grandma's pie, the purple leash Miles collected from Gibson-Gayle Park a week before, and the box Miles rigged with Patsy's double Dutch ropes practically guaranteed the stray's capture.

Now the box was a touch of genius. It would open or close depending on which side of the box Miles stood on and in which direction he pulled the ropes. The children even poked holes in the box so the dog could breathe once they caught him. But Miles's genius did not stop there. He was even clever enough to bring his dad's heavy duct tape along. Once he gave the signal, Patsy would tape the box's flaps down so quickly that their newfound friend would not have a chance to escape.

As soon as the twosome reached Kissamaine Avenue, they spotted the dogs basking in the shade behind the convenience store. Patsy and Miles decided they were not going to scare the dogs away this time. They had to move quickly, quietly, and carefully. Patience and Mr. James had put enough fear in them to be at least a little cautious.

Patsy crept down near the box. "Come here, cutie, come on," she coaxed. The little dog began to wag its tail, but the bigger dog was not fooled. He merely lifted his head so that the children could acknowledge his presence and gently laid it back down.

The little dog on the other hand, as curious as he was, wriggled forward. Patsy laid the pie in the box. As soon as the dog reached the inside of the box, *whammo*! Miles closed the box's flaps. Patsy jumped on top of the box and began taping it as fast as she could. The older dog sprang to his feet and let out a ferocious growl. Patsy had an emergency piece of pie just for this occasion. She flung it as far his way as her arms would permit. Quickly, the duo lifted the box into Patsy's old red wagon from her kindergarten days, then bolted down Kissamaine Avenue with the wagon squeaking behind them.

Now the successful dognappers knew better than to go to either of their backyards. Instead, they pulled the wagon behind Shelby Thorne High School. There was a fire hydrant there that the high school boys turned on during the summer months. Patsy and Miles figured it might be on.

Patsy lunged for the brown bag tucked in the back corner of her wagon. She had managed to scout the entire house for items before Miles rang her front doorbell that afternoon. She had thrown each item in the bag and snuck out of the house without being caught. And lucky for her, since it was packed to the brim with materials she swore they would need.

One by one, Patsy took out her trappings. First she removed a box of laundry detergent and a brush to give the dog a good scrubbing; second, a towel to dry it off; third was her beach pail to give the dog a complete rinsing; and lastly, her turquoise barrette.

When Miles saw the barrette, he exploded. "What's that for? It isn't a girl!" he scolded.

"How do you know?" Patsy demanded as she moved closer to the box.

Patamela snatched the tape off of the box's flaps and slowly pulled them open. The dog was still eating the pie, absolutely pleased with its treat. Miles carefully placed the leash around the dog's neck. Patsy crossed her fingers hoping the dog would not bite him. The dog allowed Miles to fasten the leash and continued to eat. But when Miles went to lift the dog out of the box, it snapped and began to snarl.

Miles quickly placed the dog down beside the wagon. When Patsy saw her chance, she took it. She gently slid the last piece of pie back in front of the dog. Miles held the leash tightly as the children waited patiently for the dog to finish. When the last crumb was gone, the dog sat down, crossed its two front paws, and stared at the children with anticipation.

"Come on, cutie, come on, cutie," Patsy said in the softest voice she could muster. She led the dog toward the fire hydrant, and the dog followed as if he'd known her all its life.

The hydrant was not running heavily, but it would do the job. Miles got a firm grip of the dog and held its head steady as Patsy scrubbed and brushed.

By the time the children finished lathering the dog in suds and putting it through a rinse cycle that would put the local car wash to shame, the dog almost sparkled. Better yet, it no longer smelled like dumpsters, grass, and mud.

Patsy pulled a toothbrush out of her pocket and a tube of toothpaste folded all the way to the bottom. When she finished brushing the dog's teeth, they looked as white as Patsy's.

After careful inspection, the children definitely agreed that their new friend was a boy. Trouble was, Patsy had already fallen in love with the stray and did not want Miles to sell him. Who would they sell the little mutt to anyway? And where would they keep him until he was sold? thought Patsy.

But Miles had it all figured out. They would keep the dog in his dad's tool shed in the back of his house. Patsy could not bear thinking of leaving the dog alone. He had taken a liking to Patsy too. Whenever she moved, he moved. Patsy decided she would come clean and beg her father for a chance to keep the dog.

"Patamela James!" Miles screeched, "You are not the boss you know! Either we sell this dog or I'll...I'll...I'll..."

"Aw, put a sock in it, Miles. A dog is more important than a tree house." Patsy felt she put just as much work into catching and cleaning up the dog as Miles.

Miles Malone was upset with her, but he wanted no part of Miss Patsy James. He remembered the last time he resisted Patsy's demands. She shoved him in Mrs. Tinnelmann's thorny bed of roses, and he was sore for weeks. "Fine, Patsy," Miles conceded.

Nightfall caught up to the trio as they slowly walked down Beecham Street to Patsy's home. Patsy would already be in trouble for not being in the house before the street lamps came on. She took a deep breath and walked up to the front door of her house. Miles stared intently as Patsy rang the bell. Through the front window, Patsy could see her mother walking from the kitchen to answer the door.

Mrs. James opened the door with a sudden jerk. "Patamela James, where have you been? Why are you late for supper? Why are you wet and so filthy? You know better than to ring this bell after the street lamps go on." Without taking a breath, she said, "Well, I'm waiting."

Patsy did not know which question to answer first. She stared down at her shoes, hoping a decent excuse would fall from her lips. "Mo-mo-mommy, I'm sorry, but can I ke ke-eep..." Patamela turned to look over her shoulder and could see Miles and the dog standing in the distance under the street lamp. She continued, "Miles and I, I mean

I (Patsy remembered being told to tell her part when she did something wrong instead of adding other people in hopes of lessening her punishment) caught a dog this afternoon. I didn't mean to be late. I know Dad told me not to mess with any dogs, but I cleaned him all up, and can I..."

"*PATRICK!*" yelled Mrs. James. Patsy's mom knew what was coming next and decided she and her husband should handle the matter together.

Patsy's father strolled to the door and looked down at Patsy. He had been listening the whole time from his armchair in the living room. "Patsy, look at us when we speak to you," her dad instructed. Patsy had not realized she had been staring at her shoes. Patsy looked at her parents with tears streaming down her face. She was sorry she'd disobeyed her father's wishes and hated when her parents were upset with her. "You want this dog, don't you, young lady?" her dad asked.

"Yes," Patsy answered with a voice so soft her father had to strain to hear her.

"Does this dog have an owner?" her dad continued.

"I dunno," Patsy answered, sniffling.

"Hmmmm," sighed her dad as he placed his right hand under his chin.

Mrs. James looked over to Mr. James, certain he was about to make the dog an addition to their family. After a brief moment of silence, Mr. James summoned Miles to the front door. He told the children they would spend a week posting signs all over town in search of the dog's true owner. If indeed no one called to claim the dog, Patsy could keep him. However, Patsy would be on punishment for the remainder of the week for disobeying her father's orders. She could not go outside, nor would she be allowed to play with the dog during the days of her punishment.

"Yahoo!" "Yippie!" Patsy could hear Prince and Patience from the other room. They were satisfied with the turn of events. Patsy was a little upset that they would get to play with the dog first, but she would have to get over it. She believed she had a special connection to the dog and knew the dog would not forget her.

"Hurry in and change out of your play clothes. You need to eat your supper. It's already getting cold," her dad said.

As Patsy ran in the house Mr. James yelled out, "Patsy, what will you name the dog if you can keep him?"

"His name is Puddles, Dad. Puddles," she yelped as she ran up the stairs. She believed the name summed up their first muddy encounter.

Mr. James slipped on his shoes and walked Miles home. He planned to tell Miles's parents he and Patsy were dog catching after he'd instructed them to leave the dog-catching business alone. But Mr. James noticed Miles was upset, and he knew it was not because he was telling Miles's parents. He'd walked Miles home on many occasions to update his parents on his and Patsy's shenanigans. Miles was not the type to worry. His parents expected him to be involved in all types of trouble from the beginning of the summer to the end. Mr. James figured Miles wanted the dog for himself. "Hey there, Miles," Mr. James began, "should I have flipped a coin to see who should have gotten the dog between you and Patsy?"

"Nah, Mr. James, I didn't want that ol' mangy dog."

"Then why the long face, little man?" Mr. James called all the boys in their neighborhood little man.

"Mr. James, I needed to sell that dog to get money to buy supplies for my tree house."

"Oh, I see. Well, how much do you think you'll need?"

"I'm not sure, but my dad said it would cost him a whole lot. He won't do it unless I come up with something. I'll never get the money now."

Mr. James escorted Miles to the Davis's front door and rang the doorbell. He patiently waited for one of Miles's parents to answer. When Mr. Davis opened the door and saw Mr. James, he knew Miles and Patsy had gotten into some trouble.

Mr. James informed Miles's parents of the children's latest stunt and Mr. Davis agreed to put Miles on the same punishment Patsy was given. Yet the two fathers were proud of Miles's efforts to raise money for something he wanted so badly. They figured they ought to assist him in some way.

Mr. James decided to give Mr. Davis a hand with building the tree house. He even promised to give Miles fifty dollars toward supplies if no one claimed Puddles. Mr. Davis pledged to use Miles's favorite drawing as a blueprint for the design of the tree house.

When Miles and Patsy heard what their fathers had decided, they were thrilled. That summer, no one claimed Puddles although the children and Mr. James posted lost dog signs everywhere — at the convenience store, the barbershop, the hair salon, the supermarket, and on the telephone posts on Kissimaine Avenue. After a week, Puddles officially belonged to Patsy and the James Family. Miles got his fifty dollars from Mr. James, and by the end of the summer, he and Patsy had a new hangout. As Patsy thought about Puddles and her many adventures with Miles, she got all warm inside—until she remembered what a big baby Miles was.

Patsy shook the memory of that summer out of her head. She vowed this summer would be different. Patsy was upset with Miles for refusing to share her anticipation about going to school with the big kids. When she'd asked Miles a week ago how excited he was about changing schoolhouses, he turned into a big, fat killjoy right before her eyes.

"Aw Patsy, it stinks. I'm going to miss this building. I know it like the back of my hand," he said.

Patamela knew Miles was telling the truth. After all, she'd accompanied him on many expeditions throughout the school's hallways and stairwells. Whenever Miles watched some adventurous movie on a school night, Patsy could count on a huge scavenger hunt the next day. Be it a hunt for treasure hidden away by the evil cafeteria staff (as Miles called them) or locating odds and ends for some new business idea, they had covered a lot of ground on that school's property. They had the letters home and the demerits to prove it.

"I'll miss seeing our old teachers too," Miles grumbled. "Now we'll only see them on Wednesdays when we meet for assembly. Difference is, they won't have time to talk to us because they'll be with their new students."

Patsy never thought about it that way. It was true. All the teachers knew Patsy and Miles in their school. Only a handful of teachers knew her from the other schoolhouse. The ones that did know her only knew her as the little sister of Prince and Patience. They didn't even know her name.

Patamela did not mull over Miles's feelings long before Miles interrupted her thoughts. "Patsy, we're the big kids here. All the younger kids wave to us when they see us.

When we get to the other school, we'll be dog meat. We'll be the babies of that school!"

Patsy seethed, "Dog meat! You take that back Miles Malone Davis! And who are you calling a baby? I'm no baby!"

Patamela stomped her foot down and put her hands on her waist. She really wanted to sock Miles, but she knew better than to do that—at least she did now. Barely able to hold back her tears she blurted, "Being in that school shows everyone we aren't babies!"

Patsy was sure that Miles was a chicken—a regular nine year old baby, afraid of the older boys in the upper grade school. He wasn't fooling her, and she planned to march right up to him at Sunday school and tell him they could no longer be friends.

CHAPTER 6

The Announcement

The weekend had been pretty uneventful for an adventurous tike like Patsy. After Patience's name calling and Prince's know-it-all take on things, Patsy had decided to stay in her room for the rest of the evening. Saturday was not much different and rated very low on the adventure meter. She spent the day alone playing jacks, practicing cartwheels, and rollerblading in front of her house. Yet today would be action-packed. Today was the day she would face Miles—and boy was she dressed for the occasion.

Patamela put on her white dress with the yellow and green flowers and her teal-colored socks with the yellow bowties. Patamela slipped on her white patent leather shoes. She'd made sure to ask her dad to shine them the night before and she was happy she had. They were as white as the Easter bunny in April.

Patamela had no plans to complain about looking too girly or perfect on this day. She even stood still while her mom placed one yellow and one green ribbon on each of her pigtails. That was only the beginning of Patsy's color coordinating efforts. The night before, Patsy had decided she would top her outfit off with her favorite yellow pocketbook—the one Patience picked out for her last Christmas.

Inside the purse, Patsy kept a treasure trove of keepsakes — playing cards, Prince's old digital watch with the popped wristband, and her miniature baby doll. Its secret pocket concealed any candy her mother or grandmother passed to her during Sunday school service the week before. Her pocketbook was quite roomy too. It was big enough to carry her lip gloss and her blue pad and pencil.

Patamela loved having a pad and pencil at a moment's notice. She was prepared to send a note to one of her friends at the drop of a dime. Mrs. James did not mind Patsy bringing her pen and pad. In fact, she used them quite often herself.

She often passed notes to Mr. James that read, "WAKE UP," and she passed notes to Prince that read, "CUT IT OUT AND BEHAVE!" They never got through a church service without Mrs. James fussing at least one of them.

As far as Patsy was concerned, her mother could definitely depend on her to have her pencil and pad today. She would not forget her pocketbook at home. It was part of her plan to deal with Miles. It would help her convince him she was a big girl leaving him behind. After all, only big girls carried purses and pocketbooks. Miles was no dummy. He would read her message loud and clear. In the event that he did not, the pocketbook would still come in handy. Patsy would simply use it to sock him over the head during the service.

Miles's family hardly ever stayed for both Sunday school and church service at noon. As a matter of fact, the Davis family was frequently late to Sunday school or missed it altogether. Yet they always managed to make it to church service. Although staying for church was rare for her own family, today, Patsy would make an exception. She had made up her mind.

"If that Miles doesn't attend Sunday school, I'm going to wait for him. I'll wait all day if I have to, even if it means staying with grandma for church service! *Yuck*," Patsy squirmed (as church service was too long for her tastes, but she would make an exception if she had to).

Although Patsy had business to take care of with Miles, she would still enjoy her Sunday. After all, Sunday was one of Patsy's favorite days of the week. It was the only time Patsy got her mother to herself.

On Sundays, Mr. James took Prince and Patience in his car. He volunteered each week to pick up their friends who did not have a ride to Sunday school. Patsy and Mrs. James were left to go to Sunday school alone. But Patsy looked forward to their alone time. Sundays were the best! Not only did she ride in the family car's passenger seat, but once at Sunday school, she sat with some of the older children too.

Patsy was in the Juniors Sunday school class, which was made up of second, third, and fourth graders. She enjoyed being in the Juniors class because she was able to be around fourth graders. She was even more excited about attending Sunday school in the fall. She would no longer be viewed as a member of the group's baby bunch. She was moving up in the world. She was not leaving the class, but as a fourth grader she'd demand respect. Miles was silly not to be excited over something so special, Patsy thought.

Mrs. James pulled up to the church. Patsy watched the other children bustle inside the red church doors.

"Mommy, hurry, we are going to be late for school," urged Patsy.

"Okay, Patsy, I have to park first," Mrs. James replied in an unrushed tone. But Patsy did not care about parking. She had to get to class on time. How else would she get the window seat at the end of the pew? Miles always asked Patsy to save that seat for him. She had to beat Sean Peter to it.

Sean Peter was a chubby, freckled-faced, red-headed little boy who Patsy had known for as long as she could remember. Patsy only saw him on Sundays and thank God because he always followed and mimicked her and Miles. Whatever they liked, he liked. Whatever they said, he said. Patsy knew Sean Peter did not care about the pew seat. He just enjoyed making her and Miles ask him for it. Whatever attention Sean Peter could get from her or Miles, no matter what form it came in, was all right with him.

Patamela did not want Miles to suspect anything was different from their regular Sunday routine. She wanted him to feel nice and comfortable. Really what she wanted was for Miles to be completely off guard when she told him the news.

"You can just kiss your who-cares-about-the-other-school-mister-tough-guy attitude good-bye," Patsy mumbled. Once Patsy told Miles she was leaving him with the babies for good, she knew he would sing a different tune. Patamela had not decided if she would write her announcement in a note or whisper it in his ear. But she knew one thing for sure: Today she was dropping the bomb. The last thing she needed was Sean Peter getting in the way with his peskiness.

As soon as Patsy and Mrs. James walked up to First Blessed's door, Patsy ran inside. She nearly knocked over the group of adults talking in the doorway. "Hello Ms. Patsy," said Ms. Lumley. "In a rush to hear the Lord's message today, huh sweetness?"

Patsy shot around the corner and could see her class approaching their selected pews. She tore down the aisle with the speed of a NASA rocket ship. "No running in the sanctuary," Mr. Franklin, the Sunday school superintendent, announced.

It was too late. Before Ms. Wallace could get a handle on Sean Peter's arm, he bolted off the line to beat Patsy to the punch. The two collided at the last pew near the window. Patsy squeezed to get past Sean Peter. Sean Peter squeezed to get past Patsy.

Before Sean Peter knew what hit him, Patsy snatched a huge chunk of his leg in between her index finger and thumb and delivered the hardest pinch ever. "Yowie! Yowie! You just wait, Patsy James," Sean Peter squealed, bending over to rub his sore spot. Patsy took the opportunity to scoot down to the end of the aisle and stuck out her tongue.

Ms. Wallace approached the section where the two children were seated and rolled her eyes at both of them. "I guess we know which two are leading today's lesson," she chided.

Patamela did not care if she had to lead the class lesson. Ever since Mr. and Mrs. James hired Patience's best friend, Lizzie, to tutor her in language arts, Patsy had become a whiz at reading aloud. Her main concern was waiting for Miles. It seemed like he would never come. As Ms. Wallace handed out the Sunday learners to the children, Patsy continued to look to the back of the church. By this time, the ushers were closing the sanctuary's doors and there was still no sign of Miles.

"Turn to page twenty-four children. Sean Peter, you read the first paragraph. Patsy, you will read the next one,"

Ms. Wallace instructed.

"The story of the Good Samaritan," Sean Peter began. Patsy was hardly paying attention and almost missed her turn to read. The moment she began reading her assigned paragraph she was immediately taken by the story. It was actually one of her favorites. Yet before Patsy reached the third sentence, she caught a glimpse of Miles's scrawny frame out the corner of her eye. He was crouching down to slide into the opposite end of her pew. Rats, she thought. They would not be sitting near each other this class.

"The word is *stranger*, Patsy, not *stringer*. Traveling down the road this time was a stranger from Samaria," Ms. Wallace interrupted. Patsy was not paying attention to what she was reading. She was too busy figuring out a way to break the news to Miles. She needed to get her turn over with so she could plan her next move.

"*NoOnelikedpeoplefromSamaria,theywereoutcast,*" Patsy read as fast as she could.

"Patsy, you are going to have to slow down so everyone can keep up with you...Class, can anyone tell me what an outcast is?" Ms. Wallace queried.

Patsy was finished. Her class had read that story a million times. She knew it well and the younger kids had even performed a skit about it last year.

"Exactly, Trevor. An outcast is someone picked on; it's someone that no one wants to help, be around, or even play with. Continue reading for us, Trevor," urged Ms. Wallace.

Great, Patsy thought. Now she could make her move. She dug in her pocketbook and grabbed her pencil and pad. As quickly and as big as possible, she jotted, "YOU WANT TO BE A BABY SO STAY WITH THE BA-

BIES! I AM NOT YOUR FRIEND! FOREVER AND EVER!"

Patsy was careful not to take up her entire sheet. She had to make sure she left enough space for Miles to write back and apologize. All she wanted was an apology. Then they could figure out their big kid, big shot summer plans together.

Patamela folded her note in a tiny neat square and counted the people sitting between her and Miles — Sean Peter, Desiree, Nicky Dwyer (who was always called by her last name because there were a couple of Nickys in the church and even one in their class), Hamilton, Tamia, and Jonathan. The hardest part would be getting Sean Peter not to read the note, but after their earlier run in, Patsy figured Sean Peter would cooperate.

Patsy made certain her letter's folds had hard creases before folding her note again and writing: "To Miles." She knew not to write "*from Patsy*" because of an incident this year in school. Earlier that year, Patsy wrote a note to one of her friends when she should have been doing her class work. The only reason Patsy got busted was because she wrote the note was from her.

Patsy was going to take her grandmother's advice this time. "If you're careful, you don't have to make the same mistake twice," she would say when Patsy and Patience assisted her with her garden. Patsy had been listening.

Patsy tapped Sean Peter on the elbow and slowly handed him the note. As he read its heading, he began unfolding it. Patsy held her two fingers together as if she was going to pinch him again. Sean Peter slowly raised his hand as if to get Ms. Wallace's attention. Patsy's leg began to twitch. She knew she would get in big trouble with her teacher and parents if she was caught passing notes during her lesson.

Turns out Sean Peter was just faking. He knew he had better stay on Patamela's good side. It was more important for him to sit by her and Miles when the entire Sunday school met for the lesson presentations and report readings than to read some dumb letter. He decided to pass it down. Patsy watched her note go from hand to hand until it reached Miles. Miles knew it was from Patsy as soon as he saw the handwriting. Patsy stared down the pew as Miles opened her note. She could tell he was reading it.

To Patamela's surprise, Miles shrugged his shoulders, folded the note back up, and put it in his pocket. He never looked Patsy's way. She decided to pass down her pencil so Miles could write back. He would have more to say if he had a pencil, Patsy thought. When Jonathan went to hand Miles the pencil, Miles shook his head no. Jonathan sympathetically passed the pencil back down the pew.

No? Patsy thought. She squinched her eyes tightly and imagined they were Valentine red. She counted the minutes on her watch until the entire school met in the center pews to present their lessons. I'll get to him then, she thought.

"Well, class, time is almost up. Who would like to tell the Sunday school what we learned today?" Ms. Wallace asked. Trevor volunteered as usual, and Ms. Wallace chose Tamia to assist him. Patsy, the math whiz that she was, usually tallied everyone's offering, but she would pass on her duty today. She knew Sean Peter would jump for the chance to take her place. "Patsy, are you tallying the offering today?" Ms. Wallace asked.

"No, ma'am, Sean Peter can do it."

Sean Peter reached over the pew and grabbed the offering plate. Patsy glared at Miles and watched him pitch fifty cents directly into the center of the plate. "Cheapskate baby," Patsy grumbled, as she threw in her crumbled dollar with the offerings from the other children.

"Line up, class," Ms. Wallace instructed. Patsy moved as quickly as possible. Miles would be the first to go in the third center pew and she was determined to follow right behind him.

Patsy ignored her classmates' protests as she shoved and pushed the other students to make her way to Miles. She didn't stop until she could touch Miles's back with her forehead—or at least grab a lock of his curly, black hair. But Miles never budged. Ms. Wallace decided to ignore Patsy too seeing as there were only a few minutes left to class. After the opening hymn, each class's lesson presentation, the weekly reports, and closing hymn, she would have a whole week before having to deal with Patamela again.

Ms. Wallace led the children to the assigned center pews for her class. The students quickly filed in. Patsy was seated right beside Miles. The other classes settled in and directed their attention to Mr. Franklin. "Sunday school, please lift your hymnals and turn to page sixty-five for the opening hymn," Mr. Franklin instructed.

There was a lack of hymnals for Sunday school and Patsy would have to share one with Miles. This would be her chance to really sock it to him. She grabbed her hymnal and slightly turned away from Miles, "Aw Patsy, let me see the book," Miles said.

"No! Didn't I say I am not your friend?" Patsy shrieked. "Nobody's talking, I don't hear anyone," she sang.

Miles sighed deeply and looked ahead. Mr. Franklin, noticing Miles without a book, motioned to Patsy to share her hymnal. Miles grabbed the hymnal by the other end and began to sing.

Miles had had enough of Patsy. He didn't care if she didn't want to be his friend anymore. He couldn't figure out what Patsy was even talking about. He already felt he was a big kid. He had an eighteen month old little sister and he helped his parents with her all of the time. He was the oldest and already a big kid in his parents' eyes.

Who cares about the other school? Miles thought. He had treasures to dig up in his current school. Where would he hide now before Assembly Wednesdays? Miles always hid long enough to miss most of the boring ceremony. He did not know anything about the new school. He did not know where to search for treasures, and he definitely did not know the best hiding places. More importantly, he did not want to know.

Miles decided to save all of his thoughts about the new school until he actually had to enter it. Instead he secretly bubbled with excitement over ditching bossy Patamela James this summer. He was going to South Carolina in one week and—this time—for the entire summer. He would stay with his two older boy cousins and embark on all types of adventures. No more Patsy, he thought. And as much as he loved his baby sister, Ella Jo, she got on his nerves too, always breaking his toys and inventions—good riddance to the both of them.

Patsy was trying everything she could think of to get Miles's attention. She even sang two verses ahead of him to confuse him and make him mess up. But nothing worked. She could not get a rise out of him. It was not like Patsy to give up, but she was at her wit's end. She needed to take drastic measures.

Maybe I should poke him with my pencil or stomp on his foot, she thought. She could even pull his ear or give him a pinch like she gave Sean Peter earlier. She quickly decided there were too many witnesses around to get away with any of that. Even worse, Miles might retaliate. He had never acted this way before. Might she be wrong about wanting an apology from him? Had her silent treatment made Miles never want to be her friend again?

Patsy did not pay attention to the rest of Sunday school service. She did not get excited when Prince got up to give the offering report—and that was her favorite part of the service. Not only did she enjoy the fact that Prince spoke louder and clearer than all the other children who did reports, but she would try to figure out which class gave the biggest offering before Prince announced it. But today, Miles was on her mind. She sat quietly and stared at him through the corner of her eye.

When she couldn't take it anymore, she decided to tell Miles one more time. This time she would stare straight into his spooky grey eyes to make *sure* he was not faking mad, (hoping his unibrow wouldn't throw her off too much, she couldn't help staring at it sometimes). Yet both Patsy and Miles were pros at faking mad. They could do it for long periods before busting out in laughter. That had to be exactly what Miles was doing Patsy figured. Patsy leaned over and whispered, "I am not your friend anymore Miles and I really mean it."

"Will you be quiet, Patsy! I said okay!" Miles blurted.

Patsy could not believe it. There were no traces of laughter in his eyes. He was serious!

Just then, Ms. Daye made it up to the microphone for the upcoming events report. "First and foremost I must announce this for all my darlings. Ladies, please stand. Come on, all of the beautiful young ladies in next week's dance recital from the Legends in Step School of Dance, please stand."

Patsy turned around to count how many girls were actually standing. Three girls from her class stood up, including Ms. Daye's daughter, Imani. Patience's best friends, Tamara and Lizzie, stood along with many older girls that attended the other schoolhouse at Melbourne Academy. The girls ranged in age from first graders to high school students.

Patsy was not at all interested in taking dance class. It was much too prissy and girly for her. She would rather play with Puddles, rollerblade, jump double-Dutch, practice her skipping, or even play handball with Miles. Picture me in some ol' dumb tutu hopping all over the place, she thought.

Patsy turned her head back around to face Ms. Daye and caught a glimpse of Miles staring at Imani. What was he smiling at anyway? Patsy did not want to dance at Legends, but she knew all the current dances from watching Patience, Lizzie, and Tamara. She knew the party dances that counted, not stupid twist, turns, and taps you could only do at a recital. Here she was announcing the end of their friendship and all Miles cared about was some silly announcement about Imani Daye's recital.

CHAPTER 7

·····················

Imani Daye

"I can't believe it," Patsy gruffly replied. Miles was just plain smitten over Miss Imani Daye. What a double-crossing rat fink, Patsy thought. He knew she and Imani did not get along. Although Mrs. James and Ms. Daye were pew buddies, Patsy did not believe that was reason for her and Imani to be friends. Not even Prince's friendship with Ms. Daye's eldest son, Ishmael, could make Patsy change her mind. Patsy could not stand Imani Daye. And as far as Imani was concerned, the feeling was mutual.

The girls shared a tumultuous history that stretched back to the first day of kindergarten. Patamela remembered the day clearly. How could she forget? Everyone noticed how Imani swung her head when her name was called. Patsy knew she was deliberately trying to make her twists sway and bounce. This particular day, Imani was really able to pour it on. She had long twists all over her head. Each twist had a bow-bow at the top and a barrette at the bottom. The two largest twists at the top of her head were tied with pink ribbons.

"Aww look at Imani's ribbons, their beautiful," Patsy

gushed. They were bright pink and big enough to make huge, juicy bowties. Patamela took a moment to glance over her own pink outfit and then looked at Imani's pink and white set. Who was Ms. Daye trying to kid? Patsy questioned.

"She doesn't have enough pink on to have pink ribbons! Imani would look much better with white ribbons, my white ribbons," Patsy grumbled. "Hey Imani, wanna switch ribbons? Yours match my shirt and mines match your skirt," Patsy reasoned.

"My mother doesn't let me play in my hair and I like my ribbons just fine," Imani declared.

What a showoff, thought Patsy. And each time Patsy proposed a ribbon switch, Imani turned her down. Boy is she stubborn and stingy, Patsy thought. "Who needs your cheapy, creepy ribbons," Patsy mumbled. But, no matter how hard Patsy tried, she could not get Imani's ribbons out of her head.

Even when she closed her eyes she greeted visions of dancing pink ribbons. Finally at recess, Patsy caved in to temptation. Just as Imani finished a game of tag with the other children, Patsy launched her sneak attack. "Weeee, Weeee," Patsy exclaimed, tugging at Imani's twists until they were low enough to yank at one of her ribbons.

"Mrs. Knibbles! Mrs. Knibbles! Patamela is stealing my ribbons!" Imani screamed.

Mrs. Knibbles was extremely disappointed in Patsy's behavior. She made Patamela sit inside for the rest of the recess period. She even sent a letter home to Patsy's parents. And over the years, it only got worse.

Anytime Patsy continued to chat after her teacher gave the quiet signal, she would hear, "Imani is sitting quietly with her hands folded ready to get on line." When Patsy and her classmates horsed around, failing to complete class work, she would hear, "Imani didn't have trouble with the lesson. May I ask why the rest of you don't have it?" And how could Patsy forget her teachers' favorite: "Imani, tell me who got out of their chair while I was gone?" Blah, blah, blah.

Imani was a regular pain in the neck in Patsy's world. Patamela did not know anyone who got more attention than she did for her behavior and dimples than Imani. Imani even lost her two front teeth before Patsy lost hers. Everyone made a huge deal over that.

"My, what a brilliant smile," the class photographer commented. According to the entire school, the church, and the whole world, Imani was so pretty and so well behaved.

Patsy had grown accustomed to staring at Imani while wishing she would take a long hike to some distant land. Patsy sized her up from each and every angle and still could not figure out what the big fuss was about. Imani, however, was a lot thinner than Patsy and considerably taller. "Aww who cares?" Patsy shooed. Yet their classmates thought it was a huge deal and always fought over Imani when it came time to play house. Everyone wanted Imani to play the mommy in their make-believe family.

Yet Imani did not look, or act, like much of a mommy to Patsy. As a matter of fact, Imani looked just like a miniature version of Ms. Daye and her brother, Ishmael. Her skin was the color of cinnamon spice. She had straight teeth, a pudgy nose, and dark brown eyes, which she always put to good lint detection use. Unlike Patsy, Imani managed to stay impeccably clean and tidy throughout the day, except for her raisin colored wavy hair. Her hair always seemed to frizz by the afternoon bell, but Ms. Daye stayed on top of that problem. As far as Patsy could tell, she did

Imani's hair each and every night because the next day it would always be in a different style.

Well that was good for Imani because Patsy would never go near her or her silly ribbons ever again! She wouldn't go within ten feet of the girl. And as for sharing Miles, "Humph, you can forget that Imani-eat-salami-head-like-a-zombi," she mumbled.

Patsy turned her glare to Miles as he peered forward. You think Imani Daye can take my place, I won't put up a fight, Patsy thought. I'll have different friends next year anyway.

Patamela crossed her fingers and then slapped them together in prayer. "There are three fourth grade classes in that other school...There's a chance I won't be in the same class with those two, isn't there?" she said as she looked up to the ceiling. Patsy's plea was interrupted by the second half of Ms. Daye's announcement.

Patamela folded her arms and turned off her ears, just like her mom claimed to do when Patsy was whining. She did not care about anything else Ms. Daye had to say. She was ready for Sunday school to end. Usually she and Miles ran to the corner sweet shop immediately after Sunday school. They would purchase gum and candy and then save their goodies for the upcoming school week. As far as Patsy was concerned, Miles could go by himself. Better yet, he could go with Imani! Maybe she would treat him to a bag of candy like the one Patsy always bought him.

After the closing hymn, Patsy planned to bolt out the sanctuary and wait for her mother near the red doors. She wouldn't even give Miles a chance to apologize. Tomorrow at school, he would learn how serious she really was about ending their friendship. Imani never paid him a bit of attention. "You'll see who your true friend is then Miles Malone and don't you dare come crawling back," she warned.

CHAPTER 8

Splittsville

Patsy was very proud of herself. She kept her word and had not spoken to Miles once. Even Ms. Grais noticed. "Patsy, are you and Miles having a problem?" she asked. She was surprised she had not had to send one letter home to either of their parents since the week began. "It's already Thursday, Patsy, I'm impressed," she said.

Ms. Grais seldom had a smooth ride when Patsy and Miles were around. Each day she was forced to begin her afternoon lessons late courtesy of her not so favorite duo. Patamela and Miles always made certain they were the last students to get in line after recess. Ms. Grais, frustrated and embarrassed, would chastise the children, and then walk her class inside a whole five minutes after the second bell. To her chagrin, every other grade would be back in their classrooms seated, including the kindergartners.

Ms. Grais decided not to push Patsy and Miles toward reconciliation. She decided to enjoy the last week of the school year, minus their shenanigans. She only had one day to go before the two were officially no longer her students. She was grateful for the peace of mind. After all, Patsy and

Miles were neighbors. They have their entire vacation to make up, thought Ms. Grais. If they were happy ignoring each other for the remainder of the school year, it was fine with her.

The problem was Patsy was not fine with her split from Miles. She wanted him to suffer. Instead, Miles did not seem a bit worried about Patsy's silent treatment or Imani's friendship. Patamela would catch him looking at Imani every now and then, but he never made an attempt to be her friend. He was either reading his comic books or playing with the action figures some of the boys had brought in from home.

What a waste! No class work, no homework, and no action, Patsy thought. There was never any class work or homework during the last week of school. Normally Patsy and Miles would have taken full advantage of freedom from their studies. They would have run around the school, visited old teachers, had water fights at the water fountain, and just plain cut up. Patsy was bored, and it was all Miles's fault.

That was not the only thing bugging her either. She had other friends besides Miles in Ms. Grais's class, but she was invisible to them too. She could not help but feel this way. Especially since her only other close friend in Ms. Grais's class, Destiny Taylor, was ignoring her.

CHAPTER 9

....

Yakkety-Yak

Destiny was Patsy's other best friend. They'd lived just two mailboxes away from each other since forever. But this last week of school Destiny wanted to hang around with Patsy *and* some of the other girls.

"Hey Patsy, why don't you come over here with us," Destiny encouraged.

"No thanks!" Patsy shot back several times.

Destiny could tell Patsy was pretty upset, but she decided to ignore her. Destiny had learned, just as Miles had, that whenever Patsy could not boss them into doing what she wanted, she would get angry. Anytime Destiny did not want to participate in one of their plans or do exactly what Patsy and Miles wanted to do, Patsy steamed.

Destiny would not be swayed by Patsy's silent treatment today. Patamela was her best friend and when she got ready to talk, Destiny would treat her as if nothing ever happened.

In fact, Destiny was having too much of a ball to focus on Patsy's temper tantrum. She was not at all interested in combining forces to ignore Miles. She was hanging out with Imani and all the other girls involved with the big recital coming up. It was the talk of their Melbourne schoolhouse and Destiny loved being including in the excitement even if she wasn't part of their dance group. Even Ms. Grais joined in by sharing her memories of being a dance student. All the girls thought Ms. Grais's story made her the coolest teacher at Melbourne—all the girls except Patsy, that is.

At recess, the girls practiced for the upcoming show in front of Destiny and the other girls who did not attend Legends in Step School of Dance. Destiny knew all about dance class and dance recitals since she had been attending Moves n' Shoes, a dance studio on the other side of town, since kindergarten. The girls even taught Destiny some of their routines so she could dance alongside them.

Patsy sat alone on the swing set and from what she could see, Destiny was having a lot of fun chatting it up with the other girls. Why I ought to chop off one of her cornrows, Patsy considered. "...She probably won't even care," Patsy grumbled. Destiny had not even winced when Patsy snatched up all the red crayons during the morning free art period. And red was Destiny's favorite color!

Yakkety yak, yakkety yak. That's what all that talking sounded like to Patsy's uninterested ears. "Just look at them," Patsy sneered. She knew Destiny would love to be Imani's best friend and attend Legends in Step. The only reason Ms. Taylor had Destiny attend Moves n' Shoes was because she got a single parent discount and it was directly across the street from the university she was attending on Saturdays. Destiny cried for three whole days when she found out her mom put her in the wrong dance school. "Ha, Ha, too bad for you," Patsy jeered as she thought about it.

In Patsy's eyes, both Miles and Destiny were traitors. For the first time Patsy felt a little lonely, but she refused to let them know it. She needed a break from Miles, Destiny, and the whole third grade class. "Ms. Grais," Patsy said with her most polite voice, "may I go help in the kindergarten class?"

During the morning free art period, Patsy had begun making end-of-the-year good-bye cards for all her teachers (It was a great cover up for all the red crayons she'd nabbed). Patsy decided she could take her card-making materials with her to the kindergarten class and work on them during naptime.

Ms. Grais was surprised by Patsy's request; after all, Patsy would be missing extended recess, but she agreed. Ms. Knibble was thrilled to get the help. She especially appreciated having such an energetic helper like Patsy. And as soon as it was time for the kindergartners to take their afternoon nap, Patsy worked on her cards.

"Those are very vibrant colors you're using, Patamela. It's coming out quite pretty," Ms. Knibble said.

When Ms. Grais knocked on Ms. Knibble's door and called for Patsy, Patsy's mood sagged. "*Aww*, not now, Ms. Grais."

"Well, I thought it would be nice if you could let the class know you are the line monitor and that it is time to line up. Do you think you could do that for me today?" Ms. Grais asked.

Patsy was in a state of shock. Suddenly, her luck had made a change for the better. "You bet I can!" she exclaimed. Now she could stir up some excitement. The class would have to listen to her and stop all that silly dancing. "I'll be a great line monitor!" she yelled and ran down the back stairwell leading straight to the school playground.

Ms. Grais had more than made up for her earlier chumminess with the other girls.

Patsy could not wait to burst the class's bubble. Sure she was the bearer of bad news, but who cared? They would be shocked that Patsy was even chosen to be line monitor since she was usually the one who gave the line monitor a hard time. As a matter of fact, Patsy usually ignored the monitor until she got a personal invitation from Ms. Grais to join the line. Miles would be surprised, too, and Patsy was not going to give him a break. If he came one minute after she called the class, Patsy would rush to tell Ms. Grais. That would teach him to take her friendship lightly.

Patsy approached her class. "Ms. Grais's third graders line up!" she yelled at the top of her lungs. The class, boys included, were still watching the girls perform, but turned their attention to Patsy. And there she stood, arms folded, patting her right foot on the cement. "Well, line up" she insisted.

"Wait, Patsy, we're almost finished," Destiny pleaded as the girls continued to chat about the routine.

"Yakkety-yak, yakkety-yak, Ms. Grais is waiting," Patsy demanded, but no one from her class moved. "*Boo, Boo,*" the class cried. And Patsy, after determining she heard enough hisses and boos from the crowd, decided to get even. "*Dance this, dance that, spin, twirl, jump back. Dancing is for girls and that's a fact,*" she teased. Upon hearing Patsy's song, half of the boys in the class rushed to line up. Patsy was very pleased with herself and allowed her voice to get louder, "*Dance this, dance that...*"

"That's enough Patsy," Ms. Grais chided as she approached the group. "Line up, children. You should have lined up when Patamela asked you to."

"She didn't ask," one of the students said from the back of the line.

"I did so!" Patsy protested. But before she could work her anger up into a full tantrum, she heard Ms. Grais say, "Class, we are in for a treat tomorrow."

Patsy loved treats. Maybe they were getting one of those big end of the year parties, one bigger than Patsy had ever seen, with a happy red-nosed clown to pass out treats to her and her classmates.

"Tomorrow," Ms. Grais continued," Patsy will be giving our class a very special presentation.

Special presentation? Patsy thought, perplexed. Ms. Grais had not told her about any presentation. After all, tomorrow was the very last day of school—and a half-day at that.

Patsy took a deep breath and decided not to worry. Ms. Knibble must have told Ms. Grais about the cards she was making. Ms. Knibble probably said I'm working really hard and that my cards are really beautiful, Patsy thought. Patsy felt proud and knew presenting her cards to the class would be a breeze. She had not finished Ms. Grais's card, but she would take care of it as soon as she got home.

On the other hand, maybe Ms. Grais has something else in mind, thought Patsy. She wondered if Ms. Grais wanted her to make up a little song about the end of the school year. After all, Ms. Grais witnessed how quickly she made up that dance song. She was probably impressed with how fast the boys got on line—it was faster than she was ever able to do it.

Patamela hoped Ms. Grais did not think the assignment would be hard for her. Why she had tons of practice thinking up rhymes on the spot. She learned from the best. Anytime the James family went on a road trip or down south to visit a relative, her dad would play singing and rhyming games with them to pass the time.

Although Patsy believed she had more important things to do—like figuring out her big kid, big shot summer plans—she would enjoy presenting to the class. Anything would be better than letting Imani Daye get all the attention.

Patsy hurried back to her desk. She figured Ms. Grais would give her the special assignment at the end of the day. Patsy was certain Ms. Grais was preparing to lead the class with a game of hangman or seven up. Patsy loved seven up, but Ms. Grais called Patsy to her desk right away. "Patsy, I would like you to go to the school library on the third floor and ask Mr. Jackson, the school librarian, for assistance with your presentation," Ms. Grais instructed.

Wait a minute, Patsy thought. I don't need Mr. Jackson's help making cards or making songs up on the spot. "What for?" Patsy asked.

"Well, you're going to need help finding the names of a few African American male dancers. Since dancing is only for girls and the boys in the class agreed, I thought it would be nice for you to educate the class on the subject. I'm sure you'll be able to find a number of talented African American male dancers that made a huge difference in our history," Ms. Grais said, smiling.

Oh no, Patsy thought. It's not Black History Month. It's June—and the day before school is out for the summer. "Aw man, Ms. Grais, I was just teasing. All of my favorite singers dance and they're boys."

"Patamela, you're wasting time," said Ms. Grais.

Patsy sighed and walked out of the room. She slowly went up the one flight of stairs to the third floor.

Patsy knocked on the library door. "May I help you,

Ms. James?" Mr. Jackson asked. He knew Patsy very well because she and Miles always acted as if class visits to the library meant a free period. He would have to separate her and Miles or her and Destiny every class.

This time Patsy planned to give Mr. Jackson her undivided attention. She would ask a thousand questions so she could stay extra long. She had made up her mind before knocking on the door that she would fix Ms. Grais. She would stay with Mr. Jackson one minute before the last bell and make the entire class wait for her.

"Mr. Jackson, I need help finding some dumb ol' boy dancers for Ms. Grais," Patsy mumbled.

"Who'd you have in mind?" Mr. Jackson asked.

"I dunno," she replied, shrugging her shoulders.

Mr. Jackson walked to the small bookshelf by the window and motioned Patsy to a huge album with newspaper clippings and photocopies of articles and pictures. "Everything you need should be right in here. I am certain you'll find whatever you need on any African American entertainer in there," he assured.

"What kind of book is this?" Patsy asked, frowning because of its enormity and the dust she had to brush off it.

"Oh, just some information I have collected over the years. I put it on display during Black History Month. Ms. Grais knows all about it. It's a hobby of mine, collecting articles about African American entertainers. It's a love your teacher shares with me."

If she loves it so much, she should be here looking up dancers herself, thought Patsy as she carried the huge book to one of the tables. Patsy carefully turned the book's pages. The entire book seemed as if it would fall apart if Patsy did not take her time.

The book was split into three sections: voice, dance,

and movies and television. Patsy opened up to the dance section. Some dancers were familiar to her because she had heard her parents mention their names in the past. She had seen a couple of old shows and movies with Debbie Allen and Gregory Hines. But there were many dancers she had never seen before.

There were so many names Patsy did not know where to begin. Alvin Ailey, The Nicholas Brothers, Sammy Davis Jr., Josephine Baker, Buster Brown, Billy Briggs, Katherine Dunham. The pages went on and on. Patsy almost forgot she was only there to get the names of a few male dancers.

Patsy read about any dancer whose picture sparked her interest. The articles covered the dancers' talents and some of the obstacles they faced as African Americans. "Glad you are enjoying my book, Patsy," Mr. Jackson said, breaking into her thoughts.

"Sure am, Mr. Jackson," she replied. Patsy asked the librarian for a sheet of paper and wrote down the names of a couple of the male dancers she read about. "Your book sure is cool. Thanks for letting me use it," Patsy said. Then she tore out of the library and ran back to her class. The students were just beginning to line up.

"Did you see Mr. Jackson's special book, Patsy?" asked Ms. Grais.

"Sure did, Ms. Grais," answered Patsy as she found herself a spot in line. "I'll be ready tomorrow."

Ms. Grais's class made their way to the staircase so she could dismiss them at the front door. Patsy walked quietly, forgetting all about her frustrations with Miles and Destiny. She was positively pooped and ready to go home. She was so tired that she didn't think she'd even have the energy to tell her mom about all the entertainers she'd read about.

Patsy crossed her fingers and hoped Patience was already waiting for her outside. When she got downstairs to the school's front door, Patience was standing near the doorway. "Come on, Patsy. Come on, Destiny," Patience urged.

Oh brother, thought Patsy. She did not feel like being bothered with Destiny the whole walk home. She thought Ms. Taylor would be picking her up like she had done last Friday and the day before. Patsy wanted to have an attitude with Destiny, but she was too tired to be upset.

"Want me to show you the dance the girls taught me today?" Destiny asked.

"Nope," Patsy mumbled as they trudged after Patience who was trying to catch up with a group of her friends. Patsy caught a glimpse of Imani with a group of fourth grade girls across the street. Patsy could not believe her eyes. Had Imani beaten her to the punch again—able to walk home all by herself? Patsy would not be allowed to go home without Patience until next year.

"Hey Imani!" the older girls ahead of Patience yelled. "Are you ready for the recital Saturday? Everybody's talking about it. It's going to be something!"

Imani smiled at the girls and waved. "Unh huh, you guys better come and watch me," she shouted back. "I'm staying to see you guys."

"Huh?" Patsy muttered. She was completely dumbfounded by what had just taken place. The older girls only called her and Patience to ask if Prince was around. They never talked to Patsy because of something she was doing. Patsy was busy learning about important dancers and there Imani was getting praise for some stinky recital. Patsy wondered if dancing at Legends in Step was just the thing her summer needed.

"Nah, can't be," she murmured, shaking the idea out of her head. She would be through with dance for good after her presentation tomorrow.

CHAPTER 10

No More Dancing

Patsy was happy to be out of school. Friday's presentation had nearly wiped her out, but it was well worth it. Ms. Grais had never before told Patsy she did an excellent job on an assignment. Patamela always got "Goods" and "Very Goods." She used to get "Fairs" before Lizzie began tutoring her. Yet Friday Ms. Grais was so impressed with Patsy's presentation, she not only said it was excellent work, but she took their entire fourth grade class to the library to look through Mr. Jackson's album and had the students rely on Patsy's expertise when they had questions.

Patamela loved being singled out. It was just the type of thing she expected to happen as a newly appointed big kid. When Ms. Grais gave her another compliment at 11:59 a.m. on the dot, right before dismissing the third grade class for the last time, Patsy was not surprised. After all, Patsy would be claiming her status as an upper grade-big-shot just one minute later.

But that was yesterday. Today, Patsy had a chance to be a big kid way before noon. Today was her first official day as an upper grade, big kid, big shot fourth grader from the moment she woke up until forever and ever. There would be no waiting for school to start in September. School was officially out and Patsy was ready to shock the world!

"That silly presentation was nothing," Patsy boasted out loud as she lay in her bed. "Wait until they get a load of me this summer. My big kid, big shot activity will knock their socks off."

And Patsy meant to do just that. Her big kid, big shot activity would not be worth a hill of beans if she could not brag about it. She'd made sure to get everyone's telephone number before yesterday's last dismissal bell. She did not plan to call anyone anytime soon, but the telephone numbers would come in handy when it was time to brag about her summer.

But before she could brag, she had to start by deciding how she would spend her first Saturday out of school. "I got it!" she said, leaping out of bed. She would wash up, change into her play clothes, and go downstairs for some breakfast. Then she would play with Puddles, help Mrs. James around the house, and ask her father if Prince or Patience could take her to the ice cream parlor after lunch. She loved chocolate and vanilla fudge cones. They were just the treat she needed to decide on a summer activity once and for all.

Patamela wished she could include Miles in all the summer-planning fun. It was a bit boring without him. She would even settle for taking Puddles over to his tree house and inviting him to share a cone, but she was not ready to be his friend. She would have to find something else to get into if the day got too boring. She could always write a list of ideas on how she wanted to spend her summer and hand it to her mom. If she did not hand her parents some ideas soon, they would tell her exactly how she would be spending her summer. And that was the last thing Patsy wanted.

"Good morning, Pattie Cakes," her mom said as Patsy reached the bottom of the stairs.

"Hi Mommy."

"Did you pick out an outfit for the show this afternoon?"

"What show? I'm not going to be in a show."

"Patsy, you know the recital is this afternoon and I have tickets for you, Patience, and myself. It'll be a girls' only event. We'll have fun."

Patsy wanted to faint. "No more dancing!" she yelled, stomping her foot.

"All right Ms. Lady, get a hold of yourself. You're not two years old, you're turning nine soon. Is there something you'd like to share with me?"

Patsy had been so tired Friday morning (after staying up late to write her special assignment report), she'd never had a chance to tell her mom and dad about her presentation. Actually, she did not want her parents to know. She did not want to tell them about the song she sang that made Ms. Grais give her the assignment in the first place.

"Ma, do I have to?" Patamela whined. "I don't want to see Imani or any of those girls. Yesterday at school, we already had to go to library to learn about Alvin Ailey, Josephine Baker, Sammy Davis Jr., the Nicholas Brothers..."

"I don't see why you wouldn't want to support Imani. She's in your class at Melbourne and at First Blessed. Patience is going because she wants to see Lizzie and Tamara dance," her mom interrupted.

"But those are Patience's best friends! Imani isn't my best friend. She isn't even my friend a little bit."

"Fine Patsy, but I have a ticket for you and you can go

in support of Lizzie and Tamara. They are very kind to you. Did you forget how much Lizzie's tutoring has helped you with your reading and language arts? Going will be your way of saying thank you."

Patsy was devastated. More dancing, and even worse, more Imani. It was too much for her to handle. She would have to beg her father to say he needed her help on one of his projects. That way she could stay home.

Patsy rushed through her breakfast and out to the garage to find her dad. He spent his Saturday mornings in the garage organizing or throwing out junk, as he called it. Patsy was sure she would find him there or preparing to mow the lawn. She hoped he had not left to drive Prince to one of his team practices.

Patsy quickened her pace and could hear boxes, lamps, and all kinds of stuff being moved around as she approached the garage. She opened the door to find her father and Prince carrying boxes and containers to the curb to be thrown out. "Hey Daddy!" Patsy exclaimed.

"Hey Patsy. Young lady, did you sleep at the foot of your brother's bed last night?" Her dad always asked that question when any of the children did not say hello or speak to their brother or sister.

"Hi Prince," Patsy said softly.

"Patsy, your mom already got to me. She wants you to have a great time this afternoon. Be a sport and figure out which outfit you're wearing. She's the general," her dad said with a chuckle.

Patsy hated when her father called her mom the general because it meant Patsy's dad would do nothing to save her.

"Don't give me the hound dog eyes. It is what it is. When you come back, you can tell me all about it," said her dad.

"But, Daaaaaad," Patsy pleaded. Sometimes when she dragged her dad's name out as long as she could, that was enough to get her dad talk to her mom.

"I think it will be a great show. Aren't some of your friends performing? That Imani, now she's a nice girl. You should go see her. She and Ms. Daye come to all of your birthday parties," Mr. James added.

Patsy could tell she was not going to win this battle. "Stop acting like a baby, Little Bit...*and be exposed to something new,*" Prince said, softening his voice so he could mimic their mom's tone.

It was the exact thing Mrs. James said when she was trying to "teach the children some culture and class." Mrs. James would always say that to her relatives when they teased her about some activity, museum exhibit, or show she was attending with the kids. Prince began prancing and leaping in the air like a ballerina and even did a curtsy as he held the bottom of an imaginary tutu.

"Leave your sister alone, Prince," their dad snapped.

But Patsy could tell her father was amused by Prince's performance. Patsy walked toward the door leading out of the garage. She decided to give it a little slam to show her dad just how upset she was with him. But she knew he was halfway to the curb and would not hear it. Even if he did, it was still tutus and ballet slippers for her.

CHAPTER 11

························

Disappearing Acts

Patamela ran upstairs to her room. Patience was on her bed bopping to some music and painting her toenails. She and Patience could not be in the same room for long without bickering, and Patsy was in no mood to fight. She knew Patience had overheard her conversation with Mom, and she would not give her a chance to rub it in. It was Patience's fault she had to go to the dumb recital anyway. Lizzie and Tamara were Patience's friends, not hers. Patsy did not care about seeing them twirl and whirl all night. If Patience even teased her one time, she would pour that fingernail paint all over her bedspread.

"Pud-dles! Pud-dlesss!" Patsy called. Puddles zipped around the corner to greet Patsy. She could tell he was in Prince's room lying on his bed. He would lie on any bed he could find empty, except for their parents' bed. Puddles was smart enough to know he would get more than a playful shove if he tried that.

Patsy knelt down beside her dog and gave him a hug. Puddles jumped on her, placing his front paws on her chest, and licked her cheek. "Yuck, Pudz," Patsy said as they fell to the floor. She decided to take him for a walk—and that was when Patsy hatched her plan.

"I'm going to walk so far that by the time I turn around to come home, the recital will be over. Everyone else will miss the recital too because they'll be too busy searching for me," Patsy plotted. She was an expert at picking hiding places and knew her parents would never find her.

"That's it!" Patsy yelped, struck by an idea for the perfect hiding place. She would go to Miles's clubhouse and hide. She would forget all about being enemies; she was ready to be his friend. Miles had had enough time to see it her way by now. He would run to tell her how much he was looking forward to going to school at the other building. I bet his baby days are over, she thought.

Patsy ran out of the house with Puddles. "I'll be outside!" she screamed at the top of her lungs. She could see her father standing in the driveway, waving good-bye. She didn't have to ask permission to go to Miles's house because that's what going outside usually meant. She'd gone every Saturday since she could remember—except for last Saturday when she wasn't speaking to him. Plus asking to go to Miles's house would guarantee it would be the first place they searched when she went missing. And that was the last thing she wanted.

As Patsy approached the tree house, she thought it odd not to hear any banging or hammering. Miles was usually working on some new invention or preparing for a hunt of some sort. She imagined a thousand things Miles could have been getting himself into at that very moment.

He's probably curled up in a corner sick over the loss of our friendship, Patsy mused. She didn't need anyone to tell her how preposterous that suggestion was and laughed at the thought of it. She figured he was busy thumbing through his comic books.

"Miles!" she called out. "Miles Malone! I know you hear me Miles Malone Davis!" Patsy yelled and yelled but got no response. "Okay," she said as she stomped up the stairs to the tree house, holding Puddles in her right arm. "All right Miles, I am sorry...I am sorry you are a baby!" She chuckled aloud.

"Miles Malone, you open this door right now!" she demanded. But still, she got no answer. When Patsy reached the door of the tree house, she came face to face with a posted sign that read, "Gone For The Summer." Gone for the summer, she thought. Gone where? He hadn't stopped by to say good-bye. He hadn't even told her he was going away for the summer.

This must be a joke, Patsy thought, as she marched up to the Davis's front door. She knocked as hard as she could and was greeted by Mrs. Davis, holding Ella Josephine in her arms. "Hello Patamela," said Mrs. Davis.

"Hi Mrs. Davis," Patsy said, taking no time to ask how she was feeling. "May Miles please come to the front door?"

Mrs. Davis gave Patsy a perplexed look and said, "Patsy, Miles isn't here. He left this morning. We put him on a train to South Carolina so he could spend the summer with his cousins. Didn't he tell you?"

Patsy was shocked. How could her best friend leave for the entire summer without saying good-bye? She wished she could pull a disappearing act just like the one Miles had pulled. She didn't want to be left behind to attend Imani's crummy recital alone.

"Hmmm, wait here, Patsy." Mrs. Davis gently closed the door and returned a second later. She passed Patsy a folded sheet of paper. "Why don't you give him a call tomorrow. I'm sure he would love hearing from you. He did look a little sad this morning. Maybe he forgot to stop by your house or maybe he came by and no one told you."

Patsy's face brightened. Of course that is what happened, she thought. Patsy thanked Mrs. Davis and darted back across the street to her house. She would play with Puddles until it was time to get dressed for the recital. There was no need to ask if Miles came by. Her father and Prince probably forgot to tell her. They always forgot to tell her when one of her friends knocked on the door. Miles must have come by earlier and they must have told him she was asleep. That had to be it. After all, she hadn't gotten up until eleven.

"Let's play ball, Puddles. I'll race you to it," Patsy said, now in front of her home. She grabbed the ball from beneath a bush with Puddles nipping at her heels. Patsy rolled around in the grass as Puddles tried to use his head to nudge the ball out of her grasp. Just then the front door swung open.

"Patsy, now I'll have to do your hair again. Come on inside so you can shower and get dressed. Don't forget to bring the comb and brush down when you're done. Did you find an outfit to wear?" asked her mom.

Patsy shook her head no, motioned Puddles inside the house, and ran up the stairs to her room. She wished she could stay in her play clothes but changed her mind upon seeing Patience's outfit neatly laid out on her bed. She decided to wear a similar outfit, except hers was orange.

Patamela waited patiently for Patience to get out of the shower. She never understood why Patience took so long in the bathroom. When it was her turn, Patsy showered, got dressed, grabbed the comb and brush along with two white and two orange ribbons, and tore down the stairs, leaving Patience to dance in their bedroom mirror alone.

"Patsy, did you remember to brush your teeth?" she heard her mother call from the bottom of the stairs.

"See what happens when you *rush, rush, rush* to beat me squirt," Patience yelled.

"Oh brother," Patsy sighed. She thought about faking Patience out by saying she'd remembered to brush her teeth, that is, until she realized she had forgotten to put on her deodorant and white tennis shoes too.

Patsy was still downstairs a whole ten minutes before Patience. Now both she and Mrs. James were dressed, finished with Patsy's hair, and calling for Patience to come downstairs. "She's such a slow poke," Patsy grumbled.

Patience came downstairs excited about getting a chance to support her best girlfriends' performances. Patience did not want to go to dance school, but she was a real sport about helping Lizzie and Tamara with their dance technique and steps. She would mimic their teacher, "No, do it again, no, do it again," and they would all chuckle. The extra practice helped Lizzie and Tamara a lot.

Patsy figured the Jameses would consider that when deciding whether Patience should attend the etiquette and modeling classes she begged them to pay for. What a waste of time that would be, Patsy thought.

"Riding shotgun," Patience yelled as she bolted out the door, landing in the passenger seat of their mom's car. As many times as Patsy beat Patience downstairs, she never beat her sister or brother to the shotgun call. Patsy hadn't expected this day to be any different. She was just happy to ride shotgun on Sundays.

Mr. James and Prince showered the trio with compliments as they walked them out to the car. "You look great sweetheart. You too, Patsy. And you were upset about going. You look marvelous sunshine!" her dad said.

"Yeah, Little Bit, you look like a big ol' orange!" Prince added.

"Oh hush, Prince," Patsy replied as she closed the car door behind her.

"Daddy, you forgot to tell me Miles came by," Patsy yelled through the back window.

"How could I forget something that didn't happen? I haven't seen Miles today."

"Mommy, did Miles come by?" Patsy asked.

"Not that I know of Patsy."

That's weird, thought Patsy. She remembered getting out of bed before Patience so she knew Patience could not have answered the door when he came by.

"Prince," Patsy called; but before she could finish her question, he answered, "I didn't see him."

Patsy could not believe Miles left without saying anything to her. The thought made her stomach roll. She figured she must be catching the butterflies, just like the ones Prince said he caught before each game he played. That Miles could never make this one up!

"I'm tearing up that number as soon as I get back!" she grumbled. If Patsy hadn't been feeling so upset with Destiny, then Destiny could have been her new best friend. But there was no chance of that happening—ever—now that Destiny was vice-president of the *Imani Poofawney* club.

Patsy had a hard enough time shaking thoughts of Destiny's betrayal, but she really couldn't get Miles off her brain. How much of a baby is that to just disappear and leave without saying good-bye, she thought. "I would never do anything like that to him," she reckoned. Sure, she'd told Miles she was never speaking to him, but she hadn't meant it. To make matters worse, now she had to go to this stupid recital. She did not have time to go to a recital. Didn't her mother understand that? Not only did she need to find a big kid activity to do for the summer, but now she needed to find two new friends.

CHAPTER 12

Fat And Greasy

"My goodness, it's crowded," Mrs. James said to her daughters as she pulled into a parking space in front of Gilford Mayer's Auditorium and Amphitheater at Springdale Community College. Mrs. James and the girls hurried to the steps leading up to the theater's front door. "I hope we didn't miss Ms. Taylor and Destiny. Ms. Taylor said they'd meet us here. I didn't realize we were this late," Mrs. James said, turning to Patamela and Patience. Mrs. James handed the door attendants their tickets and the girls followed their mom into the theater.

"Here we are!" a voice yelled from the front of the auditorium just three rows back from the stage. "I saved three seats for you," Ms. Taylor called out, signaling the group to look at Destiny who was seating exactly three seats down from her mother.

Patsy could already see Destiny was all grins, but she was not happy about being seated by Destiny at all. Her mother urged her to take a seat beside her old friend anyway. Patience sat beside Patsy and Mrs. James beside Ms. Taylor. Ms. Taylor had the aisle seat. "Will you be okay down there, Destiny?" Ms. Taylor asked, leaning to see if Destiny was comfortable.

"I'm okay, Mommy," she replied, before turning to Patsy. "Want a strawberry Twizzler?"

"No thanks," Patsy grouched.

The lights in the theater began to dim and Patsy allowed her eyes to close. This would be just fine, she thought. She would fall asleep like her dad always did in church. That would teach her mom to drag her to events she did not want to attend. It would also show Destiny she did not wish to be bothered.

Patsy closed her eyes, and just as she pictured herself bopping Miles over the head with her pocketbook, Patience nudged Patsy with her elbow. Patsy opened her eyes just to roll them at Patience and slowly closed them again. *BOOM-DANG-BOOM-BA-BAM-DANG...*Patsy nearly jumped out of her seat the music was so loud.

"Good afternoon ladies and gentlemen, welcome to the fifth annual Legends in Step end of the year recital. Take a trip with us this afternoon to the romping good times of the 1920s and '30s. Sit back and let your hands clap and your feet tap. Enjoy!"

Patsy had never heard a prettier voice, but she did not see anyone on the stage. Her eyes were wide and watching the stage curtains. She did not want to miss a beat.

The curtains opened. Patsy stared at a line of ten girls— all Patience's age with their faces made up. They had on huge red hats pulled down low over their eyes. Each dress was white with a hem of red sequins. The girls wore bright white tights and high red heels. Behind them stood a large juke box with a huge painting of African American entertainers like Nell Carter, Lena Horne, Nancy Wilson, Duke Ellington, Nat King Cole, and Louis Armstrong. Patsy recognized their faces from Mr. Jackson's album.

"*Five, six, five, six, seven, eight,*" one of the girls in the center of the line shouted, grabbing Patsy's attention. The girls began to tap their feet simultaneously in a thunderous roar, *ti-tap-dat-ta-ta-tap-ti-tap-dat-ta-ta-ta*. They were really tap dancing—and without music! All of a sudden, a new girl jumped from behind the curtains dressed as a big, busty woman with her hair pinned up. She had a beautiful red flower pinned to the right side of her head. She wore a sparkling red sequin dress and high heels to match.

"Oooh, fire-engine red!" Destiny yelled in delight.

Patsy loved the outfit too and could tell pillows were placed inside the girl's dress to make her look big. She was all set to lean over Patience to tell her mom the girl's stuffed dress secret until she was jolted back in her seat by the lined dancers' sudden halt. They were allowing the busty-woman-girl to dance alone.

When the lead girl finished her solo routine, the lined girls remained frozen in place. It was only after the busty woman began tapping her shoes ever so slightly that they began to imitate every tap sound she made. It was like they were having a question and answer session in tap language. Then, in an instant, the girls began jumping up and down. They jumped so high, Patsy thought one of them might fall.

Suddenly, the girl dressed as the fat, older woman, belted a huge "QUUIIIEEET!" and held it as long as she could. Patsy recognized the voice. It was Tamara! She was pretending to be the big woman! When the music started to play, Tamara lip-synced along with the record, "This joint is jumpin', it's really jumpin'!" The girls continued to jump up and down. Every single one of them were smiling and in step. Patsy even spotted Lizzie. Boy, are they good, Patsy thought.

Patsy watched number after number, outfit after outfit, and smiling face after smiling face. She was enjoying the show so much she forgot about her plan to fall asleep. During intermission, Mrs. James had to nearly drag Patsy out of her seat to go to the ladies room. Patsy didn't want to risk missing the start of the second half.

Patamela anxiously awaited the last dance of the show. It was taking much too long. She decided Patience should keep her occupied in the meantime.

Patience was busy reading a performance program she'd taken from Mrs. James a moment earlier. Patsy leaned over Patience's shoulder. Patience decided to be nice and spread the program page wider so Patsy could view the names of the upcoming acts. Patience scrolled down the page until she reached the word *Finale*. "That means the last dance of the recital," Patience said as her index finger slid to the name of the act.

"*FAT AND GREASY!*" Patsy shrieked. They had already seen Tamara dressed as a fat woman in the opening act. Patsy was not impressed and felt cheated. She knew the show was too good to be true. "That's what they always do in the end," Patsy said shaking her head. It was kind of like what Miles said about the movies he begged his parents to see that turned out crummy, "They always gyp you in the end."

Patamela decided she would ask her mother to take her back to the ladies room or ask Destiny if she was up for a game of seat tag. Miles and Patsy always played seat tag when they went on school trips to see the circus. They had seen the circus a million times and figured they would amuse themselves underneath their chairs. Neither of them would ever get far enough to escape being "it," but that is what made the game fun. Although Patsy did not wish to talk to Destiny, she knew Patience sure wasn't going to play with her.

Patsy crept down in front of her chair with her back turned to the stage. Patience sucked her teeth and reached for her arm. "If you don't get up, I'm telling Ma. You can't even sit still, big baby."

Patsy dodged Patience's reach and decided to ignore her name calling. But, before she could rope Destiny into her game, she heard a male's voice.

Watch him while he's sitting there
Chunks of fat hang over his chair
Oil just oozing from his hair
Fat and greasy like a grizzly bear

The roar of the audience startled Patsy. Everyone was cracking up. Patsy turned to the stage to see Imani Daye, Nicky Dwyer, and Nicky Lewis. They were dancing with a couple of other girls from her Sunday school class and her old Melbourne building, and all of them were in pink outfits.

The outfits reminded Patsy of the orange pumpkin costumes some of her classmates wore at Halloween. They were that plump in the middle. The only difference was their costumes were pink and instead of having a green leaf on their heads, the girls had on pink headbands with fake pig ears glued to them. They even had curly pink tails pinned to their bottoms. "They're supposed to be pigs," Patsy guffawed.

Patsy looked at the stage and noticed the entire background had changed. It looked like the girls were on a farm. There was a huge pigpen in the middle of the stage containing crumbled brown crepe paper. It looked just like real mud to Patsy. In the back of the pigpen was a huge picture of all types of farm animals. There was even a picture of an African American farmer with his wife and children.

Before Patsy could even take in each and every detail of the new scene, a group of older girls slid on stage dressed in straw hats and dungaree overalls. Each girl wore a pink shirt underneath her overalls and a pink handkerchief in her back pocket. As the older girls danced, they chased the younger girls in the pig outfits back into the pigpen. It was hilarious!

The music continued:

Ah man that fool is fat and greasy
Head to heel he's fat and greasy
Oh a big fat greasy fool.

The piglets ran frantically as the farmers slipped and fell like they could not get a hold of them. Each pig would barely escape the farmer's grasp as the farmer collided into a high haystack or fellow farmer. The pigs and the farmers even broke into their own dancing routines. Each pig partnered with a farmer to do a set of steps different from all the other pairs. By the end of the show, even after the girls were off stage, the audience, was still singing, "Fat and greasy...*Duh-da-duh-da-da-da*...Fat and greasy."

The show was over and all the girls were running from behind stage to their families and friends. The more girls Patsy got to see up close, the more girls she recognized from First Blessed and Melbourne Academy.

"Those are my girls! Make way for my best friends. *Excuse, excuse, pardon!*" Patience kidded as Lizzie and Tamara made their way through the crowd. They embraced both Patience and Patsy in giant hugs. "Thanks for coming!" they said.

"They wouldn't have missed it for the world, right

Patsy?" her mother said with a wink.

Patsy smiled.

"Wait, wait," Lizzie and Tamara exclaimed. "We want you to meet one of our teachers...Ms. Saa, Ms. Saa," they called.

Just then, Patsy caught a glimpse of a tall and slender young woman. She had a bronze-like, glowing complexion and what seemed to be dark-brown braided twists in her hair. Patsy could tell they were not quite braids or twists, she was astonished by their beauty and length. They cascaded all the way down her back. Patsy wanted to pluck one of the gorgeous bracelets traveling up her forearm. "Ladies, you did an excellent job. I am very proud of you. See what hard work does?" Immediately, Patsy knew that was the pretty voice she'd heard coming from behind the curtain at the beginning of the show.

She watched as Ms. Saa introduced herself to all the parents. Patsy was so taken by the graceful manner in which Ms. Saa walked and her beauty and warmth that she walked right up to her and said, "You're beautiful. I loved your show."

Ms. Saa gently lifted Patsy's face and said, "You're beautiful as well. Give me those dimples! Do you dance?"

Patsy shook her head no.

"I would love for you to join my summer session. It's starting soon. Promise me you'll come," Ms. Saa said. "We are going to have great fun. Our theme for the summer recital will be classic songs of the fifties – Miles Davis, Nat King Cole, Gene Kelly, and Peggy Lee. Ladies, we're going to have a ball! We're even holding the recital in our own Legends auditorium. It's been renovated and it's gorgeous."

Ms. Saa looked at Mrs. James to make certain her sales

pitch was convincing before walking away to greet the other parents. Patsy blushed, but she was truly on cloud nine. Never before had she seen a woman that beautiful close up, nor had she encountered one that complimented her dimples without digging her fingers in them. Patsy wanted to go home with Ms. Saa right then and there.

As Patsy walked out of Gilford Mayer Auditorium with her sister and mother, she was glad she'd come to the recital. Who cared if Miles did not say good-bye? She did not need him to have a good time. She could not wait to tell her father about the show. Mrs. James drove the girls out of the parking lot and up Campbellton Road as they sang, "Fat and greasy...Duh-da-duh-da-da-da...Fat and greasy," the entire way.

CHAPTER 13

Guess What, Daddy?

Patamela James woke up on Monday morning to the worst news imaginable. Not only had she still not been able to tell her father about the recital on Saturday afternoon (thanks to the fact that the recital didn't end until late evening and she'd fallen asleep on the way home and someone, (Prince), had carried her inside to bed, *and* to the fact that her dad had been gone all day Sunday at a church event leaving just minutes before Patamela awakened), but now she discovered she had to spend the day at the Davis house, helping to watch Ella Josephine. *Yuck*, thought Patsy. While everyone else would be happily enjoying their big kid or adult day, she would have to play with that slobbery baby. "Quadruple-doople hexation!" Patsy grumbled as she got dressed.

Patsy's parents (without Patsy's knowledge or consent) had asked Mrs. Davis if Patsy could help her with Ella Josephine until they decided on Patsy's summer plans. They told Mrs. Davis she would only have to watch Patsy for a couple of days.

"It won't take us very long to find her an activity for

the summer," Mrs. James said as she dropped Patsy off at the Davis's home. "I already have some ideas," she said, kissing Patsy on the forehead. Patsy got out of the car, walked to the door, and turned around to wave good-bye. Then she stood, frozen and speechless at the Davis's front door.

"Oh no!" she shrieked as her mother's words sank in. In a matter of seconds her need to find her own summer activity leaped from a *cool-as-a-cucumber, taking-her-sweet-time level one, to a full-fledged code red.* Now she was determined to choose her own summer activity and doubly determined to make her stay at the Davis home a short one.

"Of all the places they could stick me," Patsy huffed. Didn't her parents realize she would be bored out of her mind? Miles was not even there! Actually, Patsy would not have cared if he had been there. She wasn't even his friend. And Ella Jo... Why she'd rather be dragged down Kissamaine Avenue by wild gorillas than to spend a whole day with her.

Ella Josephine (Ella Jo or E-Jay as she was called) was a slobbery mess, always sucking on her coat or shirtsleeve until it was completely soaked with saliva. Patsy had heard of a baby sucking his or her thumb, but a shirt sleeve! Patsy was sure Ella Jo had cooties and as cute as everyone said she was, Patsy was not fooled. Ella Jo's shirts would be wet all the way up to the elbow from all that shirt sucking, and Patsy was sure she'd done nothing that nasty as a baby.

Yet as nasty as Ella Jo was, Patsy realized she came with the territory. She was Miles's baby sister and there was no getting around that. If you can't beat 'em, join 'em was Patsy's motto when it came to E-Jay, and Patsy had become quite the head-tilting expert because of it. Whenever she tilted her head to the left or right, Ella Jo transformed into an adorable little angel—well, in a sort of irresistibly pesky kind of way.

Ella Josephine had a bright complexion that reminded Patsy of a mixture of vanilla and lemon frosting. Her hair was as curly and jet-black as Miles's, but Mrs. Davis kept E-Jay's hair in a short ponytail at the top of her head. Her eyes were small, but her pupils looked so big that Patsy felt E-Jay was surprised to see her every time they met.

Ella Jo loved to play with Patsy, but today she would be on her own. Patsy would not waste one minute with the duchess of drool. Out on the doorstep Patsy decided that no amount of hexing, no cute game Ella Jo could want to play, and no television show Mrs. Davis could bribe Patsy into watching would coax her inside. Patsy would wait on the doorstep until her father picked her up. There was no way she would miss another opportunity to tell him about the recital. She had waited long enough.

"I've got a job to do and I will not be persuaded!" Patsy announced to herself. She would only go inside at lunchtime, and even then she would eat with the speed of a peach-cobbler-eating contest winner. Mrs. Davis could try to lure her in with goodies, but her efforts would be pointless. Patsy would simply request front stoop service. Patsy knocked on the door to let Mrs. Davis know she was there.

"Good morning, Patamela. I'm glad you're joining us today."

"Good morning, Mrs. Davis. I didn't know I was coming here today, and I've decided to wait on the front stoop for my father."

"But Patsy, he won't be here for hours."

"I know. That's okay. I just don't want to miss him."

Mrs. Davis did her best to persuade Patsy to come in, but nothing worked. Finally she surrendered and said she had things to get done inside.

A while later, Mrs. Davis stepped out to check on Patsy again. "Patsy, sweetie I hope you aren't too hot. Would you like to get out of the sun for a moment? It will be quite a while before your dad picks you up," Mrs. Davis reasoned.

"Nah, I'm fine, Mrs. Davis," Patsy replied.

"Okay Patamela, but you let me know as soon as you need something. I guess you must have something pretty important on your mind."

Mrs. Davis gently closed the screen door behind her, and Patsy continued her struggle to keep busy. She wistfully switched between playing games of jacks to playing memory pairs with her cards. Every now and then she would attempt to number a troupe of black ants vigorously mounting a barbecue potato chip Ella Jo had spit out earlier. Patsy even looked forward to Ella Jo pressing her face against the Davis's screen door and squeezing through its slash, just so she could air swat her back inside. To be quite honest, Patsy was bored to pieces.

When Patamela returned to the Davis's front stoop after lunch, she noticed a group of kids playing a couple of houses down the street. She decided the rest of her day would pass rather quickly if she watched them. When the group spotted Patsy, they asked her to join the fun. They even volunteered to walk the games over to her, but Patsy declined their offers. There was no way she was moving from her spot in front of the Davis's home. She had business to handle.

Patsy watched the kids as they played games of Red Light Green Light 123 and Mother May I, until she heard her father's horn. "Patsy, let's go," Mr. James shouted from his car.

Patsy opened the Davis front door and called out, "See ya Mrs. Davis, bye E-Jay," then she ran to her dad's car. "Daddy, I never got to tell you about the show," Patsy said.

"Hey Dad, how was your day? How was the retreat? I missed you," Mr. James said, poking fun at Patsy.

But Patsy did not get the joke. "Dad, how come you didn't wake me to ask me about the show? You forgot to wake me up Saturday night, Sunday morning before you left for church, and last night when you got home," Patsy said with a pout.

"Hey, I'm just an innocent bystander. You fell asleep, and from what I understand, girls need their beauty rest. Don't they, sleeping beauty?" Mr. James asked and gave Patsy a little nudge. But Patsy was in no mood to kid. "Aw don't worry, your mother and Patience filled me in. I heard it was jumpin'," he said, with a hearty laugh.

"Ah man, Dad, you said you wanted *me* to tell you," Patsy whined.

"It's okay, Patsy," Mr. James said as they drove up to their driveway. "Why don't you run in the house and make me a tall glass of iced tea. I'll be inside in a second. And when I come in, I'll be all ears. I want to hear your favorite thing about the recital. As a matter of fact, tell me every-thing! Do you remember how to use these?" he said, pass-ing Patsy his key ring.

Patsy snatched her father's keys and was inside her house in a matter of seconds. She washed her hands and grabbed a glass out of the cabinet and as many ice cubes as her hands could hold. She threw the cubes in the glass and poured her dad's tea. "Here you go, Daddy," Patsy said as her father walked through the door. Before Mr. James could even sit down, Patsy began. "Daddy, I want to dance this summer. Can I dance this summer? Ms. Saa said I could dance with her this summer. I want to go. Dad, she is really nice and beautiful. Do you know all the older girls go? I want to be a big kid and dance too."

"Whoa, whoa, whoa," Mr. James said, hoping Patsy would slow down, "I thought my little reporter was going to tell me about the show?"

Mr. James had not realized Patsy had been planning to reveal her summer activity idea. He thought he'd be hearing about the show, but Patsy had been beaten to the punch on that. While she was sitting out on the Davis's doorstep, she realized she would not be beaten to the punch on a summer activity. Patsy would not let anyone else make plans for her big kid summer. She would not wait another second to bring her big-shot idea to his attention. She heard what her mother had said to Mrs. Davis, and Patsy knew she had to get her idea on the discussion table first.

"I was going to tell you about the show, Dad, but Mommy and Patience already told you. Can we go to Legends now so you can sign me up? Please, pretty please. Hurry Daddy, before Mommy comes home," Patsy pleaded.

"Well Patsy..."

"Yippie! I'm a big shot! Yippee, woo-hoo!" she said, jumping up and down.

"Well, what about rollerblading, scavenger hunts, and your buddy Miles? You aren't going to Sunnyside Day Camp with him this year?" her dad asked.

"Oh Daddy, keep up. I'm a big kid now. I don't do that stuff anymore...and Miles went away for the summer," Patsy said with a tone that made her dad think he should have known better than to ask.

"Humph. Did you ask your mother about this, Patsy?"

"Nope," Patsy responded, now hopping on one foot. "It's a surprise."

Mr. James could tell Patsy was excited. He knew that she wanted her summer to be special since she was headed for Melbourne's upper grade building in the fall. Yet he also knew Patsy got bored quickly. When she took gymnastics class, she begged her parents to let her quit after three classes. She followed up with karate but dropped the lessons when she became interested in fencing. Then there were the guitar lessons and the swimming lessons. The list was long and Patsy was only eight and a half years old. Mr. James did not want this to be another one of Patsy's passing fancies. "Patsy, don't get all excited yet. I have to talk this over with your mom."

"Okay Dad!" Patsy said and ran to her room.

CHAPTER 14

Laundry Day

"*I have to talk this over with your mother,*" Patamela cracked as she placed her hand on her hip and fiercely shook her index finger at her bedroom mirror. She was so tickled by her imitation of her dad that her cackling frenzy spiraled into a face-forward belly flop onto Patience's bed.

"Ho-ho hee, ho-ho hum, Legends, Legends, here I come," Patsy sang.

She was not at all worried about her dad talking to her mom. She could not think of a better way to get her mom onboard than to have the idea come from her dad. It was not that Patsy's mom was a pushover, but her dad's approval could easily tilt the scales in favor of a Legends-packed summer. All her father had to do was give a green light to Patsy's request.

Patamela sprang to her feet and fearlessly pounced on Patience's sturdy mattress. "Chuck, we'll take a Legends summer for fifty billion-gazillion!" she roared like the contestants her mother watched on those television game shows. "Come on, Daddy, big summer, big summer," she whooped with eyes shut and fingers crossed. She imagined she was rooting for her father to draw a chance at a Legends summer grand prize. Patsy was so absolutely sure of her future as a twinkle-toed Legends celebrity that she pictured her photo in a book just like the one Mr. Jackson kept in the Melbourne library.

"*Whee!*" she squealed, leaping off the bed. She grabbed her hairbrush, placed its handle near her mouth and projected her voice, "IN-TRO-DU-CING, Legends' newest leading lady, the one, the only, Patamela 'Hot Hoofs' James. Yay, yay, Hooray!" she cheered.

Her mom could never give the thumbs down on such a great summer activity idea. How could she? Even Patsy's *ain't-afraid-to-whip-it-out, emergency-use-only, just-in-case* argument was convincing. After all, it rested on word-for-word remarks made by no other than Mrs. James herself on Saturday night.

"Those Legends girls are so talented!" her mom had said. "They really know how to put a show together. I wouldn't mind seeing them perform again. I'm surprised neither of you ever asked to attend."

At the time, Patsy would have gobbled down an entire plate of burnt jelly beans smothered in a garlicky sardine casserole before joining Legends, but that was before her mom socked her with today's humdinger of an announcement. Patsy never saw it coming. Yet her mom's big talk of activity ideas was the call to action she needed to get thinking. And since Patsy's brain worked best under pressure, the Legends idea had come to her quite easily.

"I've got her right where I want her," Patsy said with a haughty snicker. "All that fuss she made over those Legends girls—I've got it registered right up here," she professed while tapping her temple. Even if her father's efforts bombed, her mother would still be putty in her hands.

Patsy had just the weapon—her mother's soft spot for a certain someone whose name happened to rhyme with *poofawney*. That someone already attended Legends, and she could do no wrong in her mom's eyes.

"Legends must be the best in the whole wide world if Imani goes, right, Mom?" Patsy would say. "That ought to bowl her straight over," Patsy hooted.

There was no doubt about it. Patamela's activity strategy was pure genius. In Patsy's opinion, the Legends in Step summer program was just what she needed to kick off her huge summer, plus it would give her parents the peace of mind they craved. Since Ms. Daye, Mrs. Dwyer, Mrs. Lewis, Lizzie's parents, and Tamara's parents all permitted their children to attend, Legends had to be Patsy-proof. The last thing her parents would agree to was a program that let Patsy run wild. After the laundry day mishap two years ago, Patsy's parents had vowed never to leave Patsy without a tight schedule again.

Although the laundry day disaster was one cataclysmic catastrophe Patsy tried to erase from her memory, she knew her parents had not forgotten. Truth is, she'd only been trying to help out around the house. During the summer months, Patsy always helped her mom with the household chores—namely Friday afternoons when she helped her mom with the laundry. Yet this particular Friday, Mrs. James said she was too tired to move a muscle.

Patsy was great at sniffing out an opportunity, and even when she was six she knew this was a chance to impress everyone and prove she was a big helper. So on that day Patamela rushed to the upstairs bathroom. She unsnapped the shower curtains and gathered all the washcloths. She snatched the towels off the racks and scampered down the hall. Patsy brought everything to the laundry room in the basement.

Patsy spotted the washing detergent beside the washing machine. She knew she could use the detergent to wash the towels but was uncertain as to how she would accomplish her other task.

"Hmm, how do you wash shower curtains?" she asked herself. Since shower curtains were for the shower, Patsy figured you would have to use the same stuff you use to clean the tub.

Patamela ran back upstairs and grabbed the items she saw her family use when they were doing the household chores. First she grabbed her mom's yellow rubber gloves. Then Patsy reached underneath the sink to open the cabinet containing the lemony, spring breeze fresh containers of cleaning products. She scooped the items in her arms then tiptoed past her mom who had fallen asleep on the couch.

Patamela grabbed a chair, climbed onto its seat, and opened the washer's lid. There were clothes at the bottom of the washer. Patsy could see they were Prince's team uniforms. This is great! Patsy thought. Not only would she do her mom a favor by doing some of the laundry, but she would make Prince happy in the process. He enjoyed dirtying his freshly washed clothes during games because it proved he played hard and gave his best.

Patsy threw all the towels and washcloths into the washer directly on top of Prince's uniforms and grabbed her dad's goggles off his workbench. Patsy knew how to fasten goggles because she wore them whenever she helped her dad with a job. Patamela decided the goggles would come in handy because she was making one of those super concoctions she always saw Miles making. During his experiments, he would always tell her he was dealing with "powerfully explosive ingredients."

"Pass me my goggles and rubber gloves Patsy," he would say. "I need them for protection."

Patamela shook the entire box of detergent in the washer. That would cover Prince's uniforms, she thought. For extra cleaning power, she added more than half of the lemony, spring breeze fresh cleaning products and most of the white-powered tub cleaner. That would cover the bathroom stuff. After all, Prince's outfits were dingy, muddy, and stinky, and her mom always said the bathroom stuff was filthy. That was when Patsy remembered that her mom planned to wash all their sheets and comforters too.

Patsy ran upstairs to get them and quickly realized she'd need to drag them down one at a time. They were big and fluffy. When Patamela reached the washer with the first comforter, she climbed back on the chair and laid the bedspread on top of the shower curtains, washcloths, towels, and uniforms.

Patsy was all set to go. But there was a slight problem. The washer lid wouldn't close. She tried to push everything further down into the washing machine, but still the lid would not stay closed. That's when Patsy decided to sit on the lid while the washer did its job. Although some of the comforter was sticking out, she didn't expect that would make much difference. She switched the start lever on and fidgeted through a few sitting positions—until she heard the most nerve rattling sound.

Berdabur, Burr, Burr, Berdabur, Burrrr, the machine began to make a dreadful noise. The noise was so loud she jumped off the machine and when she did, bubbles started flowing out of the machine onto the floor. That was enough to send Patsy running out of the house and down the street to Miles's house where she hid under the bed.

Only when Patience and Prince arrived home from camp and heard the noise did their mom wake up and discover the problem. And it was a big problem. The basement was covered in suds. Eventually her family found her at Miles's house, hiding beneath the bed. But for all the damage, Patsy didn't really get in too much trouble. Her mom understood she was just trying to be a big helper. But her mom also understood that above all, Patsy needed a schedule and she needed strict supervision.

The laundry day disaster was the reason Patsy was sure her parents wouldn't miss an opportunity to send her to Legends. It was the perfect answer to their *"what are we going to do with Patamela?"* dilemma.

Patamela pulled out her pad and began writing the names of all the girls in the recital that went to both Melbourne and First Blessed. But before Patsy could even finish writing the second name on her list, her mom and dad were calling her downstairs. Time to eat already, she thought, and jogged down the steps.

"Hello Ms. Lady," her mom said, smiling at Patsy.

Patsy leaned in to give her mother a hug. "Hey Mommy."

"Well, your brother and sister are eating at Ms. Daye's tonight so I decided to pick up fish and chips for the rest of us," her mom said.

Patsy loved fish and chips and figured this was a good sign. Her dad must have told her mom all about Legends in Step. She knew she had nothing to worry about.

"What's new today?" asked her mom as she set a pitcher of lemonade on the dining room table.

"Patsy has something she'd like to share, don't you, Patz?" her dad said, shooting Patsy their undercover, insider's-only wink.

This isn't how it's supposed to happen, Patsy thought. She wanted her father to tell her mom first so it would seem like his idea.

"Patsy, what did I miss?" asked her mom.

"Miss? Oh nothing...it's just that Dad said...I mean, I told Dad that I want to dance," Patsy murmured, forgetting to employ Plan A—*persuade Mom by using her own words against her.*

"Really, Pattie Cakes?" Mrs. James jibed, but Patsy could not tell whether her mom was happy about the news or just faking.

Hesitantly, Patsy continued, "You always say I should be Imani's friend. If I dance at Legends, I can spend all the time in the world with her."

"All of a sudden you want to be Imani's friend? Are you sure you need dance classes to do this?" her mom said with a hint of suspicion. "You didn't want to dance before, and you definitely didn't want to be Imani's friend. What brought this on? Did your father...?"

"Nooooo, her father most certainly did not," Mr. James responded, before Mrs. James could ask the question.

Mrs. James walked over to Mr. James to offer him a plate of food and playfully nudged his shoulder and both her parents burst into a hearty laugh.

Just look at them, Patsy thought. There her parents stood, jesting and joshing as her summer's future hung in the balance. Patsy knew once her parents started kidding around that they would be laughing it up until sundown. They would forget all about her Legends summer.

"I'm not finished! I have another reason!" Patsy interrupted.

"Lower your voice, Patsy. If you have something to say,

speak up, but let's not be rude," her mom retorted.

Boy was Patsy in the hot seat now. She had to think of something to give her case legs again and fast. She had no idea her mother would rip her last-resort, if-all-else-fails, Imani-Daye plan to shreds.

"Mom, she asked me!" Patsy blurted.

"Who asked—Imani? What are you talking about? And are you sure that's the tone you want to use, young lady?" Mrs. James asked.

"She asked me," Patsy repeated. "She didn't ask anyone else but me," she exclaimed with a burst of confidence.

"Who did?" her father asked, irritated by Patsy's rash tone.

"The pretty lady, Ms. Say," Patsy said, pronouncing the dance teacher's name incorrectly.

"Oh yes, Ms. Saa. I like her." Mrs. James replied.

"She asked me, Ma, you heard her," Patsy proudly stated.

"So this is what this is all about, Pattie Cakes? You got yourself a special invitation?" her mom teased.

"Watch out! We must have a star in the making. She saw that special James glow in you, huh kid?" Patsy's father said as her parents chuckled.

Patsy did not know what was so funny to her parents. She was just trying to save her case—a case her dad had nearly flubbed. She would have never thought to say she got a special invitation. She did not see Mrs. Saa's pleasant conversation as a special invitation. She received invitations on colorful cards with balloons, bears, and cake for her classmates' birthday parties all the time. What Mrs. Saa gave was not an invitation at all, but the lifeline she needed to crossover to Melbourne's older building.

How come her parents refused to understand all the

big girls were in dance? Patsy had not finished her list, but there were many girls attending Legends in Step from Melbourne and First Blessed. They were all considered big girls and Patsy was still an "eavesdropping, little bit, baby sister."

Patsy longed to be a part of their world. She had not forgotten about the older girls who yelled out to Imani. They did not ask Imani about her brother, Ishmael; they asked Imani about Imani. Patsy was just as mature as Imani and could probably dance better too. Yet this had nothing to do with Imani, nor did it have to do with some silly invitation from Ms. Saa. This was about finding a summer activity all by herself that would prove for the last time she was the big kid, big shot she professed to be. This was about making a huge change to her summer schedule that could potentially change her life forever.

PART 2

CHAPTER 15

·····························

The Wait and the Reward

"Patsy, are you sure you'll be all right?" Mrs. James asked, letting go of Patsy's hand.

"Of course I will, Ma. I'll know almost everyone there," Patsy answered, fervently skipping to keep up with her mother's pace.

From the looks of things, it seemed Mrs. James was considering leaving her to settle into her first day alone. "*Well, all right*," Patamela gingerly pipped.

It was almost impossible for Patsy to hide her elation. She had been waiting for this day for two slow weeks. She thought she would never escape the Davis's front stoop or Mrs. Davis's constant prying into what the trouble was between her and Miles.

Each day at the Davis house Patamela faced a fierce round of questioning unmatched since Ms. Grais accused her of nibbling Imani's gingerbread man during snack time. And with each passing round, Patsy's quick wit and vivid imagination took a licking worse than the day before. Mrs. Davis seemed to determine to uncover the root of the problem between Patsy and Miles, and Patsy was just as determined to keep it covered up. She was equally determined to avoid talking with Miles when he called the Davis house. Mrs. Davis would call Patsy to the phone, but Patsy would pretend not to hear and then offer a genius excuse later. "I was busy practicing the spelling words my mom gave me," she said one day.

And each day when Miles called, Patsy would hear Mrs. Davis say, "Miles, exactly what is going on between the two of you?"

The wait had been torture. Yet during Patsy's two week stay at the Davis's, she had actually grown to like Ella Jo. Patsy taught her new words, gave her Messy Tessy (an old baby doll she no longer wanted), and taught her how to color in a coloring book. The fun almost ended when Ella Jo started sucking Patsy's black crayon, but Patsy decided to forgive and forget Ella Jo for acting like a piglet. She guessed it was better to suck a piece of the rainbow than on an already gummy shirt sleeve.

As a matter of fact, Patsy had almost completely broken Ella Jo of the sleeve-sucking habit. She did it by broadening Ella Jo's slurp repertoire to include popsicles and lollipops. And when Patsy discovered Ella Jo would suck her pacifier after it was rolled in cookies and cream ice cream, she used that trick all the time. By the time Patsy's last day with the Davis family rolled around, Ella Jo had kissed her slobbery sleeve days good-bye.

Patsy hadn't escaped Mrs. Davis's clutches a moment too soon, even if she was going to miss Ella Jo. Now here she was, heading up the sidewalk to Legends in Step. The moment she'd been waiting for.

"*Come on*, Pattie Cakes, I thought you'd be in a hurry to reach their front door...You aren't getting a case of cold feet, are you? Do I need to take your hand again? You're moving pretty slow for someone intent on collecting their just reward. Are you *sure* you deserve this?" her mom asked through a wisp of a smile.

"Don't be silly, Mommy. I've come to collect!" Patsy declared.

According to Patamela, there were a *million* reasons why she believed this particular reward was headed her way.

NUMBER ONE, it took her some getting used to, but she had finally stopped tattle-telling. *NUMBER TWO*, she had single-handedly figured out why Imani and the other girls were considered big girls. And *NUMBER THREE*, she'd been promoted to the next grade despite having to sit through Lizzie's boring tutoring sessions.

Patsy walked into Legends with her mom. She was convinced she had crossed over to the land of the big-shots. Patsy knew it was time for her mom to leave her side. She hoped her mother would trust she could find her teacher and class on her own. "Geez, it sure is getting late," Patsy said, looking at her bare wrist as if she was looking at a wristwatch. "Isn't it time for you to go to work, Mommy?" But before Mrs. James could reply, Patsy started in again. "I thought you were going to let me find my way around by myself?" she said with an annoying whine. "I'll be fine, Mommy. I have everything I need." And that she did.

That morning, Patsy had eagerly slid into her pink leotard and tights. They fit perfectly underneath her white T-shirt, orange sweater, and blue jeans. Over her right shoulder, she carried the small purple duffle bag Mrs. James bought from the dance school's gift shop. It read *Legends in Step* with a ballerina in silhouette and allowed her to carry her ballet slippers, tap shoes, and lunch. There was nothing keeping Patamela from big kid, big shot status now—except of course, Mrs. James's refusal to leave.

Patamela led the way. She poked out her chest and bravely followed the arrows pointing to the welcome desk. The program's registration sheets were visibly strewn about the table's desktop. Patsy raced to find her name.

Using her index finger she followed the entire row, *Patamela James / 8 wks / Red.* Patsy had no idea what 8 wks or Red meant, nor did she get a glimpse at the paper long enough to figure it out. She decided to ask someone who might have an idea. "Mommy, what does 8 w-k-s Red mean?"

"I'm not sure, Patamela, but I am sure we'll find out," Mrs. James replied.

"Oh, that just means the number of weeks you are registered to attend our program and the group you're in, sweetie," the woman behind the desk cheerfully stated. "As soon as you go downstairs to the performance theater, you'll see all the other children that belong to your group. Every day you'll report downstairs to meet your teacher and class before coming upstairs. There's more space down there for the teachers to get organized."

Mrs. James nodded her head as if she understood the teachers' need for space and organization.

"I'm Ms. Watkins," the woman continued, "If you have any questions, or need anything, just ask me. I'm the school's secretary."

"Well, thank you," Mrs. James said. "I'm Pamela James and this is my daughter Patamela. I must have missed you when I came a couple of weeks ago."

"I know. I took a little vacation. Chile, I had to drop my son to his father's house for a couple of weeks so I could get a breather. Today's my first day too, Patamela— well my first day back. I had a good time and I'm still enjoying myself. The boy will be back next week and then I'll be working over time. He's a terror," the woman said jokingly.

"I understand honey, I understand," replied Mrs. James with a giggle.

Patsy *did not* understand and hated when her parents were engaged in grown-up talk, especially when she had a date to be somewhere. She was ready to go downstairs and meet the other girls in her group (and she was even more ready to start her tour). Who cared about Ms. Watkins's vacation or her son? Patsy sure didn't.

Ms. Watkins handed Patsy a piece of red crepe paper then led her and Mrs. James to the stairs leading to the school's performance theater.

Patsy scurried down the steps with Mrs. James strolling behind her. Mrs. James gracefully peered through the window of one of the performance theater doors, and asked again, "Patsy, are you sure you're going to be all right? You won't be able to reach me until the end of the day. Remember Mrs. Wright is picking you up *and* taking you home."

"I know, Ma, you already told me," Patsy sharply replied.

"Okay Pattie Cakes, give me kisses," Mrs. James said.

Patsy kissed her mom good-bye and watched her walk up the steps leading back to the school's main floor.

"Yippie! I'm free!" Patamela shouted. She shoved the auditorium doors open and stood behind the last row of seats in the middle aisle. Patamela was absolutely enamored by the action. There were girls everywhere! Some girls were playing tag on the stage. Some were cartwheeling and playing patty-cake games, while others were seating in groups of four to six. The auditorium was popping with chatter and laughter.

This is my type of scene! Patsy thought. She watched as crepe paper of all sizes fluttered through the air. A few girls wore their pieces as necklaces, some tied them to their ponytails, and others pretended their pieces were kites. A couple of girls sat quietly with their crepe paper tightly crumpled in their hands.

Patsy noticed that not everyone had red crepe paper. Some girls held pink, some lavender, some baby blue, others had yellow, and some white. She walked down one of the aisles and wondered where she would sit. Just then, one of the teachers she recognized from the night of the recital clapped her hands twice. Most of the girls stopped in their tracks, quieted down, and clapped their hands in response.

"Ladies with the white flyers, I'd like you to go to the stage. Ladies with the blue flyers, please stand at the exit on the far right. Yellow flyers to the back of the..."

Patsy listened intently. She was waiting for the woman to give directions to the group with the red flyers. Patsy noticed a couple of familiar faces, but all the girls she knew were either already in line or holding pink or lavender flyers. As far as she could tell, no one she knew was holding red. Patsy gave all of the girls with the red flyers a closer look.

"*Wait a minute...*They're all babies! This must be a mistake!" she said softly with a scowl. If Ms. Watkins was not so busy running her mouth about her son, she would have given me the right flyer, Patsy thought. Patsy knew she should have had a pink flyer like Imani and Tamia or at least a lavender flyer like Nicky Dwyer and Nicky Lewis.

"Red flyers sit in the front row," the teacher finally announced.

Patsy, still shaken from her new discovery, slowly moved to the front row. "Most of you know me. Some of you may not. My name is Ms. Patterson and I am one of the founders of this school. I teach ballet, modern jazz, and technique," said the teacher. "Ladies, after today you will not be using your flyers. Please remember the name of your group and your classmates," she urged. "White flyers, you are *the Doves*. Blue flyers you are *the Hummingbirds*. Yellow flyers, you are *the Fireflies*. Pink flyers, you are *the Fairies*. Lavender flyers, you are *the Butterflies;* and Red flyers, you are *the Lady Bugs—my Ladybugs*."

"A Ladybug? Gross!" Patsy blurted. She did not want to be a stinky, plump, dotted, give-people-cooties Ladybug. She wanted to be a Fairy. Her leotard was pink and it matched the pink flyers. Imani had done it again! She had made a fool out of Patsy, just like in kindergarten when she had the ribbons that matched Patsy's outfit. Now she had the flyer that matched her leotard and she was in a better group too.

Fairies were pretty. You had the good fairy, the tooth fairy, and even Tinkerbell. And butterflies, they were beautiful. Patsy would always try to catch them when she was much younger, but a ladybug? Patsy would not stay a Ladybug for another minute! She marched right up to Ms. Patterson. "Excuse me, Ms. Patterson," Patsy said tapping her on the back, "I have the wrong flyer."

"You do?" Ms. Patterson asked. "What's your name?"

"My name is Patamela James," Patsy answered proudly, preparing herself for Ms. Patterson's apology.

"Hmmmm, let's see, Patamela James," Ms. Patterson looked on her clipboard. "No, I think we have it right. Patamela James...Red."

"I should be pink!" Patsy said rolling her eyes and folding her arms.

"Pink? I don't think you'd be pink. Isn't this your first time here?" Ms. Patterson queried.

"Yes, but Imani and Tamia..."

"Oh, I see the mix up," Ms. Patterson said as she bent

down to look Patsy square in the eyes. "You want to be with your friends and you'll miss them?"

Patsy wanted to say no, they are not my friends, but I am in their classes at Melbourne and First Blessed. Patsy decided to remain silent. If Ms. Patterson thought she missed her friends and this would get her to the Butterflies or Fairies class, so be it.

When Ms. Patterson realized Patsy was not going to answer her question, she continued, "Well, I'm really sorry, but you won't get to see your friends during class. You may get a chance to see them during recess or on Fridays."

Patsy offered a most crooked snarl and stared deep into Ms. Patterson's eyes. She did not blink once. Her fiery stance did nothing to change Ms. Patterson's tune.

"*Oh sweetie,* the groups are based upon how long each child has been dancing and what level of dance they perform on. We did not mean to split you from your friends." Ms. Patterson consoled. "It's just that they've been dancing longer than you. They already learned what you will be learning this summer. Aren't you happy they are getting a chance to move on and learn new steps?" Ms. Patterson paused and pulled Patsy in closer. "Aren't you happy you have a chance to catch up?" Patsy still did not answer. "My beginner's class isn't so bad. Don't you want to be one of *my Ladybugs?*"

Patsy glared at Ms. Patterson even harder, as if she could see straight through her. What did she mean by *my Ladybug* anyway? Patsy did not want to be a Ladybug and if she was, she would not be *her Ladybug*. She would be Ms. Saa's, wouldn't she?

Patsy looked in Ms. Patterson's eyes and asked, "What do you mean by, be one of *my* Ladybugs?"

Ms. Patterson grabbed Patsy's hand and walked over

to the front row seats where the other girls holding red flyers were seated. "Everyone, this is Patamela. She is a Ladybug. In fact, all of you are Ladybugs. You are my Ladybugs because I am your teacher. Girls, we are going to have a blast!"

The group of little girls bustled with excitement. They anxiously swung their feet and wiggled in their chairs. "We have a lot of hard work ahead of us," said Ms. Patterson.

The girls looked at each other and frowned.

Ms. Patterson continued, "I'm sure hard work doesn't scare you. You came to learn how to dance and I'm here to teach you how."

Patsy wanted to pull her teeth through her ears! She was that aggravated. Where was her mother? Ms. Watkins would have to locate Mrs. James so she could pick Patsy up early. Just wait until I tell Mommy that I'm a stinking, bottom-of-the-barrel insect and Ms. Saa isn't even my teacher, she thought.

When I see that Ms. Saa, I'm going to pull one of those braid-twist things so hard, her tongue will drop down to her ankles, Patsy thought. She's not that beautiful anyway—and she's a fibber. Patsy remembered what Ms. Saa had said, word for word. She said, "Join *my* summer session."

"...making me think she would be my teacher," Patsy griped. She never once said join *Ms. Patterson's* summer session.

Chapter 16

Ms. Patterson's Little Buggers

Patsy's eyes welled with tears. Imani wasn't one of her favorite people and neither were the Nickies, but she would give anything to be with them now. Miles and Destiny will never hear about this, she vowed to herself while bugging her eyes to keep from crying.

Just then, Patamela spotted Ms. Saa across the room near the exit. She was with the Hummingbirds! Patamela was surprised to see her and wished she could run to give her a hug. She wanted to take back all those mean things she had been thinking. If Patsy could just get in a spot where Ms. Saa could see her, she knew Ms. Saa would pull her away from Ms. Patterson. Maybe she would even make Patsy a Hummingbird.

"May I say hello to Ms. Saa, Ms. Patterson?" Patsy asked, interrupting Ms. Patterson's speech to the Lady Bugs about line safety.

"I don't think it's a good time right now Patamela. All the classes are heading upstairs. Maybe you will be able to see her later. Line up, Ladybugs," Ms. Patterson instructed.

Patamela had to think of something—and quick. She

had to get out of Ms. Patterson's line. She looked toward the exit and saw Chantal, one of the many girls who had a crush on Prince. "Hey Chantal!" Patsy yelled.

The entire auditorium turned to see who had caused such a disruption. Chantal appeared embarrassed but raised her hand half-heartedly and waved. Ms. Saa smiled at Patsy then turned back around.

"*That's it?*" Patsy mumbled under her breath. No hello, how are you, happy you made it, come over here with me? Patsy thought. How could she have pegged Ms. Saa so wrong? Patsy stared down at her shoes.

"Hello cutie-pie. Give me those dimples!" Patsy heard a gentle voice say. It was Ms. Saa! She had lined her kids up right beside Ms. Patterson's class. In fact, all the classes were lined up in the middle aisle to leave the auditorium.

"Hi Ms. Saa..." Patsy said sheepishly, "See, I came. I had my mom sign me up."

"Good for you!" Ms. Saa replied.

"Aren't you going to teach me?" Patsy asked.

"I wish I could, but I don't teach the Ladybugs. I work with the Fairies, Fireflies, Hummingbirds, and Doves," Ms. Saa said as she walked her class past the Ladybugs' line.

No fair, Patsy thought, holding back the tears that wanted to stream down her cheeks. "Bye Ms. Saa," she said softly.

Patsy really wanted to bawl now, but thought she would look like a *big* Ladybug baby if she did. What she needed was a plan.

It took only a moment for Patsy to think of one. In school, when she and Miles did not want to do a boring lesson or assignment, they asked permission to go to the bathroom. Then they would meet up and hang out in the hallway for ten or even twenty minutes at a time. She and Miles were notorious for mercilessly teasing the other students trapped in class doing work. Patsy figured even if she couldn't be in Ms. Saa's class, she could watch them whenever she wanted to.

Patsy's class filed down the hallway and up the stairs, just like the Hummingbirds. Patsy strained to look ahead and see which classroom the Hummingbirds were using. She wanted to be able to find them and Ms. Saa when she snuck out for her first spying session.

"I need a door monitor," Ms. Patterson announced, breaking Patsy's thoughts.

"A door monitor?" Patsy asked.

"*Me, me, pick me*!" Patsy heard coming from the middle of the line. Patsy turned to glare at the baby that did not know to raise her hand quietly. Every big kid, big shot knew that only quiet hands were picked.

"Great, come forward," Ms. Patterson instructed.

The little girl bustled to the door and held it open. Patsy was shocked. How could *Me Me Me* get the job?

"Let's go ladies," Ms. Patterson said as she led the class through the main floor's stairwell doors. Patsy figured Ms. Patterson needed to stop by the front office. To Patsy's surprise, Ms. Patterson led the class past a couple of closed rooms to a door not far from the front office. "Ladies, here is our room, Studio M1," Ms. Patterson said with a smile.

"Hey, where did the other classes go?" Patsy demanded to know.

"They went upstairs to their studios. We're the only Legends in Step youth class on this floor," replied Ms. Patterson.

Patsy's heart was crushed and her plan foiled. Not only was she on an entirely different floor than Ms. Saa, but the

Ladybug room was next to the front office. That meant too many grownups passing by and asking Patsy where she was headed or what she was doing in the hallway.

As the class walked through the door, Patsy scanned the room to get familiar with her new surroundings. The room seemed just as big as one of Patsy's classrooms at Melbourne. The entire room was a dull yellow and paneled with huge mirrors that took up each wall. Patsy noticed there were no mirrors on the ceiling. She thought that would have really been something to share with her parents. Each mirror had a bar running alongside it just like the bars Patsy saw ballerinas holding in her schoolbooks. She knew the ballerinas used the bars to balance themselves while doing stretches and difficult dance steps.

Patsy noticed that the floor had Xs of masking tape every few feet. There was even a cubbyhole cabinet like the one in Ms. Knibble's kindergarten classroom. A black velvet curtain hung at the back of the room.

In the front of the room was a wooden chair that looked too small for Ella Jo. A long wooden stick was leaning on the mirror beside it. On the left side of the front mirror sat a stereo with an old record player behind it. Patsy giggled when she saw the record player. She did not have one in her house, but her grandmother always played her blues records on one when Patsy visited.

Ms. Patterson instructed the girls to get in their leotards and tights. The girls whose leotards and tights were underneath their clothes were instructed to take off their outer clothes. Ms. Patterson showed them how to fold their outfits and place them in the cubbyhole with their name above it. The girls needing to change went behind the black curtain two at a time before doing the same.

"Ladies, if you're done, I'd like you to take a seat with

me here," Ms. Patterson said as she sat down on the floor. "Make a circle. I want everyone facing each other." The girls quickly took their places in the circle one at a time. Maybe this won't be that bad, thought Patsy. She'd never had a teacher who did not mind sitting on the floor and dirtying up her outfit—a pretty outfit at that.

Ms. Patterson had on a red leotard with a long red and white wraparound skirt that tied at her hip. Patsy guessed she wore it to match her class's red crepe paper and her pearl colored ballet slippers. Her hair was tightly pinned in a French roll and Patsy liked her faint red lipstick. "It's time for us to learn each other's names," Ms. Patterson announced.

Ms. Patterson pointed to the girls one at a time. She asked each girl to share her name and what she liked about dance. Patsy thought everyone's answer was babyish. "I like to spin." "I like to twirl." "I think ballerinas are pretty." "I want to tap." Patsy could tell she was the oldest in the class and could not wait for Ms. Patterson to ask her why she wanted to come. Patsy would tell Ms. Patterson that Ms. Saa personally invited her. Then she would list all the dancers whose names she knew from the presentation she did for Ms. Grais. That would show Ms. Patterson she was dealing with a dance expert who should be placed in one of the other groups.

Patsy was ready to *really* sock it to her new teacher and classmates, yet Ms. Patterson was taking forever to get to her. It seemed as if she was skipping over Patsy intentionally. Patsy looked at her fellow Ladybugs and became even more frustrated. There were eleven girls (twelve including Patsy) in her class, and Patsy thought all of them were worse than Ella Jo used to be. One girl constantly sneezed and wiped her runny nose with her hands. Another little girl interrupted Ms. Patterson every two minutes to ask if it was nap or story time and another cried about missing her teddy.

Ms. Patterson lifted herself from the floor and dusted off the back of her skirt. She then called the girls one at a time, directing them to stand on their own special X. Patsy fumed! Had Ms. Patterson forgotten she had not asked Patsy to introduce herself?

"Ms. Patterson, Ms. Patterson," the *Me, Me, Me,* girl whose name Patsy learned was Fatima (Faye, for short) shouted.

"Yes, Faye," Ms. Patterson answered.

"You forgot about her," Faye said, pointing at Patsy.

Tattle-tale baby, Patsy thought.

"I didn't forget. I introduced Patamela downstairs," Ms. Patterson replied.

"But she never got to say what she liked about dance," Faye said with a concerned look.

"Okay, please introduce yourself formally and let us know why you came to dance," Ms. Patterson said.

Patsy decided to fix Ms. Patterson for taking her sweet time. She had no right to welch on attention Patsy deserved. Ms. Patterson acted as if she'd forgotten Patsy existed.

Patsy decided she would not dare allow any of the girls to call her Patsy. Patsy, as sophisticated and mature as she possibly could, simply stated, "My name is *Patamela James*," in the same tone Mrs. James used on Ms. Watkins earlier. That would show Ms. Patterson and her creepy-crawling, red-and-black-polka-dot babies that she was way too mature for the likes of them.

When Ms. Patterson asked Patsy what she liked about dance for the second time, Patsy simply shrugged her shoulders. Ms. Patterson paid no attention to Patsy's sour attitude. Instead, she informed the girls about a handout she wanted them to take home detailing their daily schedule and requirements before graduating to the Butterflies. The rest of the day, they would go over basic technique, like posture and first, second, and third position. After lunch, they would gather with the rest of the school in the performance theater to watch a movie about Alvin Ailey and Judith Jamison, who Patsy had already learned about from Mr. Jackson. The Ladybugs were excited. "Big babies," Patsy grumbled.

CHAPTER 17

Beaten by the System

Almost a week had passed since Patsy started the summer session at Legends in Step Dance School. She tried over and over again to explain to her parents why she hated being a Ladybug, but they told Patsy she wasn't being a good sport. Even after Patsy begged to leave and go back to Sunnyside Day Camp, her parents said no. They told her she made a commitment to learning dance, at least for the summer. According to her parents, it was her responsibility to make the best of the situation. *Responsibility*, the word Patsy could not wait to hear used in the same sentence with her name, was ruining her life!

To make matters worse, Mrs. James repeatedly asked Patsy some silly question about seeing a glass half-empty or half-full. Patsy did not understand what her mom meant by the question because there was no glass around. Even if there were, she would only leave the glass half-empty or full depending on what beverage it contained. Eventually, she did get the gist of what Mrs. James was trying to say.

"Patsy, being a Ladybug isn't so bad. Ladybugs are very cute and people consider them good luck. Have you asked yourself how you could bring your class good luck? Or your teachers? Or the school? I haven't taught you to be a sourpuss. Think of all the neat steps and techniques you're learning," her mom encouraged.

Patsy did not care about lucky ladybugs or anything else her mother was saying. Her father took a different approach. "Patsy, complaining, pushing, and shoving doesn't change things. You have to think your way out of situations. I'm sure you'll come up with something."

Patsy had been thinking hard all week. In the meantime, she followed her mother's advice and gave being a model Ladybug her best shot. She tried, but she did not have the slightest idea how that would bring good luck to her class. Truthfully, she was sick of first, second, third, fourth, *and* fifth position. "Relevé, plié, elevé, blah, blah," Patsy would mock during class. It was enough to make a *Harlem School of the Arts* ballerina pick up wrestling. It was downright unbearable!

To pass the time during her vermin-infested stay, Patsy had learned to entertain herself with what she considered to be somewhat fascinating mirror games. She would either watch herself in the front mirror as she held her breath as long as she could, or she'd observe her potbelly balloon then flatten as she exhaled and then inhaled air.

"I can't take it anymore!" she would clamor ever so often.

And who could blame her? She was certain if you compared the time she spent each day at Legends to the length of the Mississippi River, it would be about even. Her day was that long. First thing each morning, Ms. Patterson led the Ladybugs through a series of tedious breathing, stretching, and technique exercises. After breathing and technique class, she walked them to the Ladybug classroom to meet the college student tutors. There, the college tutors led them through practice math exercises from their current grades and upcoming grade levels. Afterwards, they went back to Studio M1 for Ms. Patterson's ballet class, followed by lunch in the cafeteria and recess in the school's playground. After recess, they returned to the classroom for reading, then to Studio M1 for tap and modern jazz.

Sadly enough, you would have to be equipped with Miles's mega-magnifying glass to find a high point in Patamela's long day. As a big kid, big shot activity, Legends sure was lousy.

Thank heaven Patsy cherished her time in the Ladybug classroom. She loved being around the college tutors. Patsy knew that Patience thought she was a big kid; but Patience's beauty treatments, secrets, and mall outings were a drop in the bucket compared to the maturity of the college tutors. Most of the college tutors were far, far away from home. Patience, on the other hand, had a crybaby fit when their mom planned to send her to sleep-away camp. "I bet you didn't even cry when you left!" Patsy announced after some of the tutors traced how far away from home they were on the class map.

Patamela was impressed. The college tutors were fun, mature, and smart too. Smart enough to know as long as they tutored the youth dancers for a couple hours during the week, they could attend the dance school at a discount. Patsy hoped the tutors would not give up their discounts because she looked forward to seeing them each day. They brought the Ladybugs all types of treats and let Patsy tutor the other kids who were not as advanced in their studies as she was in her own. Even better were the days when the Ladybugs were allowed to do arts and crafts in place of reading or math.

Aside from their occasional arts and crafts class period, the only other activity Patsy considered somewhat of a highpoint was recess. Patsy lived for recess at Legends just as she had at Melbourne. During recess, she got a chance to see the other girls from the other classes. Even Imani had come up to her a few times during recess. Patsy thought Imani would tease her about being a Ladybug, but was she wrong.

"Patz, what steps are you guys up to?" Imani cheerfully asked. "If you need any help, just let me know. I could show you."

To Patsy's astonishment, Imani even invited her to play with her fellow Fairies. Patamela especially enjoyed watching them practice their new routines. They seemed to be having much more fun than Patsy in their classes.

Unfortunately for Patamela, recess and the time with the tutors was just not enough to keep her sane. She hated technique class, ballet, and modern jazz that much. Ms. Patterson didn't even have the decency to play music during technique class. "*One, two, three, four, and stretch two, three, four*" is all Patsy heard.

Nevertheless, Patamela preferred her teacher's counting to the music she played during ballet class. Patsy could not understand how Ms. Patterson didn't get Patsy's hint about the music. Patsy would spend the entire ballet class yawning to express how dull she thought the music was.

Whatever happened to the "Fat and Greasy" days? thought Patsy. The Ladybugs had not had tap dance yet. During the time they should have been tapping, Ms. Patterson went over steps the other girls found difficult or did a dance routine from one of her shows.

"See, girls, this is what you can dance like if you work

hard," Ms. Patterson would say.

Patsy was uninterested. She wanted to tap like Lizzie and Tamara did at the recital.

"Excuse me, Miss Patamela," Ms. Patterson would chide after overhearing one of Patsy's grunt-filled grievances, "I do know how to tap. I've just decided not to teach tap this year."

According to Ms. Patterson, two new teachers would come in for an hour each day to teach tap class instead, but they would not come for another week.

Patsy anticipated the arrival of her new teachers. Their arrival not only meant two fresh faces but a chance for Patsy to shake things up. Ms. Patterson was too boring and she was really starting to get on Patsy's nerves.

Patsy knew she'd been *beaten by the system*, (a saying she got from Miles that she knew he'd lifted from his dad). Yet, Patsy would never say it around her dad. Actually, Mr. James prohibited her from using the phrase. "The only system that can keep someone down is the one wired incorrectly in their own mind," he would say, still Patsy thought the phrase had a ring to it. But this time, Patsy decided she needed to listen to her dad's words. I've *gotta* get the wires in my mind working correctly, Patsy said with a smack to her forehead. She refused to be beaten by the Legends system.

Chapter 18

Bye Bye Babies

Patsy needed an unflappable strategy to escape Ms. Patterson's class, and she needed one in a hurry. Even though she was excited about getting two new teachers and would miss the Ladybug tutors if she went upstairs, she was ready to move on. She was sick and tired of the humiliation. Every time she introduced herself to a friend of Imani's or the Nickies, she felt embarrassed.

"How come we never see you around?" they would ask. Patamela would have to tell them it was because she was in Studio M1. She would always have to come clean about being a measly Ladybug. Patsy did not enjoy being a measly bug one bit and she still didn't have a plan to change her lowly station. There had to be a way for her to be skipped. That's it! thought Patsy. She would ask to be skipped. Ms. Patterson said the classes were based on how long you danced *and* what level you danced on. If she paid attention in class and got *really, really* good, wouldn't Ms. Patterson have to skip her? Of course she would—bye bye babies!

Patsy ran downstairs and flew through the front door.

She hoped her mom wasn't running behind schedule.

"You seem pretty excited this morning, Patsy," her mom observed, referring to her eager facial expression and the hurried manner in which Patsy jumped in the car.

"I am, Mom! I'm going to be the best Ladybug Ms. Patterson has ever seen. But not for long," Patsy added slyly.

Mrs. James had no time to listen to Patsy explain what she meant. She was too busy mapping a game plan. She would have to manage getting Patsy to Legends and herself to work after running a few morning errands. Patsy was happy not to explain herself; she didn't want any adult jinxes on her idea.

Unfortunately, Patsy's mom's errands made her slightly late for camp. "*Fiddlesticks*," Patsy grumbled as she ran into the building. Her mother's untimely errands had sabotaged her plan. Class had started and she would have to wait until recess to corner Ms. Patterson. Yet Patsy's question could not wait. It was an emergency!

"Ms. Patterson! Ms. Patterson! I can be skipped, can't I? I can be skipped to the Fairy or Butterfly group, right?" Patsy hollered as she burst through Studio M1's door.

"Patsy, settle down. You're late and we are beginning our breathing exercises. Please change and get to your X," Ms. Patterson instructed. "I won't stand for another disruption."

Patsy noticed her class was silent. Their eyes were closed and they were concentrating on their breathing techniques. Everyone, that is, except Faye, who had one eye opened in order to watch Patsy change.

Patsy slowly walked to her X, which was right beside Faye's. "How come you want to leave?" Faye asked. "Don't you like it here with Ms. Patterson? If you leave, I'm leaving too."

All of a sudden all the girls in the class focused their attention on Patsy. "If you go, I'm going." "Me too, me too." "I want to be skipped," the girls whined. Patsy had not realized how much the girls in Ms. Patterson's class looked up to her. Not only that, they believed being skipped was for special little girls and boys and they wanted to be special along with Patsy.

"Ladies, that is enough," Ms. Patterson said impatiently. "Patamela, I do not appreciate you disrupting my class. If you must know, you cannot be skipped until next year."

The other girls were not fazed by Ms. Patterson's news and resumed their breathing stances. Patsy, on the other hand, was devastated. "You have to be a Ladybug for at least a year," Ms. Patterson continued. "You can skip being a Butterfly, but you cannot skip being a Ladybug. Here you learn all of the important techniques you need in order to dance correctly. You must learn to move properly to avoid injury. That's how you learn to dance flawlessly, Patamela. You do want to dance flawlessly and properly don't you, Patsy?"

Patsy rolled her eyes with all the strength she could muster. Although her mother had taught her that rolling her eyes was rude, uncivilized, and unladylike, Patsy felt it was called for. She was furious! At least I didn't suck my teeth or sass Ms. Patterson like I could have, Patsy thought. That fact alone should make her parents proud. After all, what was a little eye roll? Hadn't she taken her disappointments pretty well up until now? Of course she had.

Patsy stared at her dance mates and seethed. If they weren't such copycat big mouths Ms. Patterson would have agreed to skip me, Patsy thought. Yet the more she tried to believe that would have taken place, the more something in her gut told her it would not have happened in a billion years. "*You're dreaming kiddo.*" That's exactly what Miles would have said about Ms. Patterson skipping her to the next class.

Patamela twirled one of her pigtails around her index finger. It was what she did when she was in deep thought. Maybe Ms. Patterson secretly wants to keep me with the Ladybugs, Patsy mused. As Patsy stared at Ms. Patterson, it all began to make sense. Though two observations in particular struck her as dead on.

The first reason was simple. Ms. Patterson was trying to punish Patsy for disrupting her class. This was not the first time Ms. Patterson was frazzled by Patsy's behavior or untimely questions. Patsy always knew when Ms. Patterson was annoyed with her because she would look down at the floor, shake her head, then take a deep breath before addressing her. "Hmmpphhh...Patamela, Patamela..." she would say.

Patsy figured Ms. Patterson had it in for her. She was fed up with interrupting her lesson to ask Patsy to get back on her X, to stop showing some student how to do a step, to quit playing with her stomach, and to stop holding her breath. Patsy only did these things to help out or to keep herself occupied. She never set out to disrupt the class. Was it her fault she learned the baby dances so quickly? Ms. Patterson's quest for revenge was unfair!

The other possible reason that Ms. Patterson refused to skip Patsy was to keep Patsy all to herself. Maybe she did not want to share Patsy with the other teachers. Patsy knew she was a better dancer than the other girls. She never had to be told more than once how to do a step. She must have been planning to tell everyone she was responsible for Patsy's smooth, twinkle-toed moves. That beastly Ms. Patterson is trying to take credit for my natural-can-keep-up-with-anything-you-throw-at-me talent, thought Patsy.

As Patsy kicked the idea around in her head, she became more and more sure that this was the reason Ms. Patterson wouldn't skip her. Truth be told, Ms. Patterson wasn't very talented as a teacher. Patsy concluded that Ms. Patterson was doing a rather poor job of teaching the Ladybugs and that she was obviously picking up the slack because all the girls came to her for assistance. If Ms. Patterson let Patsy leave, she would have to face the fact that she was having a hard time teaching the brat pack. Maybe she would even lose her job if she couldn't teach the girls how to dance well. Patsy had heard of teachers who lost their jobs at Melbourne when they did not do a good job teaching their classes. It was clear. Ms. Patterson *needed* Patsy to stay with the Ladybugs. Patsy was the reason she still had her job.

"How sad—using a kid to do her adult job," Patsy said quietly with a sigh. Yet, Patsy had to tell herself the truth. Was it *really* Ms. Patterson's fault? After all, she had been given a bunch of slowpoke baby students that couldn't keep up. Still, that was no reason to make Patsy suffer.

Patsy figured that if she was a gifted student, the whole world should know. It was just like her grandmother always said, "*Baby, don't dim your light for nobody!*"

What kind of woman was Ms. Patterson to go around dimming the lights of unsuspecting little girls? Patsy did not know and it didn't matter. All she knew was Ms. Patterson wouldn't dim her light much longer—not if Patsy had anything to do with it. Patamela was committed to finding out whether there was any truth to what Ms. Patterson had said about being skipped and she would not give up until she did. And when she did, it would be, "*Adios inchworms!*"

CHAPTER 19

Curiosity and the Cat

Just as the Ladybugs were lining up to meet the tutors for math, Patsy came upon a brilliant discovery. She realized she had access to a top-notch Legends expert. Getting to the bottom of the skip policy cover-up would take even less effort than she thought.

"That larvae-loving Ms. Patterson's no match for Ms. Watkins!" she hooted.

Ms. Watkins (secretly known as Chatty Cathy on the Legends playground for the way she cornered parents into lengthy conversations) could get anyone talking—or talk anyone into anything (including five years of Legends classes if you let her talk long enough). If anyone on God's green earth could change Ms. Patterson's mind about skipping Patsy, it was Ms. *"Lips-never-stopping, news-to-get-the-jaw-dropping"* Watkins. And would you believe her ears were just as lethal as her lips? Why if Patsy was Little Bit, Ms. Watkins was surely *Whole Lot.* She was always on the cutting edge of Legends news because her desk was smack dab in the middle of the Legends front office. If by any chance Ms. Patterson was fibbing about the skip policy at Legends, Ms. Watkins would know.

Patamela was ecstatic! After all, Ms. Watkins was a friend of the James family. She and her mom had become friends the very first day of camp. "If you need anything, just ask me," Ms. Watkins had said. Patsy remembered clearly. Ms. Watkins may not have been talking to her directly, but Patsy was the one in need! She *needed* Ms. Watkins to put an end to Ms. Patterson's unfair harassment.

Patsy was not a bit afraid to bring a case against Ms. Patterson. She was prepared to take it as far as the Supreme Court if she had to. Luckily, she only had to take it to the front office. There was no way Ms. Patterson could deny Patsy's claims, not with the mountain of evidence Patsy had stacked against her.

Patamela was a great dancer and teacher. Ms. Patterson was not. Patamela knew she was talented and should be skipped. Ms. Patterson knew this as well. It's exactly why she didn't want to let Patsy go. She wanted Patsy all to herself. Ms. Patterson saw the James glow shining in Patsy the first day she laid eyes on her. That's why she didn't let me talk to Ms. Saa, Patsy speculated. She didn't want Ms. Saa to see my glow.

Patsy believed she was on to something and now it was time to do something about it. She would ask the tutors if she could go to the bathroom. As soon as they said yes, she would sneak to the front office. Patsy didn't want to trick her tutors, but she knew she couldn't level with them. After all, they were practically grownups. They took that *responsibility* stuff quite seriously and would think the responsible thing to do was accompany Patsy to the office. She couldn't risk them reporting her every word to Ms. Patterson.

Patsy scrambled to her desk and flew through her arithmetic. She got all her multiplication tables and long division problems correct—except for one. "Ms. Lauren, may I please go to the bathroom?" Patsy asked, giving Lauren her most innocent smile (the one that made her dimples the most noticeable).

"Did you finish your work, Patsy?" Ms. Lauren asked.

"Yep, Mr. David corrected them."

"Hurry back, Patsy, we're going to do collages of dance scenes after everyone finishes."

"All right!" Patsy yelped and darted out of the room.

"No running, Patsy," the three tutors shouted in unison.

Patsy whizzed down the hallway. She sailed past a number of classrooms with their doors shut tight but stopped short when she reached a classroom door left ajar.

"That's funny," she mumbled. She knew the door was usually closed. Patamela decided she would be a Good Samaritan like the story in her Sunday reader. She would close it. But as she reached for the doorknob, some unusual sounds startled her.

Patsy looked through the cracked door and noticed a group of chairs and desks pushed to the far side of the room. They were stacked on top of one another beneath the window. That's strange, Patsy thought. She knew the desk and chairs should be set up like her classroom. Patsy inched closer and peered through the opening. Behind one desk she saw two legs with white sneakers on the feet.

Although she couldn't see the mystery person's entire body, she knew she was about to bust one of the girls playing around. Now Patsy was no longer a tattletale, but she knew a good thing when she saw one. She could tell Ms. Watkins and be skipped for being an excellent hall monitor.

Patsy inched forward. "Enrr. Ennrr. Ennrr. Powg!" she heard. "Men, back to the trenches! Their alien technology is too advanced," quickly followed.

Patsy stood in shock as she watched a little boy pretend to shoot her and then dive over a chair.

"Ugh! I've been hit! But I think I got him too. His brains are pink and white and dripping down the side of his face. Copy, copy. Can you hear me? He isn't going down, I said he isn't going down!" the boy yelled into his imaginary walkie-talkie.

"Wait a minute," Patsy said, putting her hands on her hips. "Who are you calling an alien? And stop shooting at me! Don't you know that's rude? You shouldn't play with guns—not real ones or fake ones—silly boy," Patsy reproved. "If you point your gun at me one more time, I'll come over there and you'll be sorry! I'm not an alien and I'm definitely not a boy alien!"

In fact, Patsy and Miles played fake guns all the time, but they never shot at each other. They always shot at the imaginary bad guys. Who did this boy think he was? Calling her a brain-dripping boy alien just because of her ribbons (her pretty ribbons that matched her pink leotard) was outrageous.

"I'm going to tell on you! Whose class are you in?" Patsy demanded.

The boy paid Patsy no attention and continued to fire his gun. Patsy stormed out of the classroom to go find someone in charge.

"Ooh, excuse me, Patamela," she heard as she nearly lost her balance from the woman's accidental bump. Patsy looked up. "Ms. Watkins!" Patsy said, surprised. Patsy was so bothered by the little boy she forgot about the question she'd been planning to ask Ms. Watkins. "Ms, Watkins," she continued, "there's a boy in that room all by himself with no teacher!"

"I know, Patamela. I put him there," Ms. Watkins responded.

"You did? Why would you do that?" Patsy demanded.

"That's my son. He's waiting for me to bring him breakfast."

Patsy couldn't believe her ears, "Your son?"

Ms. Watkins smiled as she lifted the two, small white paper bags in her hand from the deli across the street. "We are going to have breakfast together. Care to join us?"

"No thanks," Patsy grunted.

As far as Patsy was concerned, that little silly boy would pay. Ms. Watkins began walking to the classroom with Patsy following close behind.

"Your son has moved all the chairs and desks. He made a war zone! He was even shooting at me. AND he called me an alien. He said I had pink and white brains dripping down my face—and he called me a BOY ALIEN at that."

"He did, did he?"

Ms. Watkins was a little too calm for Patsy's taste. "Yes he did! He shouldn't play with guns you know. Not real ones or fake ones. That's what my mom says. Didn't you teach him that?"

Ms. Watkins was taken off guard. She could not believe Patamela was questioning her about disciplining her child. "Patsy, I have told him numerous times that guns are very dangerous and I do not like his war games."

"Well, he didn't listen," Patsy said, folding her arms as she stood in the doorway beside Ms. Watkins.

When he spotted his mother, the little boy scrambled to one of the desks and sat down.

"Kamal, don't even try it young man. You're busted. I asked you to sit quietly and wait for me to bring your breakfast. Why can't you follow directions? Were you shooting at this nice little girl?"

"You tattletale baby!" Kamal shouted at Patsy.

"Baby? Baby?" Patsy rolled up her leotard sleeves—which was hard to do because they were so tight. "Those are fighting words," she said as she headed in the little boy's direction. "My brother taught me how to fight and I can whip boys bigger than you!"

Ms. Watkins swiftly moved to intervene. "Now Patsy, I wouldn't want to bother your mother with a report of bad behavior, especially one about fighting.

"Aww, let her go. They don't call me Knock-'em-Out-Kamal for nothing," Kamal bragged.

His mother glared at him. "You don't hit girls, young man," Ms. Watkins said. "And you, *chile*," she said turning to Patsy, "you are too intelligent and pretty to ever lift a finger to fight. You can talk it over. Rest assured, Patsy, Kamal will apologize." Ms. Watkins turned her head to look at Kamal and waited for his reply.

"I'm sorry," he mumbled.

"You aren't as sorry as you're going to be if I can't watch you here at work. There is no one to baby-sit you. Everyone is on vacation. Don't make this a difficult summer, young man. As soon as we finish, you will put the desk and chairs back properly and sit with me in the front office, you hear? You just can't handle being left alone," Ms. Watkins said, exasperated. "Patsy baby, sit here. Have a piece of sausage and some orange juice. Rest your nerves."

Patsy sat down and stared at the little boy as she nibbled a sausage link. Knock-em'-Out-Kamal, *HA!* Patsy thought. The boy had so many scuffs and scrapes on his face, Patsy thought Kamal the Knock Down Clown would be more fitting. It was clear he lost every rumble he had ever been in. It was a shame that Ms. Watkins did not know to put cocoa butter and vitamin E on his scars like Patsy's mom did. That gook always made Patsy's scars heal better. They would probably even disappear if Patsy did not pick at them so much.

Patsy scooted her chair closer to the table to give the boy a better looking over. After much consideration, she figured the Watkins owned a mean cat with sharp claws that attacked Kamal every day. Either that, or he fell on his face a lot.

Patsy watched Kamal blow bubbles in his orange juice. His complexion reminded her of Sugar Daddies—the candy she loved so much. Patsy continued to study Kamal as if she were studying her weekly spelling words. His red cap was pulled all the way down to his brow and flipped to the back. Patsy thought Ms. Watkins should make him turn his hat to the front. Patsy would bring that to her attention tomorrow—along with her concern about the tiny, silver earring in his left earlobe. Prince had wanted an earring in his ear too, but her parents had refused. Patsy knew Kamal was much younger than Prince. How he pulled that off, she would never know.

"So Patsy, where are you supposed to be?" Ms. Watkins asked. "I'll have to take you back to class and tell Ms. Patterson you were with me for a moment."

"I'm not with Ms. Patterson now. We're in math class."

"What were you doing in the hallway? You never made it where you were going," Ms. Watkins observed.

"Oh yeah," Patsy said. "I was coming to ask you if anyone can be skipped to the next group."

"Why would you want to be skipped? Aren't you having fun with the Ladybugs?"

"*Ah*, not really," Patsy said, unable to hide her embarrassment.

"That's 'cause she's with the babies!" Kamal said, laughing.

"Watch it, Kamal," said his mom.

Patsy glared at Kamal. "All my friends are in the other classes. I already dance better than everyone in my class. I think I should be skipped."

"Good luck with that one," Kamal mumbled.

"You're that good, Patamela? Well, the problem is that it wouldn't be fair to the other girls who were good as Ladybugs. They were never skipped. Do you know Imani? She was an excellent dancer even when she was a Ladybug."

"Ugh. Not again!" Patsy whined.

"Imani, now that's a big, goofy ribbon-wearing tattle-tale goody-two-shoes!" Kamal added with a snicker.

"Kamal, Imani is not here to defend herself, and I have talked to you about name calling," Ms. Watkins snapped.

So, I'm not the only one who feels this way about Imani, Patsy thought. Imani had been kind to Patsy the last couple of days, but Patsy knew once school started she would be the same tattletale she'd always been. Patsy wasn't fooled. She didn't like Kamal, but maybe she could grow to like him. Anyone smart enough to dislike Imani just might be a friend.

Ms. Watkins got up from the table, threw out the trash, and used the towelettes to wipe the desks clean. "Put the chairs and desks back in place," Ms. Watkins said to Kamal and Patsy.

Patsy pushed the chairs and desks with her hips. She

tried her hardest to make them screech as she pulled them across the floor. She was peeved with Ms. Watkins for asking her to help Kamal when she hadn't moved them in the first place. She didn't say a word though. After all, she'd gotten to eat some delicious sausage links and was able to ditch the beetle brats for a while. Maybe Ms. Watkins could get her out of class every day. She wouldn't be in a different class, but it could still be bye bye babies—at least for a little while.

CHAPTER 20

A Two-Timing Patsy?

"So Patsy, I hear you have a new boyfriend. What's his name?" her dad asked with a wink.

"I don't have a boyfriend, Dad. I don't even like boys," Patsy said and then bit into her ear of corn.

It was the first time the James family had had a quiet Sunday dinner at home in a couple of weeks. Patsy was especially happy because her favorite aunt and uncle were joining them. Usually the James family used their Sunday dinners to catch up with the current news in everyone's lives. But lately Prince and Patience hadn't been around on Sundays—or for entire weekends for that matter. They'd been busy working on their church's Bricks of Love Project.

The project introduced them to families in the community that had lost their homes to fire. Kids and adults from First Blessed worked alongside the families to rebuild or fix the damaged homes. All the children had the benefit of making new friends and of learning how to do new things.

The program was reserved for children eleven years of

age or older, which meant Patsy couldn't participate. She envied her brother and sister. The adults from church were teaching Prince and Patience and all the other kids how to paint, plant gardens, pave driveways, and even install siding. It was just another example of the exciting summers Prince and Patience always experienced—without Patsy.

Even when the three of them had attended Sunnyside Day Camp together, Patsy felt left out. Prince and Patience's Sunnyside groups would kayak, hike, ride all the big kid rides at the amusement parks, and make homemade ice cream. Patsy's group would be left behind to create knickknacks out of popsicle sticks, hold silly bake sales, and visit the zoo—again. Every summer it was the same. Patsy would prepare herself to follow her siblings and then discover she couldn't because she wasn't old enough.

Now she'd finally chosen her own summer activity and she was doing her best to be a big kid, big shot. She wanted to talk to her favorite aunt and uncle about that—not answer questions about some dumb boy! Patsy was frustrated. Everyone was talking about Prince and Patience and their volunteer work, and Patsy wanted them to talk about what a big kid she was turning into.

"Little Bit, you know you have a new boyfriend...Ma, what's that kid's name?" Prince asked, interrupting Patsy's thoughts. He inched forward to get a glimpse of Mrs. James in the kitchen. Mrs. James looked at Patsy from the kitchen doorway and smiled.

"His name is Kamal, right Patsy?" Patience answered.

"That's not my boyfriend! I can't stand him!"

"Come on, Little Bit. You talk about him every single day. *Mommy, today Kamal did this. Patience, wanna hear what Kamal did today?*" Prince said, mimicking Patsy's voice. "That's all we hear about."

How was that all he and Patience heard about? thought Patsy. They weren't even home enough to hear her say much of anything!

Mrs. James came out of the kitchen carrying another steaming platter of fried chicken, mashed potatoes, and collard greens. She placed the platter on the table. "I don't know about him being Patsy's boyfriend. Her new trouble buddy may be more like it. Since Miles isn't around, she gets in all types of mischief with Kamal instead," Mrs. James said, looking at Patsy's aunt and uncle.

Patsy frowned at her mother. She was trying to show her aunt and uncle she had matured. Instead of helping her case, her parents and siblings were accusing her of having a crush and getting into mischief. Patsy knew what getting into mischief meant. It meant she was not behaving like a big kid.

Mrs. James tried to clean up her comment after noticing Patsy's frustration. "Patsy talked about Miles too. No one said he was her boyfriend, so leave her alone."

"Ma, that's not true. We always say she's going to marry Miles. Hey, I'd forgotten all about Miles...Patsy is two-timing. She has two boyfriends!" Prince said, placing his hand over his mouth to feign shock.

"Drop it, Prince," Mrs. James said in a stern tone.

"Don't be so serious, Pam. If the girl likes boys, the girl likes boys. It's natural, and cute," Aunt Deidre said. "Patsy, how's this new one? Is he nice to you? Does he bring you candy or write you sweet poems?"

"He better not!" Mr. James interrupted.

"How smart is the boy? That's what I want to know," Uncle John said. "'Cause that one across the street, now he's smart. Stick with that one. We'll all be rich from one of his kooky inventions one day."

"Oh hush, John," Aunt Deidre said, as the family laughed heartily.

Patsy did not appreciate being the brunt of her family's jokes. She was happy her mom had nipped Prince's and Patience's meddling in the bud, yet she hadn't corrected Aunt Deidre or Uncle John. Although Patsy found her aunt and uncle hilarious, she did not like when their jokes were directed at her.

"Can we talk about something else?" Patsy asked. "I bet those silly boys aren't talking about me at their dinner tables. And I don't want to talk about them either! It's gross!"

Everyone laughed and Patsy decided this would be a good time to ask her aunt whether they were going to have a baby soon. That's what Patsy had heard—and she couldn't wait. Finally she wouldn't be the youngest cousin at holidays and family reunions.

"Excuse me, Auntie Dee, Auntie Dee..." Patamela struggled to project her voice over her family's boisterous laughter. "Are you and Uncle John really...?" but before she could finish her question, both Aunt Deidre and Uncle John pushed away from the table.

"We've gotta get some sleep. It's some ways back to Atlanta," Aunt Deidre said.

"Yeah, we don't mean to be rude, or eat and run," Uncle John said with a hearty laugh, "but y'all know we only came to get some of Pam's fried chicken before heading back home."

"Oh, stop it, John," Mrs. James replied.

Patsy hadn't realized her aunt would be leaving so soon. Aunt Deidre and Uncle John kissed everyone goodnight, gathered their belongings, and headed for the stairwell. Just as Aunt Deidre reached the first step, she turned to Patsy and whispered, "Patsy, you're going to have to write me about this new boyfriend of yours. It'll be a secret between us girls."

Patsy was speechless. She stared as her aunt followed Uncle John upstairs to the guest bedroom. Well how do you like that? Patsy thought. She hadn't seen her aunt in months and she couldn't believe they'd spent their time talking about Kamal and Miles. She didn't get to ask about the baby or tell her aunt she was a dancer at Legends—and a gifted one at that. Aunt Deidre would have been happy to hear Patsy was doing big girl things.

Aunt Deidre was the ultimate big girl and Patsy was devastated. She desperately wanted Aunt Deidre to know that she was learning to be a performer too. Not a singer like Aunt Deidre, but a dancer. Aunt Deidre's job was to sing before the big stars got on stage to get the audience warmed up. She traveled all over the world to do so. Patsy cherished her aunt's stories and loved it when Aunt Deidre brought back pictures of her and Uncle John with all the big stars. It made Patsy feel like she had been right there with them. She often talked about the dancers that toured with her. She would have been proud of Patsy.

Patsy was fuming. Either Prince or Patience had told their dad that Patsy had a new boyfriend. And that fibbing tattletale was headed for a real bruising. Usually, Patsy didn't mind when her siblings teased her about that kind of stuff. They always teased her about Miles, but she knew they were just joking about them getting married. But Kamal was a different story. If Prince and Patience paid attention to her complaints, they would know he wasn't her best friend like Miles. He was her enemy!

"Those meddling tricksters! They messed everything up!" Patsy squawked as she stomped up the stairs.

155

If they hadn't given their dad the wrong information, he would have never asked about Kamal in the first place. It was their fault Patsy lost out on precious time she had to catch up with her aunt. "What a waste," Patsy bemoaned.

Patsy had a tremendous problem on her hands. Aunt Deidre thought she had the latest scoop, but she really didn't. The information Aunt Deidre got about her was all wrong. It was only half true. Patsy had no choice but to tell her aunt the real deal.

The real deal was that Kamal had been on her mind lately—but not in the way everyone was suggesting. She honestly despised Kamal. Patsy worked hard to keep him out of her mind, but that wasn't easy. The amount of melee he got away with at Legends was incredible, and that infuriated Patsy. She and Miles had all types of adventures together, but they got demerits and punishment for every single one. To Patsy, it seemed like Kamal never got in trouble. More than that, it seemed like he never got caught for starting trouble either. If she talked about him a lot, it was because of those reasons—not because he was her new boyfriend.

"I've got to set the story straight," Patsy reckoned. She grabbed a pencil and pad from her desk drawer and tore a piece of paper from her pad.

"*Auntie Dee,*" she began writing, "*I miss you. I am a really good dancer now. I don't like Kamal because he's bad. I don't want a boyfriend. Love Patsy...P.S. When will the baby get here?*"

Patsy folded the paper. She decided she could write "*To: Aunt Dee, From: Patsy*" on the top. She would not get in any trouble for writing her aunt. She was not passing notes at school; besides Aunt Deidre had told Patsy to write her a letter.

Patamela opened her bedroom door, got down on her knees, and crawled to the guest bedroom. She pressed her ear against the door. She didn't hear a peep, not a voice or even the television set. Patsy knew she had to hurry before someone (Prince to be exact) came upstairs and busted her with his usual, "*Whatcha doing, Little Bit?*"

Patamela opened the door and heard her Uncle John snoring. She crawled around to find one of her Aunt Deidre's shoes. Patsy figured that would be a great place to put her letter. Patsy used the light from the hallway to find her way around the dark room. "No, that's not it," she said to herself as her hand fell into a shoe. "*Phew wee,*" she squawked. It must have been Uncle John's shoe. It was big and smelled like old nacho cheese from the movie theater on Hurston Street.

Then Puddles appeared. Patsy knew his stupid panting would wake her aunt and uncle. "Get outta here, Puddles!" Patamela whispered fiercely. Puddles moved his head from side to side perplexed by Patsy's tone. Whenever she was on the floor, he believed it was time to play. "Get outta here, Puddles!" she said again. "Go on, go on," she insisted as she shooed him with her right hand. Puddles slinked away with his tail between his legs, but stood in the doorway to watch.

Just then Mrs. James reached the top of the stairs. "Puddles, get out of there." She pushed Puddles aside with her foot and closed the guest bedroom door.

As soon as Patsy heard her mother's voice, she laid flat and rolled underneath the bed. Her mother would not understand why she was in the guest bedroom. Patsy knew Aunt Deidre needed sleep and was not to be disturbed. If Patsy's mom caught her sneaking around the guest room, she would be furious. Patsy knew just what her mom would say too. She would say that Patsy should have given the letter to her to pass to Aunt Deidre. But Patsy knew her mom could be forgetful. Besides, Patsy's letter was just between her and her aunt. Aunt Deidre had said to write one and that it would be their secret.

Patsy rolled out from underneath the bed when she heard her mother's footsteps hit the bottom of the staircase.

"Patsy, is that you?"

Patsy greeted her aunt's shocked eyes.

"Girl, what are you doing? Did your mother send you in here to give us a blanket? We're fine," Aunt Deidre said.

"No auntie, I just wanted to give you this," Patsy responded, shoving the folded piece of paper in her aunt's face.

"Oh, okay." Aunt Deidre began to unfold the letter.

"No, Aunt Deidre, it's a secret. Wait until you're alone. Uncle John might be awake," Patsy pleaded.

"I don't think that's the case, but okay, Patsy. I'll read it in the bathroom, alone, when I get up," Aunt Deidre promised. "Now give me a kiss and let me get some sleep, angel."

Patsy gave her aunt a kiss. Mission accomplished, she thought. Now her aunt would know she was a dancer and that she had no intention of having a boyfriend. She wished she could have heard her aunt's latest stories or news about the baby, but it was too late for that. At least she did not let a fib about her and Kamal take the spotlight. Kamal got enough attention at Legends. Patsy wasn't about to let him get it at her home too.

CHAPTER 21

King of Legends

Patamela had met Kamal's kind before. He was an attention junkie, just like Sean Peter, The difference was Kamal could not be ignored and Sean Peter could be. The mere thought of Kamal made Patsy squirm. Whenever she heard his voice, her skin crawled and her teeth clenched. She couldn't help it.

Things might have been different between the two if Ms. Watkins would have taken Patsy out of class to share a meal every now and then, like the time she offered Patsy breakfast. Maybe then Patsy would have forgiven Kamal for calling her an alien, or maybe Kamal would have forgiven her for telling on him. Patsy figured they could have made up over buttermilk pancakes and hash browns, but that never happened.

"The nerve! Didn't even offer me one crumb...just plain ol' stingy!" Patsy would huff after spotting Ms. Watkins on her daily walk down the hall to bring Kamal his lunch.

Patsy could smell everything on Kamal's lunch menu from Studio M1. It was torture! While she was sentenced to peanut butter and jelly, tuna fish, or ham and cheese sandwiches stuffed in soggy, brown paper bags, Kamal got burgers and fries, deluxe heroes, or pizza—*room service style.*

The way Patsy saw it, she was suffering day after day as Kamal was rewarded with a delicious lunch for doing whatever he pleased whenever he pleased. He didn't even have to worry about a crew of creepy crawlers copying his every move. Nor did he have to worry about adults calling him disruptive or telling him what to do. It was unfair! Every day Kamal would do something unthinkable and get away scot-free. How could anyone expect Patsy to think her way out of the Ladybugs group with a distraction like Kamal? If he wasn't flying paper airplanes through her classroom door to smack her in back of the head, he was outside of Studio M1 mimicking the way she danced. Yet, according to Ms. Patterson, Patsy was the disruptive one.

In truth, Patsy only flew out of a lesson to chase Kamal after being provoked. If you asked Patamela, Ms. Patterson did not know what the word *disruptive* meant, because compared to Kamal, she was an angel—just like her Aunt Deidre said. Whoever heard of taking a scoundrel's word over an angel's? Well, that's just what everyone at Legends did, Patsy thought. No one seemed to care about Kamal's vendetta against the *cute little angel* in the Ladybug classroom or his despicable behavior. But Patsy could see straight through him. He's nothing but a menace! she thought, but everyone thinks he's the king of Legends!

The trouble Patsy had gotten into lately was all related to Kamal. Every time she tried to tell her side of the story she was dismissed: sent to the hallway or to the front office. She never got to see the college tutors anymore or her new tap teachers, Mr. O'Keefe and Ms. Hollingsworth.

Surviving Kamal had taken up all her time.

How could her mom call him her new mischief buddy? Kamal was no buddy of hers. He lived to make Patsy's life miserable. Just last week Patsy was sent to the front office four times because of Kamal's constant taunting—and the worst was yet to come.

CHAPTER 22

That Silly Boy!

Despite Kamal's distracting antics, Patsy had decided to become the model Ladybug her mother suggested she become. She *focused* on her tap lesson with her new teachers. She was not as focused as they would have liked, but she was as focused as she could be—seeing as she already knew the steps.

To be quite honest, Patamela was bored, but she was being careful not to do anything Ms. Patterson could label disruptive. At the current moment, Ms. Patterson was on break and away from the class, but Patsy knew that word traveled fast in Legends. If she did anything wrong, Ms. Patterson would surely find out.

Patsy figured she would keep herself occupied until the other students caught up. Normally, she would have offered to help, but not this time. She did not want her teachers to report anything to Ms. Patterson that might upset her. If there was one thing Ms. Patterson hated, it was when Patamela coached her fellow Ladybugs. Patsy guessed Ms. Patterson didn't like the idea of her star student showing her up in front of the little ones.

Patsy gazed out the classroom window overlooking Briarcliff Park. Briarcliff was always bustling with enough action to keep her eyes occupied for a while. Sometimes, if she was lucky, she could see the nursery kids from Parkside Preschool playing on the swings. She could always spot Madi, Mrs. Wright's youngest daughter out on the playground. That usually kept Patsy busy when she was bored.

But not today. Today the playground appeared empty, and that got Patsy thinking about the dreadful ride home with the Wrights. Mrs. Wright worked at the municipal building across the street from Legends, and let's just say Patsy had a bad case of *arthur-wright-us*. She wished her mother had never cut the carpooling deal with Mrs. Wright. Madi was a spy and a tattletale, and her older twin sisters (who Patsy and Miles had nicknamed Evil Doof and Evil Dumb) were even worse.

Patamela shook the thought of the afternoon's ride home out of her mind and stood on her tiptoes to see further into the park. There was still no sign of action to keep her occupied until the next dance lesson. She looked up at the clouds and decided to play one of her favorite games. She was the undefeated champ of making familiar faces and shapes out of the biggest, fluffiest clouds in the sky.

"Just a little bit to the left, yeah that's it! A teddy!" Patamela quietly mumbled as she air traced an outline of a teddy bear in the sky. But, just before she could finish the bear's right ear, she caught view of a little boy in the park. He was doing flips on top of the sliding board instead of sitting down and sliding. Patsy walked closer to the window—it was Kamal! That red baseball cap gave him away every time. He wore it every single day, whether it matched his outfit or not—and he wore it backwards at that. Patsy couldn't stand it.

"What is he doing there by himself?" she said to herself. "He needs to sit down. That's dangerous," she warned beneath her breath.

Kamal daringly flipped around the sliding board without stopping, each time faster than the last.

"I've had it!" Patsy yelped.

Kamal had gotten away with too much the last couple of weeks. Patsy was sure he was not supposed to be at Briarcliff alone. He may have had permission to be out on the Legends playground, but across the street in that huge park? "Of course not!" Patsy exclaimed. On top of that, he was not playing safely. Patsy was fed up with Kamal making his own rules. She knew just what to do. She would drag him back to the front office and demand that he be placed on punishment.

Patsy knew if she told Mr. O'Keefe or Ms. Hollingsworth what Kamal was doing, they would tell her to mind her own business. Even worse, they might tell her that Ms. Watkins would handle it. How could Ms. Watkins handle what she didn't know about? That was the problem with the Legends staff. No one ever told Ms. Watkins when Kamal was misbehaving. They simply ignored him. And the times when Ms. Watkins could have caught Kamal in some troublesome act, she was too busy getting the latest scoop on someone else's child to notice.

Well, Patsy thought, Kamal's day of reckoning is long overdue. Though she realized busting Kamal was a job for a grown-up, there was no grown-up willing to take on the job. She would have to handle things herself. Patamela raised her hand and asked if she could be excused to the bathroom.

"No problem Patamela, just hurry back," Ms.

Hollingsworth said.

Patsy's new teachers weren't as hip as Ms. Patterson was to her bathroom trick. They were always way too involved with the other girls to pay attention to how long Patsy was gone. She pulled the stunt on them a lot.

Patsy snuck past the front office. She slithered to the main entrance and carefully pushed the door open. There was no school safety guard at the front door like there was at Melbourne. Sneaking out was easy.

Patamela dashed down the steps and turned the corner. She wanted to cross the street exactly at the Briarcliff Park entrance. When the traffic light turned red, she crossed over to the park. Luckily, Kamal was still flipping around the sliding board bar without a care in the world. "Listen here silly boy! You're going to be in trouble for playing in here alone! You better come back to Legends with me, 'cause if you don't I'm going straight to Ms. Watkins!" Patsy said. Patsy planned to go to Ms. Watkins anyway, but Kamal didn't have to know that.

"Aww, make me, you big baby," Kamal taunted as he flipped around the sliding bar again.

Patsy fumed! She marched right up to the sliding board. "I'm going to count to ten. If you're not down by then, you're going to get it! One, two, three, four," she counted as she mounted the steps to the sliding board. He would have probably come down before she reached ten, but she saw a chance to get a clean slap on the back of his neck. She would be a fool to miss that.

"Hi Patsy. Whatcha doing?" Patsy heard an inquisitive voice call from the ground. She turned around to see Madi on line with her class from Parkside. "Where's your class, Patsy? Are you here all by yourself?" the little girl asked.

"Ah, ah, no, um, my class is..." Patsy did not know how

to respond to Madi's questions. She knew Madi reported everything to her mother. Patsy had no idea what to say to make Madi forget about this incident. Patsy knew if Madi told Mrs. Wright she saw Patsy in the park alone—and with a boy—Mrs. Wright would have Patsy's tap shoes on a platter.

Mrs. Wright, unlike Mr. O'Keefe and Ms. Hollingsworth, knew she had to keep a sharp eye on Patamela. She got a daily update from Ms. Watkins on Patsy's behavior so she could give Mrs. James a report. Today's slipup was just the thing Mrs. Wright was waiting for. She would ask Ms. Watkins why Patsy was in the park without supervision. Any answer out of the ordinary was sure to be reported to Mrs. James.

"Well, tell the little brat what you're doing here alone," Kamal said, giggling hysterically. Patsy froze. She could not think of anything to say.

Meanwhile, back in the Ladybug classroom, Faye was busy spilling the beans to Patsy's tap teachers. "Patsy should be back by now," she reported. "Ms. Patterson doesn't let Patsy go to the bathroom by herself, but you always let Patsy go by herself. That's why she never comes back."

The other girls nodded their heads in agreement.

"We will deal with Patsy when she comes back," Mr. O'Keefe said. "The rest of you need to worry about your shuffle step."

Just then, Faye pointed her finger at the window and hollered, "There Patamela is! There she is across the street! *Ooooh*, she's with that silly boy!"

The entire class ran to the window. Ms. Hollingsworth quickly rounded up the girls to quiet them down. Mr. O'Keefe zipped out of the room to notify the front office and then headed to the park.

Back at the park, Patsy was racking her brain to come up with a believable fib to tell Madi. She decided she would have to convince Madi she was on a top-secret mission. Prince and Patience use to play that trick on her all the time and Patsy was sure it would work on Madi. Instead of telling on Patsy, Madi would feel special to have been included in a big kid mission. Patsy was about to slide down to talk to Madi when she noticed Mr. O'Keefe quickly approaching the foot of the slide.

"Both of you come down right now! I cannot believe you children! Who gave you permission to come to this park alone?"

Patsy slowly turned her head to see if Madi was taking in everything that Mr. O'Keefe was saying. Madi looked quite perplexed as she awaited Patsy's explanation. Patsy turned to Kamal for guidance, but it was too late. He was already halfway down the slide, laughing. "It's no big deal," he yelled. "I come over here all the time."

"Mr. O'Keefe, I'm not with Kamal. I was telling him it was time for him to go back," Patsy said in an attempt to explain herself.

"Well, it seems like you were having fun right alongside of him," Mr. O'Keefe snapped. Mr. O'Keefe extended both hands for each child to grab hold of. "Grab my hand!" he ordered.

"Bye Patsy," Patamela heard a soft voice say from behind.

Patsy knew she was in trouble now. She had never had a teacher squeeze her hand so tightly in all her life. Mr. O'Keefe barged through the Legends doors with the children's hands firmly clasped in his. Patamela hoped she would get a chance to explain her side of the story. She wondered if her stomach would ever stop feeling like it had been tied around her ankles.

Kamal, on the other hand, was cool as a cucumber. It was as if he didn't care that every faculty member that happened to pass by either rolled their eyes, shook their head, or gave them a lecture. Every time someone said something to him about his behavior, he looked up in the air, hummed, or made faces behind their back. As Patsy sat in a chair in the front office, she began to feel she'd made a mistake coming to Legends. Then she heard Ms. Saa out in the hallway. Patsy slunk down in her chair and wondered if it was too late to find a closet and hide, but it was too late. Ms. Saa came in and Patsy could see the disappointment in her eyes. She said the same words Patsy had already heard over and over again.

"Patamela, we'll have to contact your parents. A car could have hit you, or worse, someone could have taken you away. We don't know if you can stay at Legends if you cannot follow the school's rules. We've spoken to you too many times," she explained with an exasperated tone. "Absolutely *incorrigible*," she grumbled, heading back into her office. Even Mr. O'Keefe and Ms. Hollingsworth were in trouble for not keeping a better eye on their class. She hadn't meant to get her new teachers in trouble. She loved them and she loved tap dancing.

How would Patsy convince Ms. Saa that she deserved to be a Butterfly or Fairy now? Each time Patsy opened her mouth to explain her behavior, she was ignored or unreasonably hushed. She had gotten in too much trouble the last few weeks and now her word was shot to pieces.

Sitting there in the front office, Patamela realized the odds were quickly stacking against her. She had learned more than she ever wanted to know about her upcoming fate. For starters, she would not be allowed to go back into Mr. O'Keefe's and Ms. Hollingsworth's class for the remainder of the day or the rest of the week. There were only three weeks left until the summer program's recital! Even though Patsy had her tap dance down pat and she knew there was no reason to panic, she would miss being in class. She enjoyed practicing the routine with her tap teachers. It did not matter that it was a routine for beginner babies. It was still kind of fun. They were taking this punishment stuff way too far!

"I disagree," Patsy overheard Ms. Patterson interject just as Ms. Saa was finalizing her punishment. "I think we need to have her sit out an additional week."

Patamela was devastated. She thought Ms. Patterson was overreacting. She hoped Ms. Saa wasn't a pushover, but by the time their conversation ended, Ms. Patterson had convinced Ms. Saa to stretch Patsy's punishment for another week. It wasn't long before they both agreed two weeks away from tap would do Patsy some good.

"It will teach her to appreciate class and behave," Ms. Patterson said. And Patsy heard Ms. Saa agree. They were certain Patsy would never risk her ability to participate in dance class again.

The frustration that Patsy had caused the Legends staff along with Ms. Saa's two-week punishment was enough for Patsy. She could have done without the long "maybe Patsy shouldn't be here for the remainder of the program" letter they planned to send home. Patsy wished she could make herself disappear.

Patamela had never encountered a group of adults more upset with her. Even Ms. Watkins was furious. She shared her disgust with both her and Kamal.

"Well, I guess you think you're grown, huh?" Ms.

Watkins said as she pulled Kamal's ear all the way to the faculty bathroom. Patsy did not want to know what happened once they got there.

When Ms. Watkins and Kamal returned from the restroom, Ms. Saa and Ms. Patterson handed out some more punishment.

"Ms. Watkins, we think it would be best for Kamal to sit in the front office with you for the rest of the program," Ms. Patterson said.

"Or, he will no longer be allowed in the building," Ms. Saa added.

Patsy knew they meant business. They ran the school and their word was final. Yet Kamal didn't seem worried at all. Patsy didn't know what Ms. Watkins did to him in the bathroom; but whatever it was, she needed to do it again. He obviously had not gotten the point. He was still acting like he was king! But even seeing Kamal get punished was not worth all this trouble.

Patsy was positively sure about one thing: Ms. Saa, Ms. Patterson, and Ms. Watkins would never have to worry about her again. If she had to be with the babies, then she would do her best to behave and put up with all the baby behavior. Trying to avoid it had caused her and everyone else way too much grief. She didn't have much longer before the Legends summer session was up anyway. After she got her big chance to show off her *light*, (a.k.a. her undeniable gift for dancing) at the upcoming recital, she would leave Legends and never return. *Stupid ol' one year to be skipped rule*, thought Patsy. They'd be sorry they mistreated such a gifted dancer and dutiful Ladybug.

Patamela was ready for Mrs. Wright to pick her up. She had a boatload of news to share with her parents. Legends was a shame and a sham. It ranked right up there with Melbourne. Just plain ol' unfair, Patsy thought. Her parents weren't going to believe their ears.

CHAPTER 23

The Boomerang Effect

Patsy could not wait for Mrs. Wright to pull up to her home. She took comfort in knowing she wouldn't get in much trouble there. Her parents would be too shocked about Legend's unfair practices and Kamal's behavior to make a big deal out of what she had done. Sure, she would get a small slap on the wrist, but it wouldn't be for crossing the street like Ms. Watkins and Ms. Patterson predicted. She knew how to cross the street by herself. Although she only had permission to cross certain streets and she had to be accompanied by Prince, Patience, or Miles, she did not expect her parents to make a fuss.

"Be safe crossing Kissamaine, you hear?" Mrs. James would call from the stoop whenever she and Miles were on their way to the 7-Eleven. And they were always cautious.

"They're making a big deal out of nothing," Patsy scoffed. After all, Kissamaine was a much bigger street than the one she'd crossed over to Briarcliff. "I won't get into any trouble over that," Patsy reasoned.

Patamela did, however, expect to get *a little talking to*

about her bathroom fib. She thought her parents might even hassle her about leaving the Legends grounds without permission—but not too much. After hearing all the unfair punishments Legends doled out, her parents would feel sorry for her. They would understand that she was only trying to help out the adults as a big kid, big shot should. They'd give her a big hug and cut her a huge slice of chocolate cake to make her feel better.

Unfortunately for Patsy, Mrs. Wright couldn't wait to get to her home either. When Mrs. Wright pulled up, she parked the car, marched in the door, and spilled the beans. Madi's Parkside teachers had told Mrs. Wright all about Mr. O'Keefe's outburst in the park. Furthermore, she had the lowdown from Ms. Watkins.

Patsy went straight up the stairs to her room without even saying hello to her parents. From the upstairs hallway she could hear Mrs. Wright. "...chasing each other down the hall, name-calling, at it everyday they said...Good teachers, nice young people, that's why she cuts up with them...Patsy knows I don't go for that *incorrigible* behavior," Patsy overheard Mrs. Wright reporting.

Any minute now, Patsy thought, believing her parents would ask Mrs. Wright how she figured she could come down so hard on Patsy with a set of twins as bad as her own. Yet, her parents never did. It was as if they were hanging on Mrs. Wright's every word.

Although it wasn't long before Patsy heard her parents trying to get Mrs. Wright to leave. "Thanks for letting us know," said Patsy's mother.

"Ooh, look at the time," her dad added.

"Oh my, I really need to get dinner on the table and you probably do too," Patsy's mom reasoned. "Thanks again for bringing Patsy home."

Patsy tiptoed into her bedroom, expecting to be called downstairs. After a few minutes she realized that her parents must have been reading the letter from Ms. Saa and Ms. Patterson. Then she heard, "Patamela James, you come down here this instant!"

So much for that huge piece of chocolate cake, thought Patsy, and she slowly walked down the steps.

"Since when do you cross the street by yourself, Patamela?" her mother inquired.

"Yeah, and do you know how quick you could have been run over by a truck or worse? You could have been snatched by a stranger," her father added.

"But, but, he was in the park all by him..."

"Let me say something, Patrick," her mother continued before Patamela could finish defending herself. "What is it with you and this boy?"

"Wait Pam, let me ask her this...Do you know how much money you've wasted spending all your time in that bathroom playing hooky? You better pray they don't kick you out," her father warned.

Mr. James promised Patamela she would work to give them back every dime they spent on her registration fee if she did. Her punishment would include doing all of her own household chores in addition to Prince's and Patience's chores—without receiving an allowance. Her allowance would be used to cover her Legend's registration fee—even if it took her all of junior high and high school to pay it.

Patsy was not only in trouble for the bathroom fib and leaving the school without permission, but for crossing the street alone. She even got punished for old incidents the Legends staff had never mentioned to her parents. Guess they remembered to put everything in that dumb ol' letter, she thought.

"Not a peep out of you this evening, young lady," her father said after they finished questioning her. "We're very disappointed in you, Patamela. Now go to your room."

And that's just what Patsy did.

"Man, Little Bit, what you'd do to get them so upset?" Prince asked her later that evening when he returned from a game of basketball at the recreation center.

"Yeah, I wanted to ask them if I could go to the movies with Lizzie, but they're on a warpath," Patience added before their mom called from downstairs.

"Patamela is on punishment," she announced. "If you have a question, you can direct it to either me or your father. Do you understand?"

"We understand. Yeah, we definitely understand," Prince and Patience answered.

"You guys come down here. Patamela doesn't have time to talk. She's busy thinking about her actions," their mom said.

Even Puddles kept his distance from Patsy. Patsy spotted him in the hallway and whispered his name, but Puddles just dropped his tail between his legs and scampered away.

CHAPTER 24

....

Feet Don't Fail Me Now

The two weeks of punishment passed slowly. Each day during tap class, Patsy was sent to sit in the front office. She never even looked at Kamal while she was there. When she returned home each evening, it was no better. Each night she had to eat dinner alone in her bedroom. Every toy that Patsy loved had been taken away too — her bicycle, rollerblades, jump rope, coloring books, treasure maps— and everything else her parents could think of that she enjoyed.

If that was not enough, Patsy had to write apology letters to Mr. O'Keefe, Ms. Hollingsworth, Ms. Patterson, Ms. Watkins, Ms. Saa, and to her classmates. She had to read each apology letter aloud in front of her fellow Ladybugs too. But that was all over now. The two weeks of torture were behind her—and now Patsy was busy with the rest of her class getting ready for the Legends recital.

"Patamela, try to keep up. Try and keep up!" Mr. O'Keefe yelled, clapping his hands each time Patsy made a mistake.

"Do you have to clap so loud, Mr. O'Keefe?" Patsy

177

asked as she stuck an index finger in each of her ears. "I'm giving my all here."

Patsy had been thrown a lightning-fast curve ball. Mr. O'Keefe and Ms. Hollingsworth had changed the entire tap routine. Patamela thought at least one of her fellow Ladybugs would have given her the heads up, but no one had, not even flap-jaw-fill-em'-in-on-everything Fatima.

"*Whew...*What happened to the other routine?" Patsy asked out of breath.

"We changed it during your stay away from us. The girls got better and we decided to add more flavor," Mr. O'Keefe replied.

Mr. O'Keefe stood in front of Patsy to demonstrate another combination of the new steps: *shuffle, shuffle, shuffle step, shuffle, shuffle, ball-change.* The steps looked easy enough, but Patamela was worried. She wasn't sure she had enough time to learn the routine changes. She knew she had better watch Mr. O'Keefe's feet with her undivided attention.

"Hey, can you ask them to be quiet? I'm trying to concentrate," Patsy said. Patsy's classmates were talking and laughing as she struggled with the new steps. "Routines shouldn't get changed, you know, that's why they call them routines," Patsy grumbled under her breath.

But Mr. O'Keefe's class was not the only class where the routines were changed. Ms. Patterson had changed her ballet and modern jazz routines too. Patsy didn't mind those changes because she'd been right there when Ms. Patterson decided to change them. Leaving Ms. Patterson's class wasn't part of her punishment because Ms. Patterson could "*handle*" her. Patsy sure wished Mr. O'Keefe would have known how to handle her a bit better a couple of weeks ago. That way she would have been front and center for all his new changes instead of in the front office with pinhead Kamal.

"Mr. O'Keefe, are you laughing at me?" Patsy warily asked before raising her left brow.

"Patamela, I told you before. I'm not here to laugh, I'm here to help. But this is what happens when you miss precious class time."

Patsy was beginning to think she had been set up. She didn't want to believe it, but it seemed likely. Her tap teachers had made the new steps difficult in a vicious attempt for revenge. Mr. O'Keefe and Ms. Hollingsworth are punishing me for my behavior during their class, she imagined. That's why they added those canes into the routine—to make sure I never catch up!

Very sneaky indeed, very sneaky indeed, Patsy thought, as she reflected on her teachers' ingenious scheme. Though, in all honestly, Patamela believed she had been punished enough. All she wanted to do was come back to class with a clean slate, but her spiteful teachers would not hear of it. They were trying to make her drop out of the recital, or worse, make her drop out of Legends all together.

Mr. O'Keefe and Ms. Hollingsworth were wrong to treat her so unkindly. "Wait a second," Patsy whispered to herself. She scrunched her face so tightly that her eyes squinted. That was always a telltale sign that she was on to something...This is all part of Ms. Patterson's plan to keep me from being skipped, Patsy thought.

It was crystal clear. Ms. Patterson had failed miserably at making the new jazz and modern dance changes too difficult for Patsy to learn. Patsy was far too talented to get left behind—especially since she was in class to learn every new step, prance, and jaunt. Patsy figured Ms. Patterson must have called upon Mr. O'Keefe and Ms. Hollingsworth for extra booby-trapping, light-dimming help.

With Patsy away for two whole weeks and a dance full of fresh steps, they knew Patsy wouldn't pick up the new routine in time for the recital. Her chances of being skipped would be blown! Everybody knew she would have to be good in all her classes to be skipped, not just in modern jazz and ballet. Her teachers had planned her downfall!

"I don't even want to be skipped anymore! Picking on me for no reason..." Patsy muttered.

"Again Patamela! Again!" Mr. O'Keefe yelled, scrambling Patsy's thoughts. But, before Patsy could pout or roll her eyes to show her disgust with Mr. O'Keefe's part in Ms. Patterson's evil plan, Mr. O'Keefe leapt directly in front of her.

"Mirror me, Patamela. Watch closely," he instructed in a most demanding tone.

Patamela followed Mr. O'Keefe's lead. He did what seemed like a thousand twirls on the heels of his shoes. After each full turn he stomped on the floor in order to break the spin, thrust his legs wide apart, spread his arms, and shouted, "Yeah!" Patsy giggled as Mr. O'Keefe made "a grin bigger than a mosquito in a bathhouse." That's just what her grandmother would have said.

Patsy thought the smile and the shouting was over the top, but she imitated him the best she could. She felt she would fall dizzy trying to keep up.

"Again, Patsy! *Spin-nnn*, break it with a stomp! Arms wide, smile for the audience, yeah!" he hooted.

Mr. O'Keefe had managed to drill his ditty into Patsy's head. She could not get the steps, but she enjoyed saying the catchy tune to herself, "Spin-nnn, break it with a stomp! Arms wide, smile for the audience, yeah!"

Although Patamela was enjoying the chance to hoot and holler during class time, she was beginning to fret. The extra attention she was getting from Mr. O'Keefe was not helping her learn the steps. And that Ms. Hollingsworth, all she did was pace back and forth and give an occasional "shame on you" shake of her head.

"What a sorry case," Patsy swore she heard Ms. Hollingsworth mumble as she held the large ruler in her folded arms. Even if she hadn't said it, her facial expression suggested it. There wasn't one drop of sympathy underneath those brows for Patamela.

"Twirl, spin, shuffle, ball-change...yeah," Patsy mimicked beneath her breath as Mr. O'Keefe led her through the step for the hundredth time. Sure, she was gifted, but this routine was too advanced for her. How did they expect beginners to pull this off?

And then Ms. Hollingsworth handed Mr. O'Keefe Patsy's latest adversary.

"Oh no. Not the cane," Patsy moaned. She lifted the back of her palm to her forehead, as if she would faint.

Patamela wanted to give Ms. Hollingsworth a swift kick right in the kneecap. Ms. Hollingsworth had witnessed the trouble Patsy had with the cane at the beginning of class. Couldn't she tell Patsy hated practicing with that *dumb ol' cane*?

At the beginning of class it had taken Patsy no time to realize the cane was trouble. She dropped it, poked herself with it, and managed to smack Faye in the fanny with its handle. Yet somehow, according to Patsy's tap teachers, it was supposed to make practicing easier. How she would ever manage dancing with the huge umbrellas they would be using for their actual performance, Patsy didn't know. She *did know* she would need to have a handle on the cane in order to control the umbrellas for their "Singing in the Rain" routine—and time was running out.

Mr. O'Keefe extended the cane and waited for Patsy to grasp it. Patamela snatched it with so much force, she nearly pulled him off his feet. "Ol' stupid cane!" Patsy fussed. She knew she was a better dancer than the rest of the Ladybugs. She just couldn't figure out how the other girls learned the new routine in so little time. They couldn't have had that many classes without me, she thought.

Patsy tried to calculate the classes she missed while sitting in the front office with the number of classes she missed when she was instructed to stand in the hallway. She added that number to the classes she missed while hanging out in the bathroom and then added the number of classes she missed while spying on Ms. Saa's class. There were too many numbers to add! Patsy lost count.

"Mr. Okay," Patsy said, exasperated, calling him by the nickname she'd given him. "I think the other routine was much better than this one."

Patsy panted heavily, wiped out from the previous shuffle-step combinations and from twirling the cane. "We should switch back to the old one. Don't you think?" she pleaded.

Mr. O'Keefe, watching Patsy struggle with the steps, shook his head and said, "Patamela you may stay after everyone leaves this afternoon to learn this routine if you would like."

"Thanks, Mr. Okay!" Patsy yelled, believing things were finally starting to go her way. "But...where will the Ladybugs have jazz and modern dance class?" Patsy asked.

"They will have it here, in Studio M1 like they always

do," Mr. O'Keefe answered, perplexed by Patsy's question.

"I didn't know Ms. Patterson would let you teach me tap while she was teaching her classes," Patsy replied.

"What do you mean, Patsy? Ms. Patterson will teach her classes in this studio as usual, at her scheduled time. You will stay with me after Legends lets out this afternoon."

Patsy's left eyebrow slowly arched. "Ah, I don't understand, Mr. O'Keefe," dropping the Mr. Okay bit because she could feel the bad news heading her way.

"Patsy, I will call your parents and ask them to pick you up an hour or two later every day this week. That way you can catch up."

Patsy's eyes opened wide. "Oh no, that's alright, Mr. O'Keefe!" Patsy said, running to the front of Studio M1's center mirror. "I think I have it now...As a matter of fact, I know I have it! *Shuffle, shuffle, tap, ball-change, spin-nnn, stomp, break it, whoa, whoa—YIKES!*"

Mr. O'Keefe leapt toward Patsy, placed his hands underneath her underarms, and managed to catch her before her bottom hit the floor. Unfortunately for Patsy, that was the only part that missed the floor. Her stockings were filthy from the slip.

"Mr. O'Keefe," Patsy said as she scrambled to get her balance, "I promise to practice all night, every night until the day of the recital. You don't have to stay with me after Legends lets out. I'll get it down pat."

Patsy smoothed her leotard and tights, which were bundled by her fall, and began dusting herself off. Mr. O'Keefe bent down and looked Patsy in the eyes and said, "Patsy, I honestly think you need the extra help, but I cannot force you to stay. A lot of Ladybugs stayed after to learn the routine, and they worked very hard. You are part of a team now. You should be willing to work just as hard to make your group look good."

But Patsy was not paying much attention to Mr. O'Keefe. All she heard was the Ladybugs got extra practice. "Mr. Okay," she said, "you guys tried to trick me. I knew something had to happen, because between you and I," Patsy leaned into Mr. O'Keefe's ear, "they stink."

Mr. O'Keefe picked Patsy's cane from the floor, handed it to her, and placed his hand on her shoulder. "Patamela, the Ladybugs love to dance and they've been willing to work very hard. I would not be so quick to say who does and who does not stink if I were you, Ms. James," Mr. O'Keefe said as Patsy recklessly swung the cane.

Patamela did not stop twirling the cane even for a moment while Mr. O'Keefe was speaking and she kept twirling it after he walked away. She made no attempt to understand what he had said. It would have never occurred to Patsy that she was anything less than a gifted dancer. Especially since the cat was out of the bag about the Ladybugs extra practices after school. The only reason they weren't having trouble was because they received extra help.

Patsy's confidence in her dancing gift soared once more. She was cheery and giddy for the remainder of the afternoon. She had no plans to practice the routine all night as she told Mr. O'Keefe she would. After all, she was gifted and it would only take another day or two before her gift won her feet over.

CHAPTER 25

The Cecret Circle

Patsy had better things to do with her time than to spend her evenings at Legends. Today she would finally break free of her parents' unreasonably long, uncompromising, and totally-unsympathetic-to-anything-she-had-to-say two-week punishment. Although Patsy believed her parents should have let her off earlier for good behavior, she was just happy her punishment term was over. She had done her time and was looking forward to her first evening of freedom, which put an evening practice with Mr. O'Keefe dead bottom on her list of things to do.

"Aaa, he'll learn. I'm a busy kid...*I have lots on my plate*," she said, mimicking a phrase she had often heard her parents use. As far as Patamela was concerned, the answer to Mr. O'Keefe's offer to stay late and practice fell somewhere between "not right now" and "probably never." Her agenda for the evening was jam-packed with things to do. And right now, her number one goal was to find the kissy-faced bandit.

Patsy had learned of the kissy-faced bandit just a few

days before her punishment ended. It happened like this. Patsy had been trying desperately throughout her punishment to keep herself occupied. Fourteen days without her adventure contraptions had nearly driven her insane. Luckily for Patsy, her creativity and dogged curiosity had stepped in to save the day. She tried everything to zap her boredom, but her favorite thing to do was to scare Patience silly. One evening, Patsy decided to lock herself in her bedroom closet. She planned to startle Patience as soon as she turned the door handle to their room. No matter how many times Patsy pulled this trick, Patience was guaranteed to jump. That's what made it so much fun.

"Patsy, this isn't playtime. I hope you aren't up there hiding again," her mom lectured from the bottom of the stairs. "I'm not the least bit thrilled with the shenanigans you've been pulling lately. This is not supposed to be a fun time for you...Don't bother Patience tonight, ya hear?"

Yet Patsy had no plans to scale back on her scare strike now. She had been patiently awaiting Patience's arrival for hours. Scaring Patience would be the highlight of her day.

Patsy had come to realize one very important fact. Any fun she expected to have while on punishment demanded Patience's involvement. Prince was too busy with his friends, sports, and girls to pay Patsy much attention. Without Miles, Destiny, rollerblading, scavenger hunting, Puddles, and double-Dutch, Patsy's days on punishment were downright dreadful. There was nothing left to do but ruffle Patience's feathers.

Patamela waited and waited, then waited some more. "Just great! When do they think their going to waltz in this place—daybreak?"

Patsy had already eaten supper. She had taken her bedtime bath and picked her outfit for the next day, but Prince and Patience still had not arrived. It was nightfall for goodness sakes! Patamela was just about to give up when she heard a couple of annoyingly giddy voices.

"Do you think Patsy's asleep?" one said.

"Maybe, but you never know with *el elefante* ears," said Patience.

"I know, she's just like my little brother."

"Yeah, what pests."

"You're a pest! And a smelly elephant too!" Patsy grumbled. Sometimes Patience and her friends really cooked her goose. They thought they were hot stuff just because they took Spanish at Melbourne, but so did Patsy. She knew exactly what *elefante* meant. She would have jumped out of the closet to give them all a grand karate chop, but she was too busy figuring out how she could rescue her failed mission.

Patsy wanted to know how Patience had gotten permission to have company on a weeknight. She had waited all that time for nothing. She wouldn't dare try to scare Patience while Lizzie and Tamara were with her.

Lizzie and Tamara had ruined Patsy's plan. It would be impossible to scare all three of them. Patience tried to act grown and sassy around those two. Instead of being frightened, they would probably point at Patsy and laugh. Worse yet, Patamela knew she wouldn't get any attention from Patience with Lizzie and Tamara there. She would have to face her night alone with no one to keep her busy. Patience had her own company to keep her occupied. "That dang Lizzie and Tamara," Patsy grunted.

Of course, Patsy would have rather been rollerblading or jumping double-Dutch than spending time with Patience, but Patsy would have never told her that, at least not while she was on punishment. There was no way she would have done anything to jeopardize the attention Patience was paying to her. While Patsy was on punishment, Patience was reading detective novels and epic tales to her each night at bedtime.

Patsy took a deep breath. She began to lift the heaps of clothing she'd piled on herself as cover while hiding on the closet floor. But boy was she achy! She'd been waiting for Patience so long that she could barely move her legs. She was still trying to get to her feet when she overheard something intriguing.

"Tell us all about it. Was it long? Did his breath stink?" one of the girls snickered.

"*Hunh, did his breath stink*? What are you talking about?" another girl asked.

Then Patsy heard quiet giggles. She managed to get to her feet and look through the tiny space she'd left open. It was big enough for Patsy to see out of, yet small enough for Patience to believe the door was closed. Patsy inched forward. She needed to find out who was doing the talking and who was doing the answering.

To Patsy's chagrin, the girls' voices were becoming more and more muffled. She moved in to get a better listen then pressed her ear to the tiny space. But all she was able to make out were a couple of very faint giggles. Patsy turned her head to the right, then to the left, then right again. She continued moving her head back and forth, ear to the tiny space, eye to the tiny space, in a desperate attempt to pinpoint the voices. Then everything went silent.

They must have left the room, Patsy thought. She cracked the door just enough to place one foot outside the closet. Yet before her foot touched the carpet, she yanked it back and dove into the pile of clothing. The girls had not left the room at all! Although the lights were out, they were at the foot of Patience's bed in a makeshift tent made from her comforter. They had even snuck Mr. James's flashlight upstairs so they could see each other under the tent.

"They're sharing secrets!" Patsy whispered with boiling envy.

Patsy knew all about the Cecret Circle meetings Patience and her girlfriends held when they had secrets to swap. She even knew Patience and her friends spelled secret with a *C* just to be different. Ever since Patsy discovered the *Code of the Cecret Circle* underneath Patience's bed, Patsy knew what was going on and felt she had one over on her big sister.

The *Code of the Cecret Circle* was a neatly written set of rules composed by no other than Patience James. The rules outlined how the girls needed to behave in order to remain friends forever. It even detailed when and how they should tell secrets.

Patamela had never wanted to be a part of Patience's Cecret Circle before, but things were different now—at least they should have been. Patsy thought that she and Patience were finally getting closer. Because Patience was paying attention to her and reading to her each night, Patsy thought they had become true sisters.

Patsy's feelings were hurt. She realized that Patience still didn't think she was big enough to be included in the ceremony. Even though Patsy was going into the fourth grade and had proclaimed her big kid, big shot status, Patience was still treating her like a baby.

Patsy was wondering just how long she'd have to hide in the closet without being able to eavesdrop on the juicy secrets when she heard the girls chime, "Patsy, you can come out now." Patsy did not move. "*Patsy, we know you're in there,*" they said in a sing-song voice.

Patsy opened the door and flipped on the light. "So what," she said to the girls, sticking out her tongue. "I heard your juicy secret!"

The girls looked at each other and chuckled.

"It's not funny," Patsy said. "Let's see how much you're laughing when I tell Dad."

"Go on and tell him, Little Bit. We knew you were in there all along," Patience revealed. "We wanted to get you upset. That's what you get for trying to scare me. Ma told me you were in here planning to scare me again—hiding in the closet."

"You're not so smart, Patience! You probably thought I fell asleep, but I heard your juicy secret," Patsy teased. "One of you kissed a boy, and I know who. Was it good? Was it nice? Was his breath all right?" Patsy sang. She was proud of the song she made up on the spot.

"Patsy, you're *incorrigible*! We made it up I'm telling you!" Patience yelped. Then the girls got up and stormed out of the room.

At first Patsy was upset with her mom for spoiling the fun, but then she decided she had no time to waste on being upset with her mom. She was too upset with Patience. Patience thought she was clever, but she wasn't as clever as Patsy. Patience always made up a quick fib to cover her tracks when Patsy caught her in some act. And this time was no different. Patsy was no dummy. If Patience was telling the truth, she was only telling half the story.

Chances were good that their mom did tell Patience that Patsy was hiding in the closet. But that would have only given Patience more reason to swap secrets before Patsy came out of her hiding place. Patience was well aware of how Patsy behaved around secret swapping. If Patsy had been lying on her bed or at her desk when they came in, the girls would have never held the ceremony. For if they had, Patsy would have eavesdropped or thrown a tantrum about being left out—and Patience knew it.

"I don't believe a single word she's saying about making the whole thing up," Patsy groused. She knew the *Cecret Circle* was no laughing matter.

Patamela walked to her desk. She took out her special black notebook that was neatly tucked all the way at the back of the drawer. Patsy's special black notepad had been her trusted pal in her tattletale days. She'd used it to write down the juiciest secrets she overheard while doing serious detective work. She even had special symbols that only she knew the meaning of—just in case somebody found it and tried to figure out what she knew.

Not too long ago Patsy had promised Prince she would never use it again. She promised to do away with it for good, but only after Prince filled her in on every detail of a secret he'd managed to keep from her. Since then Patsy had not touched her book—nor had she ever breathed a word Prince told her. But this was an emergency. Somebody had a first kiss and she was going to find out who that someone was.

"Ooooh, if it's Patience, she's going to get it," Patsy said with conviction.

Patsy knew if Patience was involved in the kiss, it was more dirt than she had ever had on Patience before. If she could put Patience at the scene of the crime, the sky would be the limit. Patsy could tell on Patience and get her in a heap of trouble. That would teach Patience to leave Patsy out of the Cecret Circle. Even better would be to hold the incident over Patience's head as a get out of jail free card. Patsy would be able to do whatever she wanted and Patience would never be able to tell on her again—unless of course, she wanted Patsy to speak to their parents about the kiss.

But more than anything, catching Patience would give Patsy an opportunity to prove she had really become a big kid, big shot. With a set of perked ears and excellent detective work, she could catch Patience red-handed, then not tell on her at all. Surely Patience would consider letting her in the Cecret Circle then. She would have proven she was trustworthy and could keep a secret. Patience would owe Patsy big time.

Patamela considered the possibilities. "Nah, I'd rather tell," she blurted in a hysterically fiendish chuckle. There was no way Patsy was going to cut Patience a break this time—because this time, Patience had really hurt Patsy's feelings.

Now that Patsy's two-week punishment was over, she was ready to embark on her mission. Ever since she overheard those juicy tidbits at Patience's Cecret Circle meeting, she had been obsessed with exposing the infamous kissy-faced bandit. Since then she'd done everything within her power to get home quicker than the day before. She had to get home and slip into the best hiding places before Patience could see her.

Patamela had been spying for the past few days, but it would be easier now that she had all her things back and her parents weren't watching her every move. Patsy had become a real pro at picking hiding places that Patience would never suspect. She hid underneath Patience's bed and in the bathtub behind the shower curtain while Patience unknowingly did her hair. Patamela hid on the basement steps too. She would crack the basement door just a little so she could listen as Patience talked on the kitchen phone.

So far Patsy had learned that Patience had a crush on Donovan Lawrence, Lizzie had a crush on Ishmael Daye, and Tamara had a crush on Prince. Furthermore, Patsy found out that all the girls shared a huge crush on Johawn Aleem, a new boy whose family had recently moved into the neighborhood.

Patsy was in hot pursuit of the kissy-faced bandit. Each day she was gaining on her. Patsy had no doubt that now that her punishment was over she would figure out exactly which girl had done the kissing. This new phase would expand her operation in a way that was sure to catch Patience James, a.k.a *Kissy-Faced Bandit Suspect #1.*

CHAPTER 26

Kiss and Tell

Over the past few days Patsy had expected to make a lot more progress than she had on operation kissy-faced bandit. The dead-end clues were beginning to get the best of her. Fortunately Patsy discovered that there's nothing like a little pressure and frustration to get her creative juices flowing. Her frustration resulted in one great plan. Now all she had to do was make it through her day at Legends and she would be free to put her plan into action.

Unfortunately, today was dress rehearsal day and Patsy totally botched her tap dance routine. Normally that would have put Mr. O'Keefe on her case like a Supreme Court Justice—making it hard to dodge an offer for afternoon practice. Luckily for her, Mr. O'Keefe did not have much time to chase her—not with all the excitement about Saturday's upcoming show.

"Patamela, I don't know what is more important than you learning this routine. Your priorities are clearly not straight," Mr. O'Keefe stated as a few of the girls tugged on his arm for his attention. "I think it would be best for you to sit..."

"I got it; I got it, Mr. Okay. Stop worrying. I'll be fine, you'll see," Patsy interrupted before Mr. O'Keefe could finish his sentence.

With all the pestering from Patsy's fellow Ladybugs, Mr. O'Keefe never got to address Patsy again. He was too busy promising the girls that he would purchase the umbrellas by Saturday morning.

Whew, that was close, Patsy thought, wiping imaginary sweat from her forehead. She didn't know how Mr. O'Keefe was going to finish his sentence, and she didn't want to know. She had too many things on her mind. Mr. O'Keefe's grievances would only take up precious memory space. She needed to focus her attention on more important things.

Patamela snatched a piece of pink thread hanging from her leotard sleeve. She hoped it was long enough to tie around her index finger. It would serve as her trusty reminder. She had to remember to fetch her special notepad before leaving the house when she got home. And she couldn't forget her dad's binoculars.

Patsy hoped she would make it home in enough time to successfully launch her new operation. She was sure this plan would give her the scoop she'd been waiting for. All she had to do was stick to the script. Instead of creeping around the house to eavesdrop on Patience like a bewildered, bush-league beginner, Patsy was planning to take a brand-new approach.

Patsy planned to head all the way to the end of Beecham Street near Mrs. Tinnelmann's house to launch her operation. She had permission to go to either end of Beecham Street as long as it was daylight and she didn't cross the road.

Patsy was sure that Patience, Prince, and their friends

cut through Mrs. Tinnelmann's yard to go home. There was nothing Patsy wouldn't be able to see from the side of Mrs. Tinnelmann's home, and Patience would never think to look behind Mrs. Tinnelmann's thorn bushes for a spy. Once they passed by, Patsy would follow them home, making sure to slink behind trees, parked cars, and bushes to avoid getting caught.

Patsy couldn't wait to spy up close. Her dynamic detective skills had already discovered that Prince and Patience were part of a group of teens that walked home together each evening. She would finally catch a glimpse of all the hand holding, hugging, and funny stuff that had been going on for who knows how long. All Patamela would have to do is go over her notes and put the pieces of the puzzle together. Then, *whamo*! She would know everything there was to know about that Cecret Circle meeting and the kissy-faced bandit.

When Mrs. Wright came to pick up Patsy that afternoon, she found herself being rushed right back to her car.

"Oh, Mrs. Wright, I have a lot to take care of at home," Patsy told her. "I need to get there as soon as possible."

"There's no need to rush me, Patamela. Trust me, I want to get to your house as much as you do."

When Mrs. Wright pulled up to the house, Patsy glanced down at the thread tied around her index finger and bolted out of the car, into the house, and up the stairs to her room where she snatched her black notepad and pen out of her drawer. She hollered for permission to play outside as she galloped back down the steps. Before hearing her mom's response, Patsy flew into the study, grabbed her dad's binoculars out of the bottom drawer of his desk, and headed for the front door.

Patsy had business to handle. "Bye Ma, bye Mrs.

Wright, bye Madi! See you guys tomorrow. Ma, I'll be back before supper," Patsy yelled.

Patamela sprinted down Beecham Street with Mr. James's binoculars flying around her neck and thumping her in the chest. It was not a short trip to Mrs. Tinnelmann's, but Patsy ran the entire way. She had to get settled before Prince and Patience turned the corner.

"Child, get away from my flowers," Mrs. Tinnelmann instructed from her window as Patsy approached the side of her house.

"*Pleeeease* Mrs. Tinnelmann. I won't bend or mess up the branches. I promise to stay right here. I won't even leave tennis shoe prints in the dirt—except for the ones that got me here. But I'll walk in the same prints on my way out. I promise."

"What are you up to Ms. Patsy?"

"It's kind of a secret. I'm waiting until Prince and Patience come around the corner."

"Are you waiting for them or are you trying to mind their business? And just what are you going to do with those peepers? They're almost bigger than you."

Patsy smiled and then crouched down as low as possible. She saw Mrs. Tinnelmann close her window drapes. "Good," she said with a sigh of relief. Prince and Patience would be on their best behavior if they saw Mrs. Tinnelmann looking out the window. Patsy did not need her scaring them away and was glad she'd gone back inside.

Just then, a car screeched around the corner of Beecham Street and stopped down the block, not far from Mrs. Tinnelmann's home. From what Patsy could see, it looked like Lizzie's older brother's beat-up station wagon. Timmy, as everyone called him, was sixteen and one of the only kids in the neighborhood with a driver's license. Patsy slithered from behind the thorn bushes. She lifted the binoculars to get a better look.

"Hold it, hold it, okay, right there," she said, adjusting the lenses the way her father had taught her.

Patsy saw Patience, Lizzie, Tamara, Prince, and Ishmael in Timmy's car. There was another boy in the front seat, but his face did not look at all familiar to Patsy. Patsy zeroed in as Timmy got out of his car and walked to a nearby stoop. He struck up a conversation with a neighborhood boy bouncing a basketball.

Patamela grabbed her special notepad out of her back pocket and the pen from behind her ear. "*T's car, Pa, Li, Ta, Pr, Is,*" she jotted. Patamela had no time to write out everyone's names. She had to keep her eye on that car—especially since her parents did not allow Prince and Patsy in Timmy's wagon unless they knew about it. Furthermore, Patsy knew it was rare for her parents to allow Patience and Prince in Timmy's car even if they asked first. Patsy's parents believed Timmy was still a young boy himself.

"How dare they get into Timmy's car without permission!" Patsy huffed.

Patsy had come to see some kissy-faced action, but instead she found Prince and Patience sneaking a ride home with Timmy. She placed her right hand underneath her chin just like her father did when he was in deep thought and let out a long sigh. What am I going to do now? she wondered.

Patamela could easily tell her parents about the secret car ride and get both Prince and Patience in trouble. She could even remain silent and have two get-out-of-jail-free cards. But when she thought about all the hard work she'd put into tracking the mysterious kiss, Patsy decided to stick to the plan.

Patsy was in no rush to involve Prince in shenanigans of this magnitude. There was nothing worse than having an angry brother on her trail. If she told her parents about the ride home, she would get Prince in trouble. Patsy knew he would come after her with a vengeance. Even holding a get-out-of-jail-free card over Prince's head was courting trouble. Prince did not take well to being bribed and would live to even the score. Patsy decided she had a bone to pick with Patience and Patience only.

Patsy noticed there was a white car parked directly across from Timmy's wagon. "That's it!" she said. If I can make it to that car without being spotted, I'll be in business, thought Patsy.

Patamela was pretty sure that car was her only hope. She could peek through its windows or even over its hood. With some skillful head ducking and a couple of well-timed bobs and weaves, she could get a perfect look at what Prince and Patience and their friends were doing. Patsy figured she could even point the binoculars directly at their mouths. She was sure she could make out some words. She did not know how much talent she had as a lip reader, but she was willing to give it a try.

The problem was she needed to make it to her lookout car without being seen. The last thing she needed was one of those meddlesome kids littering both sides of Beecham Street blowing her cover. Even if just one said, "Hey Patsy, who you hiding from?" she would be cooked.

Patsy decided to cut through the neighbors' backyards. She would jump every single backyard fence, and she would not stop until she reached the fence belonging to the house in front of the white car. Then, she would creep to the car undetected and spy. Patsy headed to Mrs. Tinnelmann's fence.

"Child, why are you going to the back of my house?" yelled Mrs. Tinnelmann. "Don't you forget to wipe those footprints! Use that broken leafy branch to brush them away."

Patsy forgot she had promised not to mess up Mrs. Tinnelmann's yard. She dropped as low to the ground as she could and squat-walked her way back to Mrs. Tinnelmann's bushes. Patsy made certain to trace her steps placing each foot in her exact footprints from earlier.

Before brushing her prints away, Patamela decided to pick up her binoculars. She would be crushed if she bent down to brush some silly footprints only to turn back around and see Tim's car pull away. Patsy peeked around the thorn bushes to make certain Tim's car was in the same parking space. The car had not moved, but Tim was on the move. He was walking back to his car!

"Wait, I'm not ready," Patsy yelped while scrambling for her notepad. She had just stuffed it back in her pocket so she could do a good job at dusting the prints. Patsy flipped her notepad to a blank page and she was ready and waiting when Patience opened the car door.

"Okay, now I've got you," Patsy said.

Just then, the boy Patsy didn't recognize walked over to help Patience out of the car. "She's not handicapped. She can get out of the car on her own mister," Patsy scolded.

The two were not talking long before Tim was back in his car, beeping his horn. "You heard the man, break it up," Patsy declared. But then, right before Patsy's eyes, the boy kissed Patience on the cheek!

Patamela pushed the binoculars closer to her eyes. "Haaaaah!" she gasped. Patsy felt her mouth drop open, but that was the only sound she could push out. She watched in horror as Patience placed her hand over her moistened cheek. Patsy could stand no more! "This can't be happening. This isn't happening!"

Patamela let the binoculars fall to her chest and turned away. She decided to count to one hundred—by tens of course—hoping that by the time she looked back the nightmare would be over. When she got to one hundred, Patsy turned back and saw Patience smiling. "I knew she was a Growny Pants!" Patsy said with conviction. "Where is that Prince?" Patsy demanded, turning her binoculars in his direction.

Prince was sitting on the far end of Tim's backseat. The window was rolled down and he was talking to the basketball-bouncing fellow. He had not noticed a thing, and it looked like Timmy hadn't either.

It was enough to make Patsy rethink giving Prince a break. He deserved to get in trouble! What kind of older brother was he anyway? Mrs. James had told Patsy hundreds of stories about how her older brothers had protected her when she was a young girl. Patsy thought Prince should have been paying more attention to those stories.

Patsy wanted to yell his name at the top of her lungs. She wanted to ask him why he let some dumb boy kiss Patience. But before Patsy could make it to her feet, Patience was back in the car and Tim's wagon was on its way down Beecham Street.

"I'll get you, Patience James! You too, Prince!" Patsy shouted, shaking her fists at the sky.

Mrs. Tinnelmann poked her head out of her window, interrupting Patsy's tantrum, "Child, are you bird watching or brushing those prints?" Mrs. Tinnelmann asked.

"I'm brushing, I'm brushing," Patsy replied as she used

her feet to kick over the prints.

"Use that broken branch with the leaves, child. Don't make me come outside," Mrs. Tinnelmann threatened.

Patsy picked up the broken branch and dusted over her prints as quickly as possible. She did not dust them up to the backyard fence because it would have taken too much time. She had to get back home. Patsy dusted the last print she was sure Mrs. Tinnelmann could see from her spot by the window and then flew down the street. She had to scram before Mrs. Tinnelmann discovered all the prints she'd neglected to cover up.

CHAPTER 27

....

This Means War!

Patamela knew telling on both Patience *and* Prince was a dangerous undertaking. Yet their behavior was more than she could stand. Between Patience's sassy-mcfrassy, boy-crazy attitude and Prince's sleeping-on-the-job, big-brother foibles, Patsy had had enough. She'd proven once and for all she was the most *responsible* junior member of the James clan. She would have never taken a ride with Timmy without permission. Yet her too-big-for-their-britches, rule-breaking siblings had done just that.

"It's high time someone brought them down to size," Patsy huffed, "and I know just the big kid, big shot for the job..."

Patamela stomped her way back up Beecham Street.

"Hey Patsy, everything alright?" a group of neighborhood children called from a distant stoop. They knew better than to approach Patsy with a bunch of silly, busybody questions. Patsy had that no-nonsense look in her eyes.

Patsy stormed passed the next row of houses, quickening her pace. She didn't want her mother granting anyone permission to attend a slumber party or a game of evening ball before she heard what Patsy had to say.

"Patsy, the street lights don't come on for another ten minutes. Wanna play?" one of the neighborhood kids asked.

"What's wrong, Patz?" asked another..

"There's a new sheriff in town! That's what!" she declared.

Even if it meant exposing herself to all types of pranks, name-calling, threats, and harassment, Patamela would stand firm and enforce the laws of the James household. She refused to allow any of her siblings' browbeating tactics to wear her down. If they turned up the heat, she would grin and bear it. Patsy had never been a sniveling, yellow-bellied coward in the past and she wouldn't start now. If the only thing standing between her and her siblings' impending doom was their front door, well then, Prince and Patience were in for it!

Patsy stood outside her house and peered in through the front window. She could see Patience gaily prancing from the kitchen to the living room. What are you so happy about, Miss Missy? thought Patsy.

"Your days are numbered too—Prince Vermin!" she growled as Prince darted in and out of view.

Patsy was ready for battle. As a matter of fact, she was ready for war. She removed her notepad from her back pocket to review her notes. If she was to be taken seriously as the family's new sheriff, she would have to know her stuff.

"Alright you grandstanding, pre-teeny-bopping delinquents...it's time to boogie!" she declared.

"Go get 'em, Patsy!" she heard her friends yell. They understood Patsy was going after her brother and sister and they sympathized. They were tired of their know-it-all, get-away-with-murder, older brothers and sisters too.

Patamela burst through the front door. In one long breath, she put it all on the line. "Ma, let me tell you what Patience and Prince did! Patience is a Growny Pants! I saw her leaning on Timmy's car door while this big ol' teenage boy that I've never even seen before..."

Patience's brown face nearly turned white as she looked on from the living room. She closed her eyes and waited for Patsy to drop the bomb.

"I'd rather hear what you did this afternoon and all the other afternoons that kept you from taking extra practice lessons with Mr. O'Keefe," Mrs. James interrupted.

"But Mommy, the boy laid a ki...,"

"Patsy, did you hear my question?"

"Can I tell you about Prince then?" Patsy bargained. Though from the look on her mother's face, she could tell she wouldn't be allowed to finish. "But...but he,"

"No buts, Patamela, I'm waiting for an explanation."

Patience's face regained its color, and she jotted up the stairs knowing Patsy had gotten into some trouble of her own. Mrs. James would not want to hear anything except the matter at hand. Patience had escaped her incorrigible little sister's wrath once again.

Patsy, on the other hand, was up to her ears in ducked tap lessons. She stared at her mother in disbelief as her latest caper threatened to ruin her career as Sheriff "B-K-B-S" James.

"This afternoon," Mrs. James began, "Mrs. Wright gave me a letter that Ms. Watkins asked her to hand-deliver. Do you want to take a guess at what the letter says, Patamela?" her mother asked.

"No ma'am," Patsy whispered.

"Well, I'll tell you. Your tap teacher, Mr. O'Keefe, personally requested that I give him a call. We had quite a conversation. As much as the poor man claimed to dislike labeling children, he said you were quite out of hand, a bit *incorrigible* to say the least. He also informed me that your chores at home and your after-school engagements were putting your participation in the tap routine in jeopardy. You wouldn't know anything about these chores and after-school engagements, would you, Patsy?" Mrs. James inquired. "Even Mrs. Wright seems to know more about this pressing schedule of yours than I do."

Patsy stared at the floor and shrugged her shoulders. She did not have anything to say. She was busted. And from the looks of things, that word *incorrigible* had nothing to do with being adventurous.

"Patsy, you do know I'll be putting all your belongings back in the garage first thing tomorrow morning, don't you?"

Patamela offered a quiet nod.

"Following supper, I want you to return to your room and wait patiently for your father. The fibbing has got to cease," Mrs. James scolded.

Patamela headed for the staircase.

"Oh, and Patsy, it's a shame your Aunt Deidre is flying up to see you in four dances, when you will only be in three. That is, if Mr. O'Keefe decides to pull you out of the dance. I assured him that we would give his decision our complete support."

Patsy fought to keep her eyes from watering.

"We teach the importance of teamwork in this household, Patamela," her mother continued. "Yet you seem to have forgotten that. Your refusal to practice and lack of concern for how that decision might affect the Ladybugs on recital night is displeasing. You *will* find another way to be of service to them, young lady."

"How will I do...?"

"Won't you, Patsy?" Mrs. James interrupted before Patsy could ask how she would accomplish the task.

"Yes, Mom, I'll find a way."

The remainder of the night was quiet for Patsy, especially since Mrs. James said she did not want to hear her voice. She silently ate her supper and never looked at Prince and Patience—unless you count that one time she managed to mouth, "This means war!" without their mother noticing.

Patamela knew Prince and Patience were getting a real kick out of her being in hot water. Patsy's voice restriction meant they were getting off scot-free—at least for the time being. I'm not out of the game yet, not by a long shot, she thought. Yet she had to admit Prince and Patience had won the battle. She was far too worried about what would happen when her dad got home to hound them. She knew her mom would fill her father in on every detail of her latest charade. He would probably wake Patsy out of her sleep to get an explanation.

After dinner Patamela returned to her room as instructed. She changed into her pajamas and hopped into bed. She shut her eyes tightly, then snapped the comforter over her head. There was nothing worse than having to wait for her father's infamous, bedtime tap on the shoulder—nothing, that is, except the sound of distant footsteps mounting the staircase. Patamela braced herself for the worst.

Instead, she heard Patience's voice. "Patsy, you didn't see or hear what you think you did."

Patsy faked as if she were snoring.

"Patsy," Patience continued. "That was Johawn Aleem

you saw near Tim's car with me. He's the same boy we were talking about in the *Cecret Circle* that night."

Patsy's eyes widened, but she continued her fake snoring, pretending to be asleep.

"Patsy, he kissed me on my hand one afternoon at the Blessed project house and called me his princess. Tamara and I were laughing at Lizzie because she asked how his breath smelled. I wouldn't know that from a kiss on the hand. But...I told Ma about it."

Patsy did not stir.

"This afternoon," Patience continued, "I didn't expect Johawn to kiss me on the cheek. I was embarrassed, and so was he. As soon as he saw my face, he apologized and said he didn't blame me if I told Prince. I told him I was only going to the sixth grade and was too young for a boyfriend. He understood and promised to keep his lips to himself. We even shook hands on it...Patsy...say something," Patience pleaded.

Patamela did not say a word. She continued to act as if she were fast asleep. If Patience would have leveled with her from the beginning, she would have saved Patsy a lot of trouble. Patsy would be in the tap dance for sure and wouldn't have her things banned to the garage for the second time!

As far as Patsy was concerned, Patience could suffer for a little while. She would forgive her and Prince later. Right now, she was too busy perfecting her snoring chorus. She decided to raise the octave just a bit. Maybe that way her father would leave her alone—at least until the morning. Patsy snored loudly as she heard her father's footsteps in the hallway.

Mr. James opened the bedroom door. "Patamela," Patsy heard as she felt her father sit on the edge of her bed.

"Patamela," she heard her father call again. "I'm not going to yell, scream, threaten, or punish you because you know what you did was wrong, and you know what to do."

That alone was enough to make a tear roll down Patsy's cheek, but her dad didn't stop there. "I am disappointed in your behavior and am curious to know what in the world was more important than practicing for this recital. Two months ago you begged to be in this dance thing."

Patsy curled up in a tight ball as her father's words wounded her already guilty conscience.

"*Hmph*," Mr. James huffed. "Pattie Cakes, do you remember that morning show special we did at the television station in the spring?"

Patsy nodded her head up and down to signify a yes, but kept her head hidden beneath the covers. Patamela clearly remembered that special April day she spent with her father. Some of her favorite memories were spent with Mr. James at Springdale's local television station where he worked as a cameraman. Mr. James always brought the children along whenever one of the station's local shows was doing a special presentation he thought they might enjoy. As long as the children did not have school, it was a date.

"Well, I've been thinking, pumpkin," he continued, "I'm going to ask if we can donate the umbrellas from the April Showers Weather Special to your class. Mr. O'Keefe told Mommy all about your tap routine. I figure this way you can be of service to your fellow Ladybugs."

Although Patsy was nestled deep beneath the covers, Mr. James was able to see the outline of a smile in her comforter. "Let's hope it's not too late for your class to use them...and I do hope you cut out all the monkey business so you can show these folks that old-fashioned James glow."

PART 3

CHAPTER 28

At Your Service

Patsy decided to make a change after her dad left her room that night. No longer would she be the Legends poster child for unruly, *incorrigible* behavior. If her father wanted her to show the people the old-fashioned James glow, that is exactly what she would do. Patamela made an oath to embrace her Ladybug status, and then she fell fast asleep.

The following day at tap class, Patsy was a new person. "Hello Mr. O'Keefe. Hey Ms. Hollingsworth," Patamela said with a big wave. It was the first time that Patsy had spoken to them so warmly. They didn't know it yet, but this upstanding, big kid, big shot behavior was Patamela's new specialty. "I'm ready to tap this afternoon!" Patamela exclaimed. "I'm free after Legends too—if you need me," she said with a playful wink before offering a radiant, dimple-chiseled grin.

"Glad you're feeling bright-eyed and bushy-tailed today, Patsy. How wonderful it is to see your cooperative spirit. We have so much work ahead of us these next couple of days," Ms. Hollingsworth replied.

Patsy believed she was back on track. That was the most Ms. Hollingsworth had said to her in weeks. She knew she would have to work harder to win Mr. O'Keefe over, but she was up for the challenge.

Patsy did everything she could think of to be of service to the Ladybugs during tap class. She volunteered to get the canes out of the cabinet and was first to get back on her X when Mr. O'Keefe asked the Ladybugs to get in place. And would you believe Ms. Hollingsworth picked Patsy to run a note to the front office? Better yet, Patsy even got the class to quiet down when they were not listening to pleas to do so. Patsy was determined to make her tap teachers forget all about her recent mistakes.

Patamela glanced at the clock over Studio M1's mirror. Only ten minutes left before tap class ended and Mr. James had not arrived with the umbrellas yet. "Come on, Daddy. Come on, Daddy," Patsy chanted under her breath. She was sure the box full of umbrellas would secure her spot in the Ladybugs' tap routine.

Patsy stared out the window, but her father's car was not in sight. "Knock, knock, can I come in?" Patsy heard her father ask.

Patamela turned toward the studio door and saw her dad standing in the doorway. Patsy ran to jump in his arms, but noticed the huge cardboard box he was carrying and settled for hugging his legs.

"Hello, I'm Mr. O'Keefe and this is Ms. Hollingsworth. We are Patsy's tap instructors," Mr. O'Keefe said, extending his hand to Mr. James.

"Oh yes, I've heard a lot about you," Mr. James replied. "I just stopped in to assist Patsy with a gift she has for the Ladybugs."

Patsy jumped up and down. "Let me tell them, Dad.

Let me tell them!"

"Go on, kiddo."

"Mr. O'Keefe, you don't have to buy umbrellas for the "Singing in the Rain" dance because we have extras. We've got you covered!" Patsy exclaimed.

Mr. James placed his special delivery on the floor as Patsy signaled the girls to come in for a closer look. The girls ran to the box. "They're huge!" Faye exclaimed in awe. She tore through the box and grabbed the umbrella that appealed to her most. There were red umbrellas, purple umbrellas, polka-dot umbrellas, black umbrellas, striped umbrellas, yellow umbrellas, and pink umbrellas. There were more umbrellas than there were Ladybugs.

"Wow, thanks man," Mr. O'Keefe said, patting Mr. James on the back. "We weren't scheduled to receive our budget money until late Friday afternoon and I was a little worried," Mr. O'Keefe confided.

"Any time man, any time," Mr. James replied.

The Ladybugs were ecstatic. Each girl gleefully picked an umbrella and no one even fought over the selections because there were two or three of each kind—well, except for one.

Patamela spotted a dazzling rainbow umbrella at the bottom of the box and knew she had found her match. She loved it so much she pledged to give it nothing less than first class treatment. She wouldn't dare treat her umbrella like she treated that dumb old cane. It was too special and the only one of its kind. She could tell the other girls wished they had picked it, but Patsy spotted it first. She would definitely master the tap routine now. She had to show everyone at the recital the beautiful umbrella she had handpicked.

"Isn't that a fancy one," Mr. O'Keefe said, smiling at

Patsy as he collected the umbrellas. Patsy kissed her father good-bye knowing he was responsible for her luck changing for the better.

Patamela was doing great! Her teachers would be happy to know she planned to uphold her pledge as a respectable insect for the rest of the program, (two and a half days by Patsy's calculations—a mere cakewalk). She had successfully gotten through her technique classes, tutor sessions, and now tap, without incident. Some other kid may have taken this feat lightly, but Patsy was thrilled to have kept her word to her dad.

When Ms. Patterson returned to Studio M1 to relieve Mr. O'Keefe and Mr. Hollingsworth of their duties, Patsy knew the look on her face was cause for even more celebration. Patsy could tell Ms. Patterson received a good report about her behavior and an update on her gift to the Ladybugs. It seemed to Patsy that in one afternoon, Ms. Patterson was nicer to Patsy than she had been in all the other days of her summer session combined.

Ms. Patterson was extremely pleased with Patsy's efforts to be an active participant in Legends again. She made sure to keep Patsy engaged at all times to prevent boredom from striking.

"Patamela, would you change the record for us please? Patamela, would you please cut off the studio lights? Patamela, would you please open the windows for us?" Ms. Patterson had a lot of requests for Patsy that day.

Patsy took pride in every duty Ms. Patterson assigned. She felt extra special when Ms. Patterson started pouring on the compliments. "Great turn, Patamela, that's going to look good Saturday. Keep that up!"

Wow, thought Patsy, Ms. Patterson's not so bad after all. Especially since it seemed she had finally moved beyond her jealousy of Patsy's naturally gifted feet. Patamela hoped she wasn't pegging her wrong. But as the compliments poured in, Patamela became more and more convinced that Ms. Patterson was ready to let her share her light with the world. She had spent enough time copying Patsy's moves and was finally ready to teach the Ladybugs without Patsy's help.

Getting skipped didn't seem like such an impossible feat anymore. If I keep up my good behavior streak, maybe she'll tell the other teachers the truth about me, Patsy mused. Yeah, that's it, thought Patsy, she'll tell them I'm the magic behind the Ladybugs' progress! Everyone will want me in their class!

After all, Patsy figured she still had today and tomorrow to master the tap routine. She even planned to practice with Mr. O'Keefe both evenings. That would be more than enough time to convince Mr. O'Keefe to get on Ms. Patterson's "let's go ahead and skip Patsy" bandwagon.

Even though Patsy did not have the burning desire to be skipped anymore (at least that is what she told herself), getting an offer would be great news to tell Aunt Deidre— and anyone else who would listen. Patsy actually blushed as she thought of how proud Aunt Deidre would be. That would surely leave Patience's and Prince's volunteer efforts in the dust, she thought. Not to mention the great story it would make for her fourth grade class. Picking her own summer activity and being skipped meant she would be the most popular, big kid, big shot girl in fourth grade.

Next stop...huge change, Patamela speculated. With school only a few weeks away, she was in a hurry to seal the deal.

CHAPTER 29

Helping Hands

When Legends let out for the day, Patamela raced to find Mr. O'Keefe. If she could show him a smidge of what she had shown her teachers during her classes, she was certain Mr. O'Keefe would second Ms. Patterson's motion to skip her. Patsy rushed up and down the halls looking for Mr. O'Keefe. She peeked in every classroom, around every corner, and into the teachers' lounge, but she could find no trace of him. Patamela decided to check Studio M1's door again. Maybe he left her a note instructing her to wait.

Patsy scurried down the corridor. She was prepared to wait as long as it took for Mr. O'Keefe to return. If he came back at seven in the evening and kept her until eleven, it would be fine with her. If that is what it took to be in the tap performance, Mr. O'Keefe could count Patsy in.

Though, to be honest, Patamela never truly believed she was in danger of sitting out the tap performance. She just went along with the hoopla everyone was making over it to keep the peace. Everyone could tell Mr. O'Keefe's letter was a grossly exaggerated account of the events. Because if she had really been in jeopardy of being kicked out of the dance, he would have mentioned it to her directly; and so far, neither he nor Ms. Hollingsworth had. Patamela was convinced her mom had told her she was getting dropped from tap to scare her, but she would never call her mother's bluff.

"Hello Patamela, shouldn't you be in the auditorium awaiting your ride home?" Ms. Hollingsworth asked, interrupting Patamela's train of thought. "I hope you're not playing in the halls."

"Nah, not me...That Patsy James is history," Patsy assured. "I've been looking all over for you and Mr. O'Keefe. Aren't we having practice this afternoon?"

"Patsy, did Mr. O'Keefe tell you we were meeting after school today?"

"Ummm," Patsy closed her eyes and replayed the highlights of her day before arriving at her conclusion. "No," she answered. "But, when I said I could stay today, you guys didn't say I couldn't. I'm ready to do my best and get that routine down pat," Patsy added.

"Oh, I see," Ms. Hollingsworth said. "Hmmph...Let's see. What can I do with you quickly?"

"Quickly?" Patsy replied bewildered. "I can stay, Ms. Hollingsworth. I have permission to stay late."

"That's great, Patsy, but the problem is Mr. O'Keefe and I didn't plan to hold practice today. Mr. O'Keefe left early to check the prices of some items we must purchase for the school's other tap routines. I'm headed to meet Ms. Watkins and a group of parents on the costume committee."

Patsy sighed heavily then picked up her Legends bag. It was time to call her mom to pick her up. She would rather go home than have two measly seconds of practice.

"Patamela, we will go over the dance twice. That's all I

can do today, and it will be quick," Ms. Hollingsworth said reluctantly. "I suggest you memorize my movements and then practice with a cane or broomstick at home."

"Okay, Ms. Hollingsworth."

Patamela fixed her eyes on Ms. Hollingsworth's every move. Yet she noticed Ms. Hollingsworth's movements greatly differed from Mr. O'Keefe's movements. The way Ms. Hollingsworth did the routine seemed to add four steps where Mr. O'Keefe only had the girls doing two.

"Ms. Hollingsworth, are you sure you're doing the steps from the Ladybugs' routine? You know, the steps Mr. O'Keefe taught?" Patsy asked with a frown. "Those steps look mighty different."

"I'm not doing them differently per se. I just do the routine in a way that works best for me. We end up in the same place and on the same count."

After five more shuffle steps, Patsy was completely lost. "Shuffle, now Patsy, break, smile for the audience." In one split second, it seemed Ms. Hollingsworth hurled a million instructions. Patsy was curious to know how Ms. Hollingsworth managed to stay on beat. It must have been hard for her to do considering the sweat that was pouring down her temples and forehead. Even the back of her leotard was streaming with perspiration.

Patsy was finding it hard to concentrate. Well, she was concentrating, but not on the steps. Patamela was too focused on keeping her distance from Ms. Hollingsworth. Once she got a glimpse of the fountain running underneath Ms. Hollingsworth's arms, Patamela feared she might smell like those hot orange peels Miles said his trumpet teacher smelled like. *Yuck*, Patsy thought. She wanted to tell Ms. Hollingsworth she wasn't learning a thing, and then bolt out the door. But Patsy did not know how to break the news to her. After all, she seemed to be working so hard.

When Ms. Hollingsworth reached the close of the routine for the second time, Patsy could tell that asking her to repeat it was out of the question. She looked so tired that Patsy doubted she would be able to make it to her car.

She's giving tap teachers everywhere a bad name, thought Patamela. Instead of writing a letter to Mrs. James, Mr. O'Keefe should have written an ad in the paper for a new dance partner. Ms. Hollingsworth was a rotten dancer! Patsy couldn't decide what was plaguing her—a case of two left feet or just one numb-to-the-bone clubfoot.

Mr. O'Keefe made dancing look easy, especially the routine's close. But Ms. Hollingsworth butchered the dance and totally rushed the ending. Patsy had no idea where her hands should end up at the close of the dance because keeping an eye on Ms. Hollingsworth's hands was an even harder job than following her feet.

"You've got it now, right Patamela?" Ms. Hollingsworth asked, using her sweater to pat the sweat from her brow.

Patsy had not broken a sweat at all. She was too busy staring in disbelief at Ms. Hollingsworth's discombobulated steps. Patsy could see now why Mr. O'Keefe was the main teacher. Ms. Hollingsworth was a beginner. She's the one that needs to be a Ladybug, thought Patsy.

Ms. Hollingsworth turned to lead Patsy out of the studio. Patamela followed as far behind as possible while squeezing her nose with her thumb and index finger. If Ms. Hollingsworth smelled half as bad as her dancing looked, one whiff and Patsy would pass out.

"I hope that helped," Ms. Hollingsworth said, trying to comfort Patsy by wrapping an arm around Patsy's shoulder. Patsy cringed. It felt like her leotard was absorbing all of Ms. Hollingsworth's perspiration. "I'm very proud of you, Patamela," she said, pressing her wet check against Patsy's face. She used her arm to pull Patsy in tighter. "I bet you want to see how the costumes are coming out, don't you, Patamela?" Ms. Hollingsworth asked.

"Sure do, Ms. Hollingsworth! Can I help too?" Patsy asked anxiously.

"I'm sure we could use a helping hand."

Boy, am I lucky, Patsy thought. She was happy to be getting a sneak preview of the finishing touches on the costumes. "Yippee!" she cheered, startling Ms. Hollingsworth. She would even be allowed to help with costume alterations!

Actually, this is a thousand times better than some silly evening practice, thought Patsy. *Shucks*, after my latest good deeds, I'm a shoe-in for the tap performance and for being skipped, she thought.

"Oh brother, not her again!"

It was Kamal. He was giving Patsy his meanest grin while effortlessly balancing the wooden chair he sat on. The chair's front legs were high in the air. Its back legs were tilted just enough for the chair's backrest to lean against the radiator below the window. He began rocking just to annoy her, but caught himself before crashing backward.

"*Boy, don't make me come over there,*" said his mother. "Hello Ms. James," she continued, turning to Patsy.

"Hi Ms. Watkins," Patsy answered. "I'm here to help with the costumes."

"We'd love to have your assistance. Let's see. You can glue the rhinestones on the seams of the Fireflies' costumes. Kamal will offer you whatever help you need," Ms. Watkins continued while glaring at Kamal.

"I wouldn't take any help from him if he was the last..."

Ms. Hollingsworth interrupted Patsy. "Patsy, you're doing so well. Don't mess it up now."

"Yeah Patsy, don't mess it up now. You might need me one day," Kamal said, puckering his lips to blow her a kiss.

"Cut it out, Kamal!" Ms. Watkins insisted.

"That's what you tell me, Mom: *Be nice, you never know when you are going to need folk,*" Kamal mimicked.

Everyone in the room laughed. Patsy wished everyone would stop clamoring over Kamal and get on with the business of costume primping. Fortunately, Patamela's wish was granted before she had a chance to say something she shouldn't or get herself in some other trouble with Kamal. As soon as the group recovered from their laugh attack, they got right down to work. Patsy quickly discovered that she had an instrumental role to play in the costume designs. The parents seemed to trust her with their most perplexing costume decisions. When the parents couldn't make up their minds, Patsy decided they should leave the belt buckles off the Doves' costumes and shorten the collars for one of the Hummingbirds' outfits. Patsy even suggested they spray paint the Ladybugs' white tap shoes the color of their rain ponchos. The women raved about Patamela's helpfulness.

Patsy had given the committee a huge helping hand. She was certain Ms. Patterson would be pleased after hearing about her work with the costume committee. Come tomorrow morning, she would treat her even better than she had this afternoon.

Mr. O'Keefe would be pleasantly surprised as well. In turn, he'd make practicing with Patsy his top priority. Patsy could see it now. Both Ms. Patterson and Mr. O'Keefe would escort her to the front office and demand that Ms. Saa skip her. She would return to Legends next summer not as a Butterfly, but as a full-fledged Fairy! Friday was going to be great!

CHAPTER 30

A Telephone Pick-Me-Up

Friday didn't go quite as planned. As a matter of fact, Patamela considered it to be a disaster! Not only did Mr. O'Keefe disappear at the end of the day—for the second day in a row—but this time, Ms. Hollingsworth disappeared too. Even Ms. Watkins and the costume committee parents were heading out early. They decided they would rather work in the comfort of their own homes than be cooped up in a stuffy classroom all evening. They decided to handle any surprise costume mishaps when they met the next morning before the recital.

"*Legends Dance School*—what a joke! It's more like Legends ghost town," Patsy grumbled. Although, Patamela had permission to stay after Legends let out, there was no one around to care. It was a shame too, since she had been looking forward to evening practice. After yesterday's backwards hokey-pokey lesson from Ms. Hollingsworth and today's cake and ice cream celebration that cancelled all afternoon classes, Patsy believed her involvement in the tap performance depended on spending an evening with Mr. O'Keefe.

How could he run out on me now? Patsy wondered. He had to know he hadn't practiced with her since Thursday afternoon's class. He owed her at least one more day of practice before Saturday's recital. Hadn't she earned it after donating umbrellas to the Ladybugs?

"Railroaded again!" Patsy shouted at the top of her lungs. She fumed that Mr. O'Keefe had not kept his end of the bargain.

"Honey, ain't no use crying over spilt milk or whatever you're fussing about," Mrs. Wright said from the curb. She had been watching Patamela the whole time as she helped Ms. Watkins load some items into her car.

"*Aint that right...*Now go on and get in Mrs. Wright's car, Patsy," Ms. Watkins instructed. "Your teachers are gone for the day. Makes no sense for your mom to come and get you when Mrs. Wright is standing right here."

By the time Patamela got home she was practically dragging herself through the front door. "Hey Patsy, guess who's on the line?" Mrs. James said with a huge smile. Patsy knew it had to be Aunt Deidre and bolted to pick up the kitchen phone.

"Hey auntie, are you really coming?" Patsy said with a hint of disbelief.

"I wouldn't miss it for the world, Pattie Cakes. I hear you have performances in ballet, jazz, modern, and tap. You know tap is my favorite. Your mother and I used to take classes when we were girls."

"Really auntie?" Patsy asked.

"Sure did, but we weren't any good," Aunt Deidre said with a boisterous laugh. "But I know my baby is the star of the show, aren't you, angel?"

"See you tomorrow auntie! Tell Uncle John I said hi."

Patsy could not sit still the rest of the night. Her aunt's

words had rejuvenated her winning spirit. It was just the pick-me-up she needed after Mr. O'Keefe's backdoor exit. She scrambled from room to room gathering the items mentioned on her Ladybug costume checklist.

Patamela packed, unpacked, and then repacked her Legends bag three whole times. She didn't want to forget a thing. Luckily Mrs. James suggested she use her book bag on wheels to carry some items. By the time she finished, both her Legends bag and her book bag were packed to the brim.

"*Ugh*! Her you go, Little Bit," Prince said as he dropped her bags beside the front door.

"Patsy, I wanna help," Patience added from the sofa. She had been trying to help Patsy all evening. She hoped Patsy wouldn't hold her grudge all night, especially since Patsy had forgiven Prince yesterday.

Patamela finally gave in. She knew she had better make up with Patience if she wanted to count her as part of her standing ovation squad. The last thing she needed was Patience convincing her friends to sit on their bottoms and refuse to clap because Patsy hadn't been her friend. Plus no one on this earth could make Patsy more "Eartha Kitt, Judith Jamison, Debbie Allen, fabulous dancer" beautiful than Patience could.

That evening Patsy received Patience's special beauty treatment. It started with a manicure and pedicure, rounded off with a foot massage, and then ended in a jelly face mask. Patience promised it would make Patsy's skin glow. Normally, Patsy would have refused Patience's jelly mask, but after her two-week stint on punishment, she had grown accustomed to being Patience's beauty shop guinea pig. The entire treatment tickled Mrs. James until Patience spilled the grape jelly all over the kitchen floor.

"Patience, don't you start another refrigerator, or cabinet-raiding treatment," Mrs. James warned.

"Okay Ma," Patience answered before she and Patsy giddily snickered, "we're done..."

The only thing left to do was Patsy's hair, and that was her mom's job. According to the Legends checklist, each group had a choice of hairstyles they could wear and Patsy chose to put a bun on the crown of her head. Mrs. James had to redo it several times until Patsy felt it was perfect. Then Patsy asked her mom to tie her headscarf as snuggly as possible so her bun would stay in place as she slept.

At bedtime, Patsy had difficulty keeping her eyes closed. The idea of being on stage with her beautifully striped umbrella and Aunt Deidre in the audience thrilled her. Patamela pictured herself receiving standing ovation after standing ovation until she fell fast asleep.

CHAPTER 31

A Deal's a Deal

When Patsy woke up, she sprang out of bed determined to make the day better than the one before. She had it all figured out. First, she would arrive at Legends before all the other students. Then, she would corner Mr. O'Keefe and double- or even triple-dare him to pull that ducking stunt he had been getting away with all week. "*Fool me once, fool me twice, fool me three times, I won't be as nice,*" Patsy proudly sang.

As an expert on the art of ducking and dodging, Patamela was understandably agitated. She couldn't believe she'd been ditched by an amateur like Mr. O'Keefe. Normally she could detect a wet-behind-the-ears, wanna-be ducking specialist a mile away. There had to be a glitch in her radar. Otherwise, a beginner like Mr. O'Keefe would never have been able to dodge her for so long.

Although Patsy considered Mr. O'Keefe an amateur, she was certain he was strutting around Legends claiming to be the Grand Emperor of Escape. Patamela was convinced Mr. O'Keefe believed he had successfully thrown her for a loop. Yet it was that type of uppity, rub-it-in-your-face gloating that really roasted her insides. Mr. O'Keefe gave her no other alternative but to take action. He's got some nerve thinking he can offer help and then duck out of the deal, thought Patsy. "A deal's a deal!" she yelled out in her quiet house.

Mr. O'Keefe had volunteered to stay after, point blank, end of story! No matter how many times Patsy turned down his offer, he had no right to take it back, and that's just what Patsy planned to tell him when she saw him that morning. "Mr. Okay, the offer still stands!"

Patamela had been duped for the last time. She had naively allowed Mr. O'Keefe to throw her off his trail two evenings in a row. Whether Mr. O'Keefe knew it or not, yesterday marked the last evening she would wander Legends like a lost puppy in search of its master. Her teacher-chasing days were over.

Patsy would demand that Mr. O'Keefe keep their deal. He could do so by providing her with a private lesson. The lesson would have to be at least four hours in length and take place before the recital that evening. Patsy felt that was the only way he could honor his commitment to her. When that was added to the day's regularly scheduled tap rehearsal, it would give Patsy more than enough time to convince Mr. O'Keefe she deserved her spot in the dance and to be skipped.

My glow will be unstoppable with that kind of time, Patsy thought. Her private-lesson idea guaranteed a flawless, James-glow performance for her father and for Aunt Deidre.

"Now that's how you turn around a bum deal!" she said to her reflection in the bathroom mirror. Patsy went downstairs and prepared a bowl of cold cereal and milk. She decided she would pass on her mother's famous pancake and sausage breakfast. It would take too long to pre-pare and the clock was ticking.

"Let's go, Mommy!" Patsy shouted after finishing her meal and dressing for the day. "I have places to go, teach-ers to see, and a show to put on!"

"Choose your words *and* your tone wisely, Patamela."

"I mean, good morning, Mommy...Can we go now?"

Yet for all Patsy's pushing and prodding, Mr. O'Keefe was nowhere in sight when she and her mom arrived at Legends.

"Hey lady!" Ms. Watkins exclaimed before hugging Mrs. James. "Mr. O'Keefe? Oh no, he's not here. He called in to say he was running a little late. He won't be here until at least nine thirty or ten o' clock."

"*Somebody catch me!*" Patamela wailed before swoon-ing at her mother's side. "Everyone will be here by then."

"Come on, Patsy, stand up. Stop kidding around," said her mom as she propped Patsy on her feet.

"*Boy*, people sure don't keep appointments like they used to. Whatever happened to good old-fashioned, *put-it-there-partner*, deal making?" Patsy said as she shook hands with an imaginary business partner.

"Darling, I'd be more than happy to make a deal with you," Ms. Watkins said. "If you promise to pick that pretty face of yours up off the floor, I promise to crown you the costume committee's alterations model for the day."

"It's a deal!" Patsy hooted.

"Is that right, young lady?" Mrs. James jokingly asked.

"Please, Ma, can I?"

"Alright, you can stay. I'll be back around five to help you get ready for the show."

"Don't even worry yourself. We have a group of par-ents that handle all of that. She'll be fine," Ms. Watkins assured as she hustled Patsy from the front office to the costume committee's classroom.

Patamela flew into the classroom and stripped down to her leotard and tights. Ms. Watkins tossed the first outfit to be tailored across the room. Patsy leapt in the air and caught the jumpsuit in her arms. Within seconds, Patamela was standing in the jumpsuit with both straps fastened. Ms. Watkins tacked a few butterfly brooches on each leg, and then moved on to the next outfit. They were a great team.

"You were right, Ms. Watkins!" Patsy hooted. "I'm having a ball!"

Patsy must have tried on twenty costumes after her mom left. She was turned and spun in so many directions she imagined she was the star of her favorite *Adventures of Elastic Girl* cartoon. And when Ms. Watkins wasn't thrashing her about, she was pinning down every hem, fold, and crease on Patsy's frame.

"You got some type of goose loose in your caboose chile? Stay still before you leave here chock full of holes. I've got to get this hem straight."

Usually, bossy, have-it-their-way adults ranked terribly low on Patamela's lists. Yet the more Ms. Watkins ordered her to model, prance, and leap in her costumes, the more Patsy grew to like her. She made Patsy feel like a princess, a beauty pageant princess at that. Patamela was living out a true big kid, big shot fantasy (the type of fantasy some of her Melbourne classmates would chop their ponytails off for—and Patsy couldn't wait to tell them). In fact, Patsy was having so much fun being a model she forgot just how quickly the clock was ticking.

"Sure wish other grownups could stick to their deal making like you do, Ms. Watkins," Patsy said in a most flattering tone.

"Really?"

"Yeah, maybe you should give lessons. I know a couple of teachers that could use your help. For starters, that Mr...."

"Hey there dragon breath!" Kamal rudely interrupted as he swaggered into costume headquarters. "How come you're not following the warden around like the other Ladyboogers?"

"Mr. O'Keefe and the Ladybugs are here?" Patsy asked, puzzled. She had almost forgotten that Warden Warthog was Kamal's codename for Mr. O'Keefe ever since that day he busted them in the park.

"Yeah, they've been here for a while," Kamal reported. "They're stomping the floor like an army sent by pest control. I sure hope they don't call that practice," he cackled.

Patsy hopped off the wooden chair, tightened her headscarf, and tore off the latest costume. "Gotta go, Ms. Watkins!" Patsy was in a rush to get to the auditorium. She snatched her Legends bag from the floor and ran out of the classroom. "Watch my suitcase, please!" she yelled.

"What happened to our deal?" Ms. Watkins called out as Patsy disappeared down the corridor.

CHAPTER 32

It's Curtains!

Patsy burst through the double doors of the auditorium. And there, onstage (just as Kamal had reported), surrounded by a troupe of teeming Ladybugs, was none other than Mr. O'Keefe. "I'm here, Mr. O'Keefe, I'm here! I was waiting for you in the classroom with Ms. Watkins," she shouted, running toward the stage.

"It's okay, Patsy. We added a couple of finishing touches here and there, but there's still time to help," Mr. O'Keefe assured. "We've got a stack of props and scenery boards that need work."

"Okay ladies, let's break for lunch," Mr. O'Keefe proposed as he jumped off the stage. "Let's see," he said, tapping his wristwatch, "we'll take an hour for lunch, grab the paint brushes, go over..."

"An hour lunch? You just got here!" Patsy snapped.

"Actually I've been here for a while. Besides, it's nearly two o'clock and we're hungry. Right guys?" "You can't stop now!" Patsy wailed, but no one paid her any attention.

Patsy watched in awe as Mr. O'Keefe and the Ladybugs

took their seats in the reserved rows for their group. She could tell Mr. O'Keefe was getting a real kick out of rubbing his break idea in her face. He slouched down in his seat and propped his feet on the chair in front of him. "*Way to honor a deal, Mr. O'Cheat*," Patamela griped. And when he crossed his legs and all the Ladybugs attempted to prop up their feet and do the same, Patsy thought she would die. Didn't anyone care about Mr. O'Keefe's broken promises?

Patamela slowly made her way to the Ladybug section. "Well I care, and that's more than enough," she said. She slid into the row directly behind Mr. O'Keefe and crept to his chair. "*Mr. O'Keefe*," Patsy gently called while tapping his shoulder. "*Mr. O'Keefe*," Patsy said a bit louder. "When will I get *my* practice?" she asked as a drove of dancing insects filed into the theater. The commotion sweeping the auditorium muffled her question to a faint whisper.

"Mr. O'Keefe!" Patsy shouted above the noise. "When do I get to practice?" she hollered as the remaining groups poured down the aisles.

Mr. O'Keefe turned his attention to Patamela. "Ms. Patterson is holding her practice for ballet, jazz, and modern from two thirty to four thirty."

"I'm asking about tap!" Patsy screamed.

"Patsy, the Ladybugs know the tap routine like the back of their hands. We even did a little work with the umbrellas when everyone first arrived. I will hold an hour practice from four thirty to five thirty—and that's it."

"But I need...Will you be able to give me a practice by myself?" Patsy demanded.

"I'm not sure we have time for that, Patsy. It'll be crazy in here for the rest of the day. I just don't have time."

Patamela rolled her eyes and held them shut as long as

she could before opening them. They better not ask me to work on their stupid props, she thought. Her cooperative spirit of service had checked out for the day. Instead of working on their scene props or joining their lunch party, she would sit in silence—and as far away as she possibly could. "And you better not follow me!" she threatened before grabbing her bag and stomping off to a distant row.

Patamela was in quite a snit. She dropped her bottom lip and plopped into a seat to give Mr. O'Keefe the deadly Patsy James stare. But Mr. O'Keefe was busy telling stories to make the Ladybugs laugh and doing his best to rope Patsy in at the same time. "Didn't it happen like that, Patsy? Patsy was there. Hey, Patsy, come in closer!" he summoned.

He sure was making it hard for her to zap him with her dirty looks. Patsy didn't answer him though. She was aggravated and pooped. She doubted if zapping Mr. O'Keefe was worth this much effort—especially since he was deflecting her attempts with a force field straight out of a comic book. When the Ladybugs' pizza arrived, she decided that zapping Mr. O'Keefe with her deadly stare wasn't worth any more effort.

Although Patsy was determined to keep her distance from her deal-breaking opponent, she quickly wormed her way from the back of the auditorium into the circle of Ladybugs surrounding him. She needed to be close to her group—or more importantly, to the stack of pizza pies heading their way.

Patamela scampered to the food line, thanked the parent volunteer for her plate, and took her seat. Although the Ladybugs were cackling hysterically at Mr. O'Keefe's comedy act, Patsy slowly chomped her pizza slice and made certain to contain her amusement to a soft-pitched giggle. She did not want Mr. O'Keefe to mistake her merriment as a peace offering or as an apology for rolling her eyes. After all, he deserved some form of punishment for his stupid hour-long lunch idea and wishy-washy answer to her private lesson request.

I bet *their* teachers would practice with them if they needed it, Patsy thought to herself, as she turned her attention to a nearby group practicing their routine. Just then, Ms. Patterson cheerfully paraded down the middle auditorium aisle. "Are there any Ladybugs in the house?" she yelled. "I said, are there any Ladybugs in the house?" Patamela inhaled the rest of her pizza slice, guzzled her fruit juice, and joined her dance mates.

All the Ladybugs were glad to see Patsy finally participating, but they wondered if Ms. Patterson had bopped her over the head with a magic, frown-be-gone wand. That's just how quickly Patsy's sour attitude disappeared. She turned and swayed her hips and pointed her toes, just as they'd learned. Patsy made certain to stress every technique Ms. Patterson had taught her since the first day of class. She would not let Mr. O'Keefe's wobbly, jellyfish of an answer get her down.

"Excellent, Patamela! Yes! Yes! You must do just that for the recital tonight," Ms. Patterson cheered.

Even Faye looked at Patsy's renewed dedication with astonishment. "You're on fire, Patz!" she yelled.

Patsy was ready for Mr. O'Keefe to bring his Ladybug rehearsal on. She knew he'd agree to a private lesson if she showed him the same fire she had just shown Ms. Patterson. She wished Ms. Patterson would stay to watch her practice tap but guessed she had last minute scene props to purchase.

Unfortunately, the fire that Faye and the other girls

had witnessed was no where to be found once tap rehearsal started. Patsy was suddenly overcome with anxiety. If that wasn't bad enough, her imagination kicked into overdrive causing her to feel as if chunks of hot lava were sputtering from her tap shoes one goopy chunk at a time.

"Are you alright, Patsy?" Faye asked.

Patsy closed her eyes and tried brushing her tap shoes against the stage floor. She gave a tip, then a tap. But in her mind all she could hear was her glow oozing from the tip of her shoes—*Blobbit, blobbit.*

When the girls surrounded Patsy for her turn to dance alone in the semi-circle, she couldn't determine which tap style she knew better, Mr. O'Keefe's or Ms. Hollingsworth's. She was so confused she could not tell her right foot from her left. She tripped over her umbrella, pushed two girls in the circle to their knees, and then slid to the edge of the stage, face first.

Patsy scrambled to her feet to catch up with her two tap partners, but she had already missed her cue. They were already on their way offstage. Mr. O'Keefe looked at Ms. Hollingsworth in the front row seat and Patsy could tell the look meant trouble. Ms. Hollingsworth signaled for the music to stop, though Patsy wished she would have kept it on.

"She's going to ruin our dance."

"She's terrible."

"She doesn't know what she's doing."

Without the blaring music Patsy couldn't avoid hearing the Ladybugs' comments, and then things got worse. Mr. O'Keefe and Ms. Hollingsworth broke their huddle to call her forward.

Patamela trudged down the stage steps. She could feel the glares coming from the older dancers standing throughout the auditorium. She was certain they caught the pose she struck when she reached the edge of the stage but hoped they missed the crash landing that got her there.

"Patamela," Mr. O'Keefe said as he placed his hand on her shoulder, "Ms. Hollingsworth and I have decided to put you on the light and curtain committee. During the Singing in the Rain performance, you'll assist that team with the lights and curtain closings. You can even remind the Ladybugs when it's time to do their solo dances and break off into pairs."

Patsy was no dummy. She was not fooled by the old switcheroo. Miles had taught her to watch out for it. His parents were known for pulling it on him. "They'll take something you want away and then put something that isn't half as good in its place—but they'll try to make it seem like it measures up," Patsy recalled Miles saying. And that's just what Mr. O'Keefe was doing.

"Curtains? I don't want to touch those dirty curtains! I can't even reach the lights backstage. I don't want to be on the light and curtain committee," Patsy grumbled. "Does this mean I'm not in the dance, Mr. O'Keefe? You promised to stay after with me, but you never did! I want a private lesson right now!"

"Patamela, I just can't give you that. I do, however, apologize for any misunderstanding. I had errands to run the last couple of days, but how many times did I offer to work with you after class before this week? See how things happen?" he explained. "Look, with a little practice, you'll have the routine down pat for the Christmas show. Maybe we can do a version of it then."

"Christmas? That's too far away! I want to be in this dance!" Patsy demanded with a stomp of her foot.

"I'm sorry, Patamela, you just aren't prepared."

Mr. O'Keefe walked back toward the stage as the Ladybugs prepared themselves to go through the routine again—this time, without Patsy.

"Mr. O'Keefe, can I have Patsy's umbrella?" Faye asked.

"Of course, I'm sure Patsy won't mind."

Patsy stuck her index fingers in her ears. She must have missed a huge gob of wax this morning because her hearing was obviously on the blink. When she saw Faye bend down to retrieve her umbrella, she realized she'd heard exactly right.

What a kick in the teeth, Patsy thought. What injustice!

"Okay Girls, let's take it from the top," Mr. O'Keefe instructed.

Patsy struggled to fight the tears that wanted to roll down her cheeks. She'd never been so hurt or so furious, and she wouldn't stand for it. Patamela headed straight back to the auditorium stage. Mr. O'Keefe wondered why Patsy was getting back on stage. "May I help you, Patamela? The girls are in the middle of rehearsing. We'll talk after I'm done," he said with authority.

Patsy never answered. Instead, she pawed the floor like a bull in a bullpen. She charged straight toward Faye. "My daddy bought these umbrellas! Get your own!" she screamed as she snatched the opened umbrella out of Faye's hand. Patamela walked around the stage and collected as many umbrellas as she could before fumbling them all.

"Patsy, is this the way your mother told you to be of service and display team spirit?" yelled Mr. O'Keefe.

"I don't care! My daddy bought them and they're mine! Get your daddy to buy you your own umbrella!" she said to all the Ladybugs. Patsy ignored the umbrellas she'd dropped and started trying to grab the remaining umbrellas.

"Stop it this second, Patamela James!" Ms. Watkins called from the back of the auditorium. "I'm appalled by your behavior. You were doing so well. *Chile*, you better get over here!" Ms. Watkins rushed to Mr. O'Keefe's side. "Lucky thing I came when I did, huh? I just came to tell her I didn't need anyone to help with the costumes anymore."

Ms. Watkins quickly looked over her shoulders to make sure no one else was listening. "I made the boy do it," she whispered. "He may never recover," she softly chuckled.

Patsy shuffled to the steps leading off the stage, struggling with an armful of umbrellas. "And drop those umbrellas!" Ms. Watkins snapped. "Mr. O'Keefe, please finish your lesson. Patsy will not interrupt you again."

Tears were gushing down Patsy's face by the time she made it to the bottom of the steps. No fair, Patsy thought, and after all my good deeds. Patsy just couldn't understand how Mr. O'Keefe could kick her out of her own dance and give Faye the okay to nab her umbrella. He was holding a grudge after all.

Patsy was sure Mr. O'Keefe had never forgiven her for that day in the park or for ducking his practices. It's all clear now, she thought. He never planned to stay after, and he never wanted me in the dance. What an underhanded, deal-breaking, umbrella-heist phony, thought Patsy as she folded her arms and followed Ms. Watkins out of the auditorium.

CHAPTER 33

The Big Payback

"Patsy, since there's only an hour or so left before the recital begins, you'll sit here with me until it's time for you to get dressed," Ms. Watkins instructed as she motioned Patsy to sit down. "And to think you've been so good lately. I just don't understand what got into you.

"They're my umbrellas!" Patsy shouted. "If I can't dance, they can't hold them! *Don't even deserve...that Faye... just not fair*!" Patsy grumbled in a sentence too muffled for Ms. Watkins to put together.

"Girl, how much time did you have to learn those routines? *You* got on punishment and then *you* ducked practice, no one else. To me, it's very fair. Let me ask you this: How fair is it for you to dance when you don't know the routine?"

"I do so know the routine!" Patsy interrupted.

"Patamela, you can't expect to get congratulated for last minute efforts. A good sport would happily help with the lights and curtains *and* lend their umbrellas. It's the fair thing to do, if you ask me. Chile, quit acting like it's the end of the world. You're still in three other dances."

Patsy was not convinced. She would get her umbrellas back if it was the last thing she did. "This isn't over. They'll see," she vowed beneath her breath. Patsy swung her legs around so she could stare into the hallway as Ms. Watkins droned on about the consequences of bad choices.

Just then the sound of faint laughter caught Patsy's attention. With Ms. Watkins busily pinning up announcements and discount flyers on the bulletin board, Patsy could investigate without alarming her. First Patamela stuck out her tongue, jammed her thumbs in her ears, and wiggled her fingers. She had to make sure Ms. Watkins didn't have eyes behind her head or some trick mirror like she once heard Mr. Piccirillo carried. Ms. Watkins never turned around. The coast was clear.

Patsy lifted her body slightly off the chair and peeked out the door. The corridor was stark empty, except for three Ladybugs heading for Studio M1. They're carrying my umbrellas! Patsy thought.

As their faces met Patsy's, they stopped giggling and stared at the floor.

"Where do you think you're going with those umbrellas?" Patsy demanded in a sharp whisper.

"Mi-Mi-Mister O'Keefe said to bring them up here until it's our turn. There's no space backstage," one of the girls stammered.

"Ooo, you're not supposed to speak to her," one of the other girls said as she pulled the stammering girl toward Studio M1.

Patamela's nerves sizzled as she watched the girls open Studio M1 with Mr. O'Keefe's key. She could tell it was the long black key chain he always wore around his neck.

"No room backstage. Like I'd fall for that," Patsy grunted.

"Okay, where is he?" Patsy wondered, peering down the hall. If anything, Patsy figured the trio was secretly meeting Mr. O'Keefe for a private, pre-recital lesson—a lesson they desperately needed.

Yet not even two seconds later, Patsy was startled by the girls' abrupt (and surprisingly empty-handed) departure from Studio M1. They ran straight past her, skillfully zigzagging their way through a crowd of parents filing into the show. It was clear they weren't going to return anytime soon, and although Patsy didn't want to admit it, neither was Mr. O'Keefe.

Patsy wanted to get even. I'll never let those thieving termites get the last laugh, thought Patsy. They deserve payback.

The idea hit Patsy like a bolt of lightning. She would hide the umbrellas. They'll look pretty silly trying to do a "Singing in the Rain" routine with canes, thought Patsy.

This was the best, bubble-busting revenge plot ever. She pictured each phase of the plan just so she could see how perfectly diabolical it was. First, she imagined finding an undiscoverable backstage hiding place. Then she would wait quietly with a huge bucket of water. Finally, she would climb a super tall ladder to the very top rung and as soon as the Ladybugs pranced on stage, she would pour ice-cold water on their umbrella-less heads.

"They'll be all wet!" Patsy laughed. "That'll teach them to throw me on some stupid curtain committee."

Patamela chuckled even harder as she pictured the Ladybugs slipping and sliding offstage in their tap shoes. Patsy realized the ladder, bucket, and ice-cold water part of her plan was far-fetched, but she knew getting her hands on those umbrellas was not. A pair of keys was already within her grasp. All she had to do was hide the umbrellas and then stand by as the Ladybugs and Mr. O'Keefe met their ruin.

Patamela turned her attention back to Ms. Watkins, who clearly had her hands full. Ms. Watkins was up to her nose in registration packets. Each time she put a batch of freshly copied registration leaflets together, she was back at the copier to pick up another. Patsy couldn't have asked for a better break. Now where does she keep that extra set of keys? Patsy asked herself.

On many occasions, Patsy had been instructed to ask Ms. Watkins for Studio M1's duplicate key after Ms. Patterson had misplaced her own. And there, hanging on the wall, to the right of Ms. Watkin's desk, were eight sets of keys. Above each was a typewritten label listing the door it opened.

Patsy strained her eyes in order to make out the key labels. "There it is!" she quietly gasped.

"You called, chile?" Ms. Watkins asked without raising her head from what she was doing.

"No, I was just remembering something," Patsy said in her most innocent voice.

Patsy decided it was the perfect time to make a run for it. If she moved quickly, she could grab the key ring without Ms. Watkins noticing. Patsy leaned out the door to make certain no one was coming and then turned to check on Ms. Watkins.

Patsy tiptoed away from her seat until she reached the closed gate on the left side of the welcome counter. She quietly opened the gate, crouched down until her knuckles hit the floor, then scrambled like a wild chimpanzee to Ms. Watkin's desk. "*Ready...set...go...*" she whispered, popping her head slightly above the desk to track the latest whereabouts of Ms. Watkins, although her tracking system wasn't the only one on duty.

You see, as Patsy's eyes rose above the desk, Kamal's eyes greeted her from the opposite end of it. He had been watching her every move. "Need some help?" he asked.

Patsy wasn't sure she could trust Kamal. But Kamal had been looking for some action since his two-week punishment ended. Earlier in the afternoon he had been so completely bored that he agreed to be his mother's dress-up doll. The last thing he would do is risk a chance to stir up some excitement. Patsy could count on him to be a most loyal ally.

Patsy snatched the key to Studio M1 and scurried back to the gate. She squeezed through the gate's cracked opening then slid into her chair just as Ms. Watkins turned around.

"I was wondering where you went," Ms. Watkins said as she gave her son a suspicious glare.

"I was in the auditorium being an usher for Ms. Saa. I even helped Ms. Daye collect tickets at the front door," Kamal replied. "I just came back because Ms. Patterson asked for Patsy. She said it's time for her to change. I came to tell her and help her with her bags."

"How kind of you, Kamal. I appreciate you keeping busy—because these packets have just about wiped me out," she stated. "I know one thing, I better hurry up and relieve Ms. Daye at the front door."

Patsy could not believe how quick Kamal could fib. He definitely ran circles around her in that department. She was happy he decided to help.

The children grabbed Patsy's belongings, left the front office, then crept toward Studio M1. "I told you you'd need me one day," Kamal snickered. "What are you trying to get in there for anyway?"

"My umbrellas!" Patsy snapped.

"Oh yeah. I heard you got kicked out of the dance."

"Watch it!"

"I'm just teasing, Patsy."

Kamal motioned to Patsy to pass him the keys and opened the door to the studio. Patsy dashed to the cabinet. She was in luck! The girls had forgotten to lock the cabinet door. Patsy swung the cabinet doors open, grabbed as many umbrellas as she could, and told Kamal to grab the rest.

"What's the plan?" he asked. "Where are you going to hide them?"

Patsy had not thought that far ahead. She had been too busy thinking about ice water and buckets.

"I have the perfect place," Kamal said. "Come on, follow me."

The children scurried to the other end of the hall. Kamal turned the knob to a classroom door Patsy would have never thought to enter. "I don't know about this," Patsy said when she spotted the *Do Not Enter* sign taped to the door. If the sign wasn't enough to make her keep her distance, the jagged splinters of wood above and below the doorknob were. The room was obviously off limits. Kamal ventured further into the room, but Patsy did not follow. After all, she could read. The sign said not to enter.

"Come on, fraidy cat."

Patsy stayed put.

"Will you relax!" Kamal ordered.

Patsy inched closer to Kamal and surveyed the room. She could hardly see the floor. There were dingy white sheets splattered with green colored paint in almost every direction. The sheetless parts of the floor were even worse—covered in mounds of sawdust. Patsy was certain she was about to sneeze and began backing her way to the door.

"We're not supposed to be in here," Patsy said.

"And?" Kamal shot back as he walked over to close the door behind her. "We're not supposed to be hiding the Ladybugs' umbrellas either. Don't get all goody-two-shoes on me now."

"Why is it so dusty in here?" Patsy asked, following Kamal to the room's closet.

"They're pulling up the floors, repainting the walls, and repairing the ceiling. It's all part of the renovation project, but the men never show up when they're supposed to. I hide in here from my mom all the time. She never finds me."

Patsy believed Kamal was telling the truth because most of the chairs and desks were set up like the fortress he'd built in the other classroom. Patsy was certain Kamal had found a secret hideout of his own. No one else would dare come in.

"Stand back," Kamal instructed as he prepared to open the closet at the back of the classroom.

Patamela jumped behind him just before a slew of mismatched shoes, socks, lunch boxes, book bags, toys, and sweaters fell off the top shelf of the closet and plummeted to the floor. Patsy was astonished. She immediately recognized the items were belongings she and the other girls had reported lost or misplaced during recess.

"You scoundrel! You just wait. You are going to get it!" Patsy said.

"Do you want to hide these umbrellas or not?"

Patsy didn't reply.

"Well, don't just stand there. Make yourself useful," Kamal snapped, fetching a dusty chair from the corner of the room.

"Hurry up and pass me those umbrellas," Kamal demanded with his left hand out to grab the first one.

Patsy handed him the umbrellas as quickly as she could, although she made sure to pass her umbrella last. She wanted to twirl it one last time.

"Wee, wee," she sang, twirling and swinging the umbrella back and forth.

Kamal sprang off the chair and snatched the umbrella out of Patsy's hands. He skillfully leapt back onto his makeshift ladder and threw her umbrella to the back of the shelf before the other items could tumble down. In a matter of seconds, Kamal jumped off the chair, kicked it out of the way, and slammed his body against the closet door to close it. "I'd hate to be the one who opens that door," he said. "Let's get out of here."

CHAPTER 34

Keep a Lid On It

Patsy and Kamal sprinted out of the classroom then tore down the hall like a pair of Olympic-gold hopefuls. Although the two were moving fast enough to smash any hallway-dash record, neither one of them was on the look-out for a stool pigeon named Faye. Though as soon as they got wind of her, the pair reacted like a couple of quick-thinking spies and slowed down to a smooth, innocent-looking stride. Just in the nick of time too—since Faye didn't appear to suspect a thing.

"Ms. Patterson said you need to get into your costume, Patsy," Faye announced.

"Oh, thanks, Faye," Patsy said. "C'mon, let's get going."

Kamal and Patsy tried to quickly rush Faye away from the front office where Ms. Watkins was still busy working. They didn't want Faye's message to expose Kamal's earlier story as a bold-faced lie.

"Wait a minute. Why are your bags so dusty? And why are you with *him*?" As far as Faye was concerned, Kamal was their archenemy.

Patsy, on the other hand, wanted to give Faye a good, down-home knuckle sandwich *to go*. She had not forgotten about Faye's ruthless power play for her umbrella. Covering Faye's mouth, Patsy dragged her back to the staircase leading to the auditorium.

"Patamela, what are you up to?" Faye asked as she peeled Patsy's fingers from her lips.

Though Patsy wanted to punch Faye square in the kisser, in her heart she knew Faye couldn't help it. She was just a chronic copycat, never to be cured. So Patsy simply said, "I'm not up to anything. You're just too loud..."

"Yeah, too loud!" Kamal interrupted.

"...and Ms. Watkins told us to stop making noise in the hall—or else," Patsy threatened.

"Girls, no one has all day to wait for you!" Ms. Saa interrupted. "The Doves are on their way offstage. Didn't Ms. Patterson tell you it was time to get dressed? Hurry up backstage—now!"

Patsy and Faye did as they were told, leaving Kamal behind. As they walked away, Patsy could hear Ms. Saa chastising her new pal. "Kamal, either you're going to be a troublemaker or an usher. You can't be both..."

"*I got you*, Ms. Saa. I'm an usher!"

"Well then, where's your blazer? Come here so I can wipe that dust off of you. How did you manage to get so dusty?"

Patsy trudged down the corridor and wondered if she could trust her new pal. Would he go down defending their secret, or would he be a tattletale too? She didn't have much time to think about it before Ms. Patterson interrupted her worries.

"Chop, chop ladies!" scolded Ms. Patterson. "What took you so long?" She scooted the girls to the parents in charge of hair, costumes, and makeup while the other La-dybugs patiently waited on the procession line for their cue.

"*Girl...*" said one of the moms to Patsy. "Do you know what I could do with those dimples? A little rouge *and* some glitter? Let me get a closer look."

Patsy surrendered to the makeup and hair committee and hoped the powder-puff armed parents wouldn't girly her up too much, but when she looked at herself in the mirror, she thought she looked like a young countess preparing to attend the prince's ball.

"Ladies, we're about to go on without you," called Ms. Patterson.

At the last second the girls slipped into their tutus and ballet slippers and jumped on line.

"Now!" Ms. Patterson cued as the girls waltzed through the curtains. "*Go, go, go...*"

Patsy whirled on stage, daintily flowing into first, sec-ond, and third position. She pranced and leapt across stage just as Ms. Patterson had directed and each Ladybug fol-lowed her lead. Patamela imagined it was 1937 and she was one of the *American Negro Ballet's* first ballerinas. *Here goes everything*, she thought before flitting into a series of stunning pirouettes, arabesques and grand pliés.

When Patsy's slippers delicately touched the ground, she knew she belonged with the dance greats. She closed her eyes and *believed* she was Janet Collins (the first African-American ballerina in the *Metropolitan Opera Bal-let*) and Raven Wilkinson (the first African-American bal-lerina in the *Ballet Russe de Monte Carlo*) rolled up in one.

"You were marvelous Patsy!" Ms. Patterson gushed as Patsy ran offstage and into her arms. She gave Patsy a huge kiss and hurried her to get ready for the next number as the Butterflies took their place on stage.

"Patsy, *you're missing it*," Faye whined, peeking at the Butterflies from the stage wings.

It was unlike Patsy to miss an opportunity to watch Nicky Dwyer and Nicky Lewis dance, but she and the other Ladybugs were too proud and excited to bother gawking at them. With two more Ladybug dance numbers less than ten minutes away, it was more important for Patsy to prepare. Although she had been too busy concentrating on her steps to make out any of the faces in the audience, she knew she had an entire cheering section awaiting her return.

The Ladybugs' next two numbers went just as well as the first. "We did it!" Patsy and Faye both said, giving each other a high five. "Did you hear all that hooting and hollering?" Patsy asked.

"Yeah, both times," Faye said.

All the Ladybugs were convinced they had given the best performances of the night thus far—especially after realizing they were one of the only groups celebrating.

"What's eating them?" Patsy asked, referring to some sobbing Butterflies.

"I think they messed up—AND BAD," said Faye.

To Patsy's surprise, the awful news did not stop at the Butterflies. She learned some of the Fireflies and Hummingbirds had forgotten their steps too. But not her. She had not forgotten one step in any of her dances and she'd smiled the whole time. Patsy was certain her father would be proud of her James glow. And she knew he enjoyed the modern dance because it was set to one of his favorite songs. Once they heard that song and saw me jump into my split, they must have jumped out of their seats, Patsy thought.

"*Ladybugs, Ladybugs,*" Ms. Patterson said, disrupting Patsy's musings over her remarkable split. "I do be proud!"

As Ms. Patterson showered the girls with kisses and hugs, Patsy crept toward the curtains.

"Patamela, get back here," snapped Ms. Patterson.

"Just a quick peek—please? I don't know where my family is sitting."

"They're out there, Patsy. I'm sure they're even more proud of you than I am. And I'm so happy you volunteered for the lights and curtains committee too. Why don't you walk to the other side of the stage and see if they can use your help now? Make sure you stay behind the curtain."

"Ooo, I wanna help. Can I go too?" Faye pleaded.

"*No,* your last number is coming up right after the Doves come offstage. You need to get ready for your tap dance. Patsy's not in it, *remember?*"

Patsy had nearly forgotten about her dishonorable discharge because she was still glowing from her earlier performances. After dancing three dances without messing up, Patsy wasn't about to let anything bring her down. She figured she would be a fool to pay Ms. P and her troupe of gnat burglars any mind—especially when their tap routine had no chance of being as big of a hit as their earlier numbers.

"You don't even have umbrellas," Patamela taunted in a whisper. "Ha, ha!"

"Patsy, let's keep a lid on it," said Ms. Patterson. "Performances are still going on. Whisper while you wait."

"You're the boss," said Patsy with a sinister smile. She was sure that Ms. Patterson and Mr. O'Keefe would face tantrum-filled chaos as soon as the bugs realized *their* (and

Patsy used that term loosely) umbrellas were missing. "Let's see you keep a lid on that," she grumbled under her breath.

CHAPTER 35

How Do You Spell Revenge?

Patsy secretly crossed her fingers. "Break a leg guys! Knock 'em dead!" she said to her fellow ladybugs. She was positively certain no one would suspect her of hiding the umbrellas after such a display of support.

"Patsy, you'll come back for me—*won't you?*" Faye asked as Patsy waved good-bye and backed away from their group. Patsy didn't answer Faye. Instead she quietly mocked her as she slipped away. "Will I be back? Is a ladybug red? Does a caterpillar crawl? Of course I'll be back! I wouldn't miss the look on your 'down-in-the-dumps, couldn't find the umbrellas so our routine stunk faces for all the tater tots in Idaho."

Patamela may have shared a sentimental moment with Faye over their flawless dance routines and she may have even appreciated Faye's news about the Butterflies' disastrous performances, but none of that, at least in her mind, did a thing to change her feelings. Patsy thought Faye was a treacherous tattletale, a chronic copycat, and an underhanded umbrella thief. And now to make matters worse, Patsy was adding show-off to Faye's long list of offenses.

"Whoever heard of volunteering to be part of a dumb ol' lights and curtains committee when you have a tap dance to perform?" Patamela mumbled to herself. "What a show-off."

"Come on, Patsy, we're waiting for you," a male voice beckoned in the distance.

Patsy turned her head, looking for the voice that had spoken to her. She saw a teenage boy gesturing her closer while a group of tutors untangled a bundle of cords behind him. "Hurry, I want to show you something," he said.

Patsy looked up and noticed the group of tutors waving to her from an elevated platform above the stage—a platform even higher than the jungle gym at Briarcliff Park. Suddenly, she wanted nothing more than to be a part of their group. No matter what tedious tasks she was assigned and no matter how angry she was over being stuck on the light and curtain committee in the first place, she wanted to be on that platform. If that was where she was headed, Patsy planned to be the best, curtain-wrangling lightning bug they'd ever seen. She'd be a superhero and the platform would be her hideaway.

"Do those guys need help—*up there*?" Patsy asked, pointing to the tutors waving from above.

"Patsy, you spoiled the surprise. That's exactly where we're headed. We need your *expertise.*"

"*Expertise*? But I've never done lights *or* curtains."

"It's simple, Patsy—at least it will be for you. Mr. O'Keefe told us you're Legends' top helper. I'm William by the way," the teen said as he led her onto the platform.

"Willy, how come I've never been invited up here before?"

"You didn't need an invitation."

"Wow, there's a whole 'nother world up here," Patsy said in awe. "A secret floor! *Cool.*"

William chuckled. "It's certainly no secret, Patsy. And you don't need an invitation. You were just too busy practicing to ever look up, but who can blame you? Our job is to be quiet. Neither seen nor heard, that's our motto. We want the people to enjoy the light and sound effects, but we sure don't want them to know where the magic is coming from."

"So this *is* a secret hideaway!"

"Hey now, don't blow our cover. *Quiet on the set.*"

Man, I could have done my ice-cold revenge scheme on those lawless Ladybugs after all, Patsy thought. But then Patsy looked around and realized that although the platform was hidden from the audience, anyone standing backstage below or working on the platform would have spotted her almost immediately.

Yet there was something about that platform that would not let her imagination rest. The missing umbrella plan was brilliant, but Patsy figured there had to be a way to add the platform in the mix for *double payback power.* That's when Patsy's light bulb went on.

Patsy knew there was nothing the Ladybugs loved more than to fill their polka-dotted bellies with juicy tidbits of information. She could see it now. Once she told them about the secret platform, the Ladybugs would regret having had to tap without their precious umbrellas, while she had a chance to explore unknown territory. It was the one-two, knock-out punch she had dreamed of. Not only would the critters be weeping over their missing umbrellas, but they'd also be weeping over the missed opportunity to be Patamela's secret-territory-exploring sidekick. Patsy wondered how she would get the Ladybugs to take the bait.

"Am I the only Ladybug helping you guys up here?"

"Yep, you sure are, Patsy," said Maxine, who was working the lights. "Matter of fact, you're the only Ladybug who's ever had permission to come up here. And you're getting a job assignment. I'm *positive* that won't happen again. You're pretty special..."

"*HOT DOG!*" Patsy roared. Maxine and William both told her to quiet down.

Now that Patamela was certain no other bug was given platform honors or their very own platform job, she had all she needed to fill the other Ladybugs with regret. Patsy was sure the platform was the best addition to her revenge plan she could have ever asked for. Not only was she personally invited to work on it, but none of the Ladybugs would ever be able to copy what she had done. According to Maxine, the secret hideaway platform only had room for one bug and that bug was Patamela James.

Patamela was now leading the Ladybugs by *three* successful dances, *one* missing umbrella prank, *one* shot at light and curtain committee history, and *eleven* chances to gloat as each Ladybug wished to be as lucky as she was.

"Way to sock it to them, PJ! *Now that's how you spell revenge.*"

CHAPTER 36

You Give Me Fever

Patsy's sense of satisfaction didn't last for long. She quickly realized there was no real job for her on the platform after all. While all the teenagers rushed around performing important tasks, Patsy was ignored—except when she was being too loud. Finally she was assigned the task of holding an enormous spotlight in place—at least that's what William told her. "Now hold this right here. And don't move, okay?" William said. He carefully placed her hands on the light's huge handle. "It isn't too heavy for you is it?" he asked, but he turned away before Patsy could reply.

Patsy decided she would never tell William the lamp was too heavy—even if it felt like it weighed a ton. She eagerly positioned her hands for a better grasp, but something didn't feel quite right. Patsy slowly stepped back from the lamp then stretched out her arms until only her fingertips were touching it. "Rats!" she said. This was nothing more than a bum assignment—a real joke of a job. Even a preschooler would have been able to tell the light did not need her to hold it steady.

"It's showtime, people!" William shouted, signaling everyone to their posts. "Ready Patsy? *Now!*" he shouted again, as the auditorium lights dimmed.

"What? Showtime? *Now?*" Patamela hoped she had not missed some secret platform committee signal. What exactly was she supposed to do? Then Patsy realized the gigantic spotlight she was pretending to operate was shining a crimson beam directly on a little girl standing center stage. Patsy decided her plan was back on track. She would tell everyone that was her work.

The theater was completely silent. Everyone was awaiting the girl's next move. But there the girl stood, motionless, and completely surrounded by the dark—except for Patsy's lone, red light beaming down on her frame.

Suddenly, the young girl put her right hand in the air and began to snap her fingers. Patsy widened her eyes to make out the girl's costume. She was dressed in an all white nurse's outfit with a white nurse's hat to match. "You can't dance with that stuff. It's against the rules," Patsy said, referring to the clipboard in the girl's left hand and the stethoscope around her neck.

Pop, pop, pop, pop... The audience was so quiet you could hear each snap's crisp sound: *pop, pop, pop, pop...*
Never know how much I love you
Never know how much I care
When you put your arms around me
I get a fever that's so hard to bear
You give me fever
The young girl tapped her shoes lightly, *click, clack, click, clack*, identical to the rhythm of the song. She spun her head to the left then spun her head to the right. She slowly moved her head to the center of her shoulders then bopped it from side to side. She made sure her head's

movements kept the same beat as her fingers then peered into the audience. She abruptly snapped her head back to look straight up at the ceiling. Patsy got a good look at the dancer. It was Imani—on stage all by herself!

"*Woooooo*, Imani!" Patsy heard Ishmael call from the audience.

Just then, a group of the college tutors, wearing white T-shirts and pants, rolled from underneath the back curtains onto the stage. Then Patsy spotted some adults gently pushing hospital gurneys on stage from the wings. The college tutors gracefully leapt to catch the gurneys and rolled the gurneys around the stage until they surrounded Imani in a semi-circle. Then they joined Imani in one of the best Legends routines Patsy had ever witnessed. When they were done, the tutors slid down to the floor and rolled back offstage. Patsy noticed that Imani still hadn't budged from center stage, so she knew there was more in store.

Fever!

One, two, three…Heads were popping up everywhere! It was like trying to track a family of gophers on a golf course…*Four, five, six*…From underneath the sheets of each gurney, a Fairy reared her cute, little head. At once, the theme of the dance was clear to everyone. Imani was the head nurse and the other Fairies were her ward of patients!

The Fairies leapt out of their hospital beds and began to dance beside them. They were dressed in sky-blue gowns and wore white tap shoes. They even sported white bands around their wrist like real hospital patients.

"*Why didn't Mr. O'Keefe think of that?*" Patsy whined. She was so envious of the Fairies' unique costumes that she nearly missed Imani scooting away from the glare of her lamp. Patsy hoped Imani's part in this routine had come to an end, but it was not to be. Imani yanked a thermometer from her dress pocket and walked around the circle pretending to check each Fairy's temperature until she had done a routine with every Fairy on stage, each different and better than the one before it.

When it was clear Imani had completed her final dance number with the last Fairy left on stage, the Fairy jumped on her gurney just like the other Fairies had done before her and pulled the sheet over her head. Just then, the tutors sprang back onto the scene and carted them offstage.

Patsy could tell the Fairies had just had the time of their lives. Not only did they get to do an exciting dance, but they also enjoyed rides on rolling scene props.

"This must be the longest dance in history," Patamela grumbled. Imani was grooving onstage alone—again. She swayed and jaunted across the stage doing a combination of shuffle hops, scuffles, chugs, brush backs, and cramp rolls.

Patsy had heard Imani was good, but now that fact was staring Patsy straight in the face. Imani was *proving* she was good—good enough to have an entire dance to herself.

Patamela's stomach began to knot. Her shoulders hunched over and her knees weakened. "Beaten by Imani again," she mumbled.

Patsy had wasted so much time crusading against the Ladybugs that she'd totally missed her archenemy of old. Imani would be the star of the Legends recital and the fourth grade too once school started. She would be able to say she'd performed a dance solo. Who would care about Patsy choosing a summer activity on her own or being a superhero with a hidden hideaway? That malarkey would be forgotten about as soon as everyone heard Imani's huge summer event.

I'll never be much of a big shot with Imani around, Patsy thought. Imani is the big kid, big shot champ *and* the princess of Legends. A solo performance tops a dancing group's performance every time. Even Aunt Deidre knows that, Patamela thought.

Fever was the right word for Imani's dance because Patsy was burning with envy. Not even her new superhero identity could cheer her up. After all, she couldn't really fly and her hideaway was just a dumb platform with spotlights. She didn't even have a real platform job she could brag about. She was only pretending to operate Imani's light.

Patsy decided that Imani's performance was good but not flawless. And good was not the same as gifted. Patsy knew her own performances had been flawless and that there had to be a way to bust Imani's plans to steal the show. If she could add a solo tap performance to her already spectacular night, she could ruin Imani's plan. And more importantly, then no one, not even Mr. O'Keefe, would be able to deny the magic of Patsy's gift. If she could pull this off, all of Legends would be eating out of her hands and the kids at Melbourne would be too. Why after three group dances, one solo, and the privilege of being the first Ladybug to ever be skipped, she would be the greatest, big kid, big shot, beauty-pageant-princess fourth grader to ever walk the halls of Legends and Melbourne.

Patsy looked around the theater. She looked in the faces of the college tutors, the backstage mob below, and into the audience. Everyone seemed absolutely riveted by Imani's performance. "*Big deal*," she grunted as Imani pulled off her closing combination of paddles, riffles, and ball-changes. "I've seen better fevers on runny-nosed kindergarteners in the nurse's office."

CHAPTER 37

T♀ the Dressing R♀♀m!

Patamela was convinced her plan would be a cinch to pull off. While Mr. O'Keefe and the Ladybugs frantically tried to locate the umbrellas, she would sneak onstage to perform her tap dance solo. "That'll show 'em who really holds the big-shot crown—won't it, *Imani Poofawney*?" Patsy taunted under her breath. Patsy was done worrying about the Lady-bugs. She had to pay attention to more mature pursuits—like wowing the Legends community and the James family once and for all. And Patsy knew just what she had to do first. "*I quit,*" she announced, releasing the spotlight's handle, and then she stormed off the platform without bothering to look back.

Patsy figured she did not have much time before William and Maxine noticed she had abandoned her post. She had even less time to prepare for her solo debut. She needed a quick-witted game plan for retrieving her things from Kamal's hiding place. Finally she would be cutting out the monkey business as Mr. James had asked. Even Aunt Deidre would be proud. She would get to see the tap performance she so desperately wanted. "You know tap is my favorite,"

Patsy recalled her saying.

Patsy was certain that when she carried out her plan, she would not only be Aunt Deidre's favorite tap-dancing niece but she would be Legends' favorite tap soloist as well. With no other pattering feet to get in the way of the audience's view, everyone would agree Imani's *fever* was no match for the James glow. Patsy was certain Mr. O'Keefe would be begging Ms. Patterson *and* Ms. Saa to change their skip policy halfway through her performance.

Patsy raced through the backstage area looking for the place she'd left her bags. Unfortunately, when she spotted them, she also spotted Ms. Patterson just a few feet away.

"Ms. Patamela, what are you doing over here?" Ms. Patterson asked.

"*Uh, um*...Mr. O'Keefe said I could help the Ladybugs with their cues and stuff."

"Well, I suggest you get to the side entrance. That's where the Ladybugs are stationed now. Chop-chop Patamela! Imani's dance ends in a couple of seconds and then there is only a seven minute intermission before the Ladybugs are on...Must you take those bags?" Mrs. Patterson asked, shaking her head.

"I've got to Ms. Patty! My mom packed extra stuff the parents might be able to use."

"That's quite thoughtful. Now off you go," she said, and she watched Patsy make her way through the crowd until she was out of sight.

Patamela sprinted from the backstage area straight down the hidden corridor. Patsy heard the Ladybugs bickering at the end of the passageway and she knew she was getting close. She watched as a parent cracked the hidden door and allowed each bug a chance to locate relatives seated in the auditorium's rear section.

Patsy hoped her group would be too occupied to notice her—at least until she reached the door. By then it would be too late to stop her.

"Patsy! You came back for me!" Faye yelled. "I can't go with you now, but I'll be ready as soon as we finish our performance. Are you going to get a seat—*so you can watch us?*"

"Um yeah, I mean no. Uh, I'll be right back, Faye," Patsy replied, hoping to make it through the door before a parent got suspicious. Though to Patsy's surprise, one of the parents actually held the door for her and helped her through the exit as she struggled with her bags.

Kamal spotted Patsy as soon as she came through the door. It took him less than a second to realize Patsy was up to no good. He was sure she had no business being near the Ladybugs or with those bags of hers. In one split second Kamal decided he would be by Patsy's side to help her in whatever escapade she was struggling to pull off. What else was a first-time usher bored to tears and in need of some action supposed to do?

Kamal, king of mischief, knew just what to do. He dashed toward Ms. Saa who was talking backstage with a group of parents and offered a warm hug. He was willing to do everything in his power to keep Ms. Saa's eyes on the group (and off of Patsy)—even if it meant suffering as her long locks brushed against his face and tickled his nostrils. As soon as Kamal was sure Ms. Saa couldn't spot Patsy, he signaled his friend to proceed.

Patsy trudged down the hallway and headed for the front door. She hoped Ms. Watkins had taken a break from collecting tickets at the front door because there was no way she could pull a fast one on her. If anyone could see through her cockamamie help-the-Ladybugs story it would be Ms.

Watkins.

Patamela slithered down the hallway toward Kamal's secret hideout. She slowly opened the door and carelessly plunked her bags in a mound of sawdust. She peered at her dusty bags and considered brushing them off, but decided she had better shut the classroom door first.

Upon shutting the door, a heap of plaster flurried to the floor. Patsy looked up at the ceiling, figuring the sudden movement had upset the hole above her. She carefully tiptoed passed the ceiling's opening to prevent more plaster from trickling down and decided she'd brush off her bags once she reached backstage.

Patsy looked around for a chair tall enough to boost her to the closet's top shelf. That'll do, she thought, spotting a chair near the window. Just then, Ms. Patterson's words rang in her head, "...*seven minute intermission.*" Patsy grabbed the wooden chair and darted toward the closet door. She set it down, opened the closet door, and then.... *Sczoom, Boom, Crrr, Crash-Bam-Plunk*! An avalanche of Kamal's lost and found items tumbled to the ground.

Patsy shot to the classroom door. She poked her head in the hall to make certain no one heard the crash. *Whew,* That was close, she thought. She closed the door softly, tiptoed passed the hole in the ceiling, and then sprinted across the room to retrieve her tights, poncho and tap shoes out of her bags.

After peeling out of her modern dance costume and stuffing it back into her suitcase, Patamela pulled her purple poncho over her head and put on her tights. She shoved her feet into her purple spray-painted tap shoes and tightly fastened the buckles.

Patamela ran to the back of the room to search the mound of items that had tumbled out of the closet. It was easy to spot her umbrella's bright yellow handle. Patsy pulled the handle toward her, yet the umbrella would not budge. "*Oh no it's stuck*," she moaned. Patsy gave the handle a strong yank but only managed to hurt her arm. "*Ouch*," she cried. Patamela took a deep breath. She tightened her lips, rubbed her palms together and then focused her attention on the handle. She gave it one more tug, "*Unh*," she grunted, pulling the handle with all her might...

"*Whoooaaa!*"

Patsy's forceful pull had backfired! Once the umbrella broke free from the items it was stuck under, the umbrella sprang into her arms with whirlwind force! Patsy fumbled the umbrella, flew off the mound, crashed bottom first into the seat of a wooden chair, and went sailing a couple of yards back into the classroom's tall cabinet...*Chsssss...Chssssss.* Before she could recover from the calamity, a heap of dust from the cabinet's crooked shelf spattered onto her head.

Patsy wanted to feel sorry for herself. More than that, she wanted a watch. Patsy had no idea how much time she had left, but she knew sitting still in that wooden chair would only waste more time. Patsy sprinted toward the door hoping her tap shoes would glide over the sawdust.

At the door, Patsy could hear the intermission music playing in the distance. She wished that Legends didn't have any dumb rules about dancers wearing watches. Didn't they understand it was the only way for a girl to stay on schedule?

Patsy slowly cracked the door. She didn't want to upset any holes, known or unknown, in the ceiling above. She slithered around the door's edge and was almost home free with one foot in the hallway—when suddenly she realized her poncho was caught on the door's splintered edge. Patsy tried to push forward, but that just caught the poncho more.

Patsy closed her eyes, lifted on the balls of her feet, and

slowly inched forward. *Crrrchhhhh*…that one lift coupled with her slight tilt forward was too much for the thin poncho to bear! Instead of lifting off the crook, the poncho tore, sending Patsy careening toward the floor. Patsy didn't even feel around the bottom half of her poncho to determine the length of the rip. She hadn't planned to dance with her back toward the audience anyway. "*It's nothing*," she told herself.

Patsy sprung up and ran toward the auditorium.

She heard a voice coming from behind her. "Is that you, Faye? What are you doing up here? Isn't your class on stage? Stop running in the hallway! And pull that poncho down while you're at it. I had no idea they had huge slits up the back like that."

Patsy knew better than to turn around and show Ms. Watkins that she was not Faye. She simply put her poncho hood up and waved.

CHAPTER 38

Can I Get an Encore?

When Patsy reached the auditorium, she rose on her tip-toes for a quick peek through the auditorium door's window. She hoped to get Kamal's attention and not Ms. Saa's. Patsy would need his help getting past the gatekeepers again. Yet Patsy saw no sign of her partner. She gently pushed the door open, poked her head through, and then quickly jerked it back, afraid someone would notice her.

"That silly boy, where is he?" she huffed.

Seconds later the door opened. "What took you so long?" Kamal whispered, leaning on the door and twirling his flashlight.

"How'd you know I was here?"

"I've been watching the door waiting for you to come back, slowpoke. I saw your big ol' head sticking out the door."

"Zip it, Kamal."

The intermission music lowered and Ms. Saa's velvety voice invited the audience to take their seats for the next act. "*I've got to get on that stage,*" Patsy said, heading for the side entrance.

"You can't go that way!" Kamal shouted, yanking Patsy's arm. "It's a zoo back there. Everyone's looking for those umbrellas you hid."

"*We* hid."

"Oh yeah, that's right," he chuckled. "But you'll never get to the stage that way. You'll be caught as soon as you open the door—and Ms. Saa's about to find out too." Kamal shook his head as if he felt sorry for Patsy and her half-baked scheme.

"What should I do?" Patsy whined.

"I thought you'd never ask."

Kamal gave his collar a quick tug to adjust his blazer's fit, signaled Patsy to flip up her hood, and turned down the intensity of his flashlight. Patsy flipped up her hood hoping it would give her enough time to reach the stage before being recognized. Kamal led Patsy to the other side of the auditorium and down the far right aisle.

"Go ahead, Patz, go ahead..." Kamal whispered. The two of them were standing in front of the side steps that led directly on stage.

"But the curtains aren't opened and the music isn't playing."

"Don't worry about that!"

Kamal ran up the steps and behind the curtains. Patsy figured he was either going to pull the curtain ropes open himself or tell the committee it was time to begin. This was Patsy's chance and she was not going to let it get away.

Patsy snatched her umbrella from underneath her poncho and shook off her hood. The audience quieted down. Parents nudged their children to be quiet and pointed in Patsy's direction.

> *I'm singing in the rain*
> *Just singing in the rain...*

That was Patsy's cue! She pushed her shoulders back, lifted her chin, and shuffled center stage—right in front of the curtains. Patsy did not know what Kamal had said or done, but the curtains opened behind her at just the right moment. Patsy widened her grin to a brilliant smile then hopped back a couple of paces. *Hoppity hop, hoppity hop.* She wanted to dance directly in the middle of the stage so everyone would have a perfect view.

"*Psst, hey Patsy!*"

At the side curtains the Ladybugs were trying to shoo Patsy off the stage, but she acted as if she could not see or hear them. Unfortunately she *could* see them and hear them, and they were interrupting her efforts to decide which routine she would perform—Mr. O'Keefe's, Ms. Hollingsworth's, or the routine from the first tap dance they taught and later changed.

Patamela decided to do a combination of each and zealously tore into her revised routine. *Spin, break it with a stomp! Arms wide, smile for the audience, yeah! Shuffle, shuffle, step back, step forward, shuffle, ball-change.* Patsy knew she was winning the audience over with her fancy footwork because of all the laughter she heard coming from the floor. They were really enjoying themselves!

Patsy figured dancing harder might even get her a standing ovation and she zipped across the stage. She was ready to imitate the leaps that Imani did during her routine, but she only managed to wobble into a series of stiff leaps and awkward skids. The last leap was the worst by far, lifting no more than a foot off the floor. Nevertheless, Patsy continued to smile and dance.

I'm laughing at clouds
So dark up above
'Cause the sun's in my heart
And I'm, ready for love

The music told Patsy that the dance should end soon. She gleefully stumbled into her last shuffle combination: *shuffle, shuffle, shuffle step, shuffle, shuffle, ball-change.* To Patsy's surprise, the audience was not out of their seats. I know, I'll give them something they can't resist, she thought, deciding the only way to get a rise out of the audience was to pull off something worthy of an encore.

Patamela figured she would climb on one of the park bench props and jump off into the three-quarter split she perfected in her modern dance. That was sure to give her the height she needed to flawlessly launch into a split. Not to mention, it would send the audience to their feet for a standing ovation.

Patsy shuffled her way to the back of the stage until she was certain the park bench was within reach. For the first time Patsy took complete notice of the beautiful scenery behind her. The stage was set up like a park with a group of clouds hanging in front of a sun from the ceiling. There were cardboard flowers, trees and squirrels set up all over the floor.

Patsy lunged for the park bench. She threw her right leg on the park bench while gripping the bench's backrest with her right hand. Just as she lifted her left leg atop the bench, the sound machine rattled off makeshift thunder. The sound startled Patsy, but, worse yet, the bench collapsed under her weight. It was just a prop thrown together at the last minute and it wasn't meant to hold anyone. Patsy flew backward onto a patch of daisies and two friendly squirrels. Even parts of the bench went for the ride.

As quickly as she could, Patsy threw the bench pieces aside and scrambled to her feet. "Grab that *incorrigible* youngster!" she heard a parent yell from the wings of the stage as the audience howled.

Patsy felt a strong gust of air on her bottom and reached behind her back. *What happened to my poncho—and my tights?* she wondered. She looked over to the side of the stage and could see Ms. Saa's hands flailing about. The jig was up.

Patamela turned to the audience to accept her encore, but instead she saw Mr. O'Keefe plunging forward with open arms to scoop her off stage. *Uh oh*, she thought. Good thing Patsy paid attention to Prince's fancy football moves. She dropped on a slant and used her elbow to slide between Mr. O'Keefe's legs. Unable to get to her feet in time, Patsy scurried on her hands and knees to the steps at the side of the stage and plopped down to the floor. She got up and sped down the aisle with the two flaps of her torn poncho lifting in the air. This gave the audience a full view of the huge, ever-expanding hole in her tights.

"Go baby go," a silvered-hair woman cheered as Patsy ran by her seat. Patsy flew out of the auditorium's double doors with her mom, dad, Prince, Patience, and Aunt Deidre on her heels.

CHAPTER 39

Come Out, Come Out, Wherever You Are

Patsy didn't leave her room for a week after that fateful night. Her parents didn't actually punish her; Patsy just didn't want to see anyone. Mr. and Mrs. James decided that this time Patsy was punishing herself more than they possibly could.

In fact, each time Patamela thought about her tap performance, her stomach rocked back and forth as if she were seasick. As if that wasn't enough, her ears burned and her toes got clammy too. The entire James family felt sorry for Patsy, but there was nothing they could think to do, except to try and cheer her up.

"Hey Pattie Cakes, we've got good news. You *earned* *THREE* certificates for your flawless performances," her parents said through her bedroom door.

The news didn't help. Even the citizenship certificate she received for being an exemplary helper during her last week at Legends did not lift her mood. When Mr. O'Keefe stopped by to bring Patsy her "Sunny Side Up" plaque, Patsy refused to budge from bed.

Patsy felt like the plaque was a joke. She hadn't been a good sport after learning she could not be skipped, nor had she been happy about getting kicked out of the tap routine. Mr. O'Keefe knew that more than anyone else. The award only managed to make her feel worse. She certainly did not deserve it after what she did to the Ladybugs' tap routine.

"It's no big deal, Patsy, the Ladybugs still got to perform," Patience had reported one afternoon, hoping to lift Patsy's spirits.

Patsy, unmoved, responded with a disheartened, "*Hmph*, good for them..." Deep down she was glad to hear that Ms. Saa had called an emergency intermission to give everyone a chance to calm down. She was not at all surprised to hear the show went on as planned. Ms. Saa was not the type of teacher to let Patsy—or anyone—ruin things.

Interestingly enough, *Imani* could ruin anything she wanted, even Patsy's attempts at a peace of mind. Patamela could not understand why her mother told her that Imani won a huge trophy for excellence in dance. "*Imani, Imani, Imani*," Patsy mimicked.

"That's enough, Patsy," Mrs. James said. "Imani has her talents and you have yours. Be happy for her."

Yet Patsy could not be happy, not with pictures of Imani's trophy dancing in her head. It's probably big and shiny with her name in glossy letters, thought Patsy. She imagined it stood five feet tall. Patamela wanted to rip her own certificates to shreds and throw her itsy-bitsy plaque out the bedroom window.

Not even Aunt Deidre had been able to cheer her up, and Patsy had hidden under the covers each time she came to her room to try. How could she face her Aunt Deidre? She was not a tap star. Instead, she was the laughingstock of Springdale.

"Well, at least we know which side you got your tap shoe magic from," Aunt Deidre teased, reaching under the bed to give Patsy a tickle.

"That's not funny!"

"Patsy, cheer up. You weren't that bad, and that was just one dance out of four. You knocked them dead with your fancy ballet, modern, and jazz moves. I was shocked. I didn't know you were that good. Your father and I were screaming, '*Show 'em that glow girl!*' the whole time. Didn't you hear us?"

But Patsy would not take comfort in her aunt's words. Her father and aunt may have chanted for her during her ballet, modern, and jazz performances, but Patsy was sure they hadn't done so during her tap stint.

"Patsy, you must have forgotten how hard your mother and I struggled with tap dance. It's no big deal. You handled it a little differently than I would have, but that's what makes you so special."

Patsy's parents hadn't been happy when Patsy refused to leave her room to say good-bye to Aunt Deidre. But Aunt Deidre had defended her. "She just needs some rest. It's been a rough weekend for her," Patsy heard Aunt Deidre pleading on her behalf. That was exactly why she was Patsy's favorite aunt.

CHAPTER 40

Springdale Day!

One week had passed since the recital and Mrs. James could tell Patsy was no closer to ending her pity party. Yet Mrs. James had news for her youngest daughter, "Patamela, we have let you stay inside for an entire week now. I'm sorry to tell you, but it's time to stop feeling sorry for yourself."

Mrs. James pulled the covers off of Patsy's head.

"Patsy, you made a choice that had very harsh consequences, but I think you've learned your lesson. As much as I sympathize with you, honey, I cannot let you hide from the world." Mrs. James walked over to the window on Patsy's side of the room and opened the curtains.

"Aww, Ma, that's too much light!" Patsy shouted.

"Good! Today is Springdale Day. You're going to get out with the rest of the neighborhood kids and enjoy it. School starts next week and you need to end your summer on a good note." She walked to Patsy's closet to find her an outfit to wear for the day.

"But, Ma, I don't want to. Now everyone knows I'm *incorrigible*—and that's not a good thing!" Everybody will laugh at me," Patsy whined.

"Maybe they will, maybe they won't. You'll never know if you're hiding in here," her mom replied. "And who cares about someone laughing? People have laughed at me and your father too. Trust me, it will pass. You will live to see another day."

"No I won't, not with everyone calling me incorrigible. It's not a compliment!"

"Oh, that's just another way to say you're a *free spirit*. You just need a bit more action and freedom than the rest of us to be happy."

Mrs. James pulled a pair of orange capris out of Patsy's closet with a hot pink and orange shirt to match. "Patamela, you can't ignore all the good that happens to you the very minute something not so good happens. Let's go. Get up and get dressed."

As Patsy considered nestling even deeper into her covers, her mom passed her a folded sheet of loose-leaf paper and closed it in her hand. "Someone asked me to make sure you got this." Mrs. James kissed Patsy's forehead and walked out of the room.

Patsy opened the palm of her hand and read the top of the folded paper. *"TO: PATSY,"* it read in block letters. Patsy did not feel like reading a letter and tossed it to the floor. She imagined the letter included some mean-spirited ditty like, *"Ha! Ha! You got two left feet. We're all laughing 'cause you can't dance to the beat!"*

"Open the letter Patsy," her mom called from the hall.

"Oh brother," Patsy huffed, as she bent over to retrieve it. She took a long, deep breath and slowly unfolded the letter.

"Dear Patsy,

I was at your show. I'm sorry everybody laughed. I hope you come outside soon.

Miles ♥

P.S. Destiny says hi, Ella Jo too. The heart was their girly idea"

Patsy's stomach churned and she felt herself begin to sweat. The thought of Miles seeing that tap dance made her feel faint. There would be nowhere she could hide from the dreadful night at Legends—not in her neighborhood, not at her school, not even at her church. Nowhere, she thought. Now that her own mother was determined to feed her to the lions, she was surely doomed.

Patamela struggled to think of a way she could escape going outside, but her mind was blank. She hoped something bad might happen to her before she reached her front door. Maybe she would slip on a bar of soap in the shower. Even better would be to fall down the stairs and break an arm and a leg.

Since none of that was going to happen, Patsy decided to rush to get dressed. The sooner she left the house, the sooner she could turn around and come back, she figured. "*I'll go outside*, but you can't make me have fun!" Patsy yelled as she slammed the front door. She would sit on the stoop for twenty minutes then go back in the house. That should get her off my back, Patsy thought. She opened the door and took a seat on the stoop, resting her elbows on her thighs and her fists underneath her chin.

Patamela looked on from her stoop. Her neighborhood was bustling with activity. She hadn't realized so much action was taking place right outside her door. Music was blasting and every home had balloons flying from their front stoops.

Beecham Street was blocked off with a sign that read, "*No cars permitted.*" Patsy watched as adults walked their children in the direction of the neighborhood park. Every child seemed to have an ice cream cone in one hand and a balloon in the other.

Patsy's stomach stopped churning and began to growl. She tried to keep her nose from inhaling the aromas, but she could not resist. Everyone was barbecuing. Patsy smelled hamburgers, hot dogs, and barbecue chicken. She knew there would also be fried chicken, baked macaroni and cheese, potato salad, and macaroni salad. Suddenly she wished her stomach could expand ten sizes just so she could sample each dish.

The problem was Patamela didn't want to participate in

Springdale Day. She dropped her head in between her knees and tried desperately to keep the aromas out of her nose and the sounds of music from penetrating her ears.

All the kids who passed by said hi to Patsy, but no one asked her to come along with them. She wished someone would. That way she could tell her mom that she hadn't agreed to have fun but was dragged into it. Yet Patsy had no such luck. Everyone waved from across the street or passed her stoop, but no one asked her to join them.

Patsy figured no one wanted to be seen with the laughingstock of Springdale. Her eyes began to water, and she got up to go back inside.

"Hi!"

"Hey there, Patsy" Destiny and Miles were crossing the street and coming her way.

"Hi guys," she stammered, fearing they would mention the recital.

"What took you so long?" said Miles. "I've been waiting to see you for a whole week!"

"I thought you weren't my friend."

"Aww, Patsy, cut it out. We're going to be fourth graders. We're too old for that baby stuff."

"You want to be a fourth grader now?" Patsy asked Miles jubilantly.

"Yep! My cousins told me all about the fun they had in fourth grade."

Patsy was elated over Miles's new attitude and walked down the steps toward her friends. "Good grief, Patsy, I called you a million times this summer. I thought you weren't my friend for sure," Destiny added.

"No, I've just been busy with Legends."

"I sure hope we're all in the same fourth grade class this year," said Destiny.

"Yeah," said Patsy. "Me too."

"Ugh!" said Miles. "Let's not talk about school anymore. It's Springdale Day. Let's go play some games!"

CHAPTER 41

There's No Ditching Them!

The park was filled with the kind of games you only find at carnivals and amusement parks. Destiny and Miles were ready to jump right in line and get started. "Come on, Patsy," they urged.

But Patsy had already spotted too many children she was sure would give her a hard time about the recital. She decided to sit down on an empty park bench and just watch.

"Hey Patamela, where you been?" Patsy heard.

Patsy turned her head and saw Kamal and Faye coming toward her.

"Hi Kamal. Hi Faye," Patsy murmured.

"Did you get in a lot of trouble?" Kamal asked.

"Yeah, I thought I'd never see you again," Faye added.

Oh brother, when did these two become buddies? Patsy asked herself.

"I tried to cover for you as much as I could," Kamal said. "But I had my own batch of trouble. They figured I was the one who opened the curtains, *so* I kind of told them I knew where the umbrellas were stashed. I got in hot water for being the school's lost and found bandit though. I heard they might

make me take ballet next year as punishment. I really did try
to keep a lid..."

"Me too," Faye interrupted.

"No you didn't. You didn't even know what was going
on," Kamal said.

"Did too," Faye insisted.

Kamal glared at Faye. "I think I hear your mother calling
you. Why don't you get out of here!"

"No! Make me!" Faye protested, and Patsy realized the
two weren't friends at all. They just had nothing better to do
than to poke into her business.

"*Ol' busybodies*," Patsy grunted.

"I didn't think you were going to stay on stage *that* long,"
Kamal said.

"Me either," Patsy said.

"You got to admit, Patamela, you looked funny," Kamal
recalled.

"She looked just fine! You only helped her to get her in
trouble—didn't you?" Faye shouted, cutting Kamal off. Faye
looked as if she was going to charge at Kamal, but because
she only came up to his elbow, Kamal paid her no mind.

"Oh be quiet. I just wanted to see some action. It was
dead in that place."

Patsy was too embarrassed to continue with the conversation. "Well, I guess I'll see you guys later," she said and
she headed back to the park's entrance. Patamela hoped they
would say good-bye and go back wherever they came from.
Patsy was not really going to leave the park; she just wanted
Kamal and Faye to believe she was leaving. Patsy could see
Miles and Destiny were headed her way with some cotton
candy and the last thing she wanted was for them to join a
discussion about the worst night of her life.

"Patsy, wait up! Why are you leaving?" Miles called out.

"You're Patsy's friends from Legends—right?" Miles said to Kamal and Faye.

"Friends?!" Patsy belted.

"Yeah, you're her friends from Legends," Miles said, continuing to talk to Kamal and Faye. "I saw you guys the night of the show. We all live next door to each other and we go to school together."

"I'm her best friend at Legends," Faye said.

"You are not," Kamal said.

"I am too! You sure aren't!" Faye shouted.

Destiny ignored Kamal and Faye's nitpicking. "Patsy, the relays and stuff are about to start."

"Yeah, they are going to have a potato sack race, a relay race, and their first ever rollerblading derby. You should enter, Patz," Miles said. "I'm going to enter the regular relay race."

"You're going to enter a rollerblading derby?" Kamal said, pointing at Patsy as he giggled hysterically.

"Yeah, Patsy loves to rollerblade," Destiny added.

"She'd probably beat you, monkey boy," Faye said to Kamal.

"You should do it, Patsy," said Miles. "You haven't done anything all day."

Patamela ignored Miles and Destiny's pleas to enter the derby. She loved to rollerblade, but she figured going anywhere near the races would put her too close to the kids from Legends. She already had run into Kamal and Faye, and worse yet, she couldn't shake them. She knew if Kamal and Fatima were there, others had to be too. Destiny and Miles may not have mentioned her performance, but the other children would. "Nah, I don't feel like it," Patsy said, trying to sound as convincing as possible. "I'm still sore from all that dancing."

"Yeah right. That dance was ages ago. You just know I'd clobber you," Kamal said, snickering. Patsy let Kamal's comments roll off her back. She was not about to risk being ridiculed by the other kids just so she could prove Kamal wrong.

Miles frowned at Patsy, knowing it was unlike her to turn down a challenge. "Have it your way, Patsy," he said. "I'm going to run back home and get my brand new tennis shoes. They'll give me super-duper speed."

"I'm going to go get a temporary tattoo on my arm. I saw a girl get a pair of dance slippers on hers and I want the same one," Destiny said.

"I want that one too," Faye said. "And a butterfly."

"Well, I'm going to sign up for the rollerblade derby," Kamal said. "I brought my blades and everything."

Patsy didn't want her friends to leave her behind again, but she didn't want to face the huge crowd of people either. Having to duck and dodge Legends students all afternoon was not her idea of fun. Patsy decided she would stay but she wouldn't participate in any activities or competitions, nor would she go any closer to the action. She would simply blend into the scenery. Patsy tried to convince herself that watching everyone else have a good time would be just as fun.

CHAPTER 42

Patsy Gets the Glow!

Patamela sat on the bench pleased with her decision to stay. Although keeping her eye on her buddies—and Kamal, was challenging. She'd lost track of him when he ran off to sign up for the races. Patsy could see the tattoo table in the distance, but Destiny and Faye were no where in sight. Patsy stopped looking for them when the sack race started.

Patsy's feet were itching for action. Usually she and Miles never missed a sack race, but Miles hadn't returned from fetching his sneakers. Patsy mounted the park bench to get a better look at the starting lineup of neighborhood kids. She didn't know who she was going to root for, but she stood on the bench anxiously awaiting the announcer's signal.

Patsy was laughing at how ridiculous the sack racers looked when her mom tapped her on the shoulder. "What are you doing here, Ma?"

"Miles told me you were rollerblading in the derby."

"How could we miss that, Patti Cakes?" asked her dad.

"I'm not entering any derby!"

"Patti Cakes, you wouldn't make me walk all this way to see the *James glow* in action for nothing, would you?" said her dad.

Patsy let out a huge sigh. Miles was back to his old tricks. He was standing there with her rollerblades, helmet, and pads. Patsy wanted to bop him in the head, but she snatched her skates off his shoulders instead. She didn't want to disappoint her dad.

Patamela sat down on the park bench and put on her rollerblades. "I'm ready," she muttered, and Miles and her parents accompanied her to the sign-up table.

"It's too late for me to sign up!" Patsy exclaimed when she saw the sign on the table. "It says, 'Derby Registration Closed.'"

"You're already signed up," Miles said. "I told Destiny to do it. We weren't gonna listen to you. You love to rollerblade."

"*Why you little...*" Patsy mumbled under her breath. But it was too late to turn back.

Mrs. James pushed Patamela toward the starting line. Destiny popped out of the crowd and handed Mrs. James a white plastic bib with the number twelve written across it.

"Hurry up and put your number on, Patsy," said Miles.

The announcer welcomed the participants to the first annual Springdale Rollerblade Derby then described the length of their race. At the sound of the whistle, they would skate the entire width of the park. They would head straight until they reached the children's playground and hang a right behind the little red house that housed the bathrooms. After passing the red house, the skaters would go up then down the steep hill that made the biker's trail. They had to skate past each pair of stone tables and chairs set up for chess tournaments before reaching the finish line or risk disqualification.

The race would be a cinch for Patsy to complete. She skated that far whenever she followed Prince and his friends on their bikes. And anyone silly enough to skate with her would always be left in the dust.

Patsy adjusted her helmet and pads.

"Hey Patsy, good luck," Imani shouted from her place on the starting line. She was about four children down from Patsy.

"Congratulations on your trophy," Patsy muttered before noticing the words that fell from her lips. *Nooooo*! Patsy screamed in her head. She could not believe she had just congratulated her archenemy. No matter how hard she tried to dodge *Little Miss Poofawney*, it never worked. *Rats*, Patsy thought.

"Hey girls, I'll probably be home sleeping by the time you get to the finish line. So I guess I'll see you tomorrow," Kamal hollered.

Patsy panicked. Kamal wasn't the problem though. Imani was. Imani had already showed her up in dancing. Patsy didn't want all of Springdale to find out Imani was better than her in everything! She had to get out of the derby.

"On your mark...Get set..."

It was too late. There was no way out of it.

"Go!"

The whistle went off and Patsy took off racing. She crouched down low, swiftly moving her arms back and forth. She clutched her hands into tight fists as she caught up to the boys and girls who got off to a quicker start. *"One down, two down,"* Patsy said as she passed them one by one. Patsy could hear the crowd cheering, but their applause began to fade as she reached the red house. Patsy noticed the crowd had not walked down that far and figured everyone would meet the skaters at the finish line.

Patamela didn't look to either side as she turned the corner at the red house. She carefully placed her right foot over her left to balance her sharp turn. She came out of the turn and just kept flying. *Kablam, Oooh, Ehh, Smack*! Patsy heard a huge thump and then a scream. Patsy looked around, yet no one was beside her. She gently glided into a T-stop and turned around completely. Patsy hadn't realized how far ahead she was of the other racers, although the pack of boys and girls were catching up to her.

Patamela skated toward them.

"Hey, you're going the wrong way!" shouted one of the skaters.

"Turn around shrimp!" shouted another.

Patsy would have thought about revenge, but she decided to keep going. She could hear someone crying near the red house.

Patamela turned the corner by the red house and saw Imani against the side of the house. Before a *"well, well, well, what do we have here, Poofawney?"* could fall from her lips, Patsy found herself racing toward her sworn enemy!

"See you at the finish line, losers!" yelled Kamal as he whizzed by. Some of the other kids were even laughing and pointing at Imani as they passed.

Patsy bent over to look at Imani's knee. It was oozing blood. "It hurts, Patsy," she said, crying. Patsy extended her hand to help Imani up. As soon as Imani was on her feet, she lunged toward the wall to steady herself. "I'm not very good at rollerblading, but you're great, Patsy," said Imani. "Thanks for helping me up."

"Aww, it's nothing," Patsy replied. "Maybe you should take your skates off."

"And walk in my socks? No way. I just needed help getting up. You should go ahead Patsy. You looked like you were going to win."

"Are you sure you're okay?" Patsy asked.

"I'm sure. Hurry Patsy!"

Patsy turned around hesitantly. She wasn't sure she should leave Imani behind. "I'll come back for you!" Patsy shouted as she sped off.

Patamela flew around the corner of the red house. She allowed each leg to stretch as far as it could with each lunge forward. She knew she would really have to work her arm and leg muscles to catch up to the others, but she was certain she could catch them at the hill. Patsy's arms and thighs began to burn. She could not remember ever skating faster than she was at that moment. She pressed forward. She could see that no one had made it up the hill yet. Patsy zeroed in on the top of the hill. "*One-my-baby, Two-my-baby, Three...*," she grunted. She drove her legs to mount the hill's incline, using her chant to encourage her legs to move.

Patsy began passing the kids stalled on the middle of the hill. Some of them looked like they wanted to cry. Others had stopped completely and were bent over panting. When they saw Patsy advancing, they tried to start skating again, but found it impossible to keep up with her. She could even tell the skaters in front of her were running out of steam. Patsy moved her arms faster and faster. By the time she reached the top of the hill, she had passed Kamal and was approaching the three skaters leading the pack.

Patsy tore past one boy, then the girl, until she was neck and neck with the last boy. Patsy squatted down as far as she could, hoping that would be enough to propel her down the bike trail. The red finish line ribbon was less than fifteen feet away.

"*Go Little Bit!*" Prince and Patience screamed from the finish line as Patsy passed the chess tables.

Patsy mustered the last bit of energy she had and broke through the ribbon with the boy on her heels.

Patamela spotted her father and sprung into his arms. "*You got the glow kid, you got the glow,*" he said as he pecked

Patsy's cheeks and forehead. Prince, Patience, and Mrs. James broke through the crowd to shower Patsy with hugs and kisses. Miles, Destiny, and Faye flew from the sidelines to congratulate Patsy's victory too.

When Kamal passed the finish line, Miles ran up to him and patted him on the back. "Don't worry, you'll get used to it. She beats me in stuff all the time."

Kamal, barely catching his breath, skated over to Patsy. "Con-grat-u..."

"Spit it out already! Congratulations Patamela! Is that enough action for you monkey boy?" Faye shouted.

Eventually, Imani managed to make it through the commotion as well. She limped forward, using Ms. Daye as a crutch. "I told you you'd do it, Patsy! Congratulations! You think you could teach me how to rollerblade like that one day?"

Patsy looked at her mom and then turned to Imani. "Only if you promise to teach me how to tap like you."

"Everybody told me you quit Legends and weren't coming back," said Imani.

"Ah, I'm coming back—well, that's if they'll have me back," Patsy said bashfully and the two began to chuckle.

"I'm sure there is a place for you, Patsy," Ms. Daye added.

Everyone applauded and cheered when Mr. Barclay called Patsy on stage to present the huge trophy. Her prize stood more than three feet tall and it was so shiny that Patsy believed it was made of real gold. There were two golden skates on top and it read, *"First Place, Springdale's First Annual Rollerblade Derby."* It was too heavy for Patsy to carry, but she watched it bounce up and down in her father's arms the entire walk home.

CHAPTER 43

The Biggest Big Shot of All

Patsy asked her mom if she could keep her trophy beside her chair during dinner. She did not want to take her eyes off of it for one minute. She could not believe she'd won something so huge all by herself. As Prince and Patience joked about the day's highlights, Patsy's mind began to drift. She wondered if winning the trophy finally made her a big kid, big shot. She didn't feel different, but a trophy that big had to mean something.

"Mommy, would you say I am a big kid? Right now—with this trophy and all? I mean before I even get to Melbourne's other building?"

"Well, Patsy, let me see." She wanted to come up with the perfect answer. "Actually, I would say you have taken up a lot of *responsibility* this summer. You didn't know I knew, but Mr. Jackson stopped me in the supermarket and raved about the black entertainers presentation you gave in front of your third grade class. I thought that was absolutely marvelous and very mature of you. Not to mention you taught Ella Jo how to stop sucking her sleeve…"

"You chose your own summer activity," Prince added.

"And you volunteered to be an outfit model for the Legends costume committee. You had an excellent performance in jazz, modern, and ballet," her mom continued.

"You forgot about winning the race to help Imani when she fell," her father interjected.

"And you made her a friend by agreeing to teach her how to skate," said her mom. "You even made peace with your *incorrigi*...ah, I mean your *free* spirit," said Mrs. James. Turning to Patsy's dad, she said, "Patrick, how proud are we about Patsy's decision to return to Legends and take tap lessons from Imani? We were just talking about that in the kitchen. We think that shows big kid initiative."

Mrs. James walked over to Patsy and gently lifted her chin, "Pattie Cakes, the key to being a big kid is not winning a race or participating in a million activities to prove you're as big as the rest of them. It's not even about trying to act like a big kid every second..."

"Because sometimes you won't," Mr. James interrupted.

"The key to being a big kid is learning to act like one when it really counts. I think you've done that. You made some really *huge* changes this summer," she said as she kissed Patsy's forehead.

"And don't forget, Patsy. You were inducted into the *Cecret Circle* too," said Patience.

"Now Patience, does that really matter after everything I just said?" asked their mom.

"*Inducted*, what does that mean? Wait, I'm in the *Cecret Circle*? When did you let me into the Cecret Circle?"

"You know, Johawn...Timmy's car," Patience said in a voice meant to jog Patsy's memory, before winking her eye. "You've kept it a secret, so we decided you should be in!"

"Johawn's car? Timmy? Secret? What?" asked Mr. James.

"Not Johawn's car, Timmy's car, and anyway it's a secret Dad. *Shhh*," Patsy said as she put her finger over her lips and winked her eye at Patience.

Patsy found comfort in her mom and dad's words, but they did not come close to what she felt about her trophy and her *Cecret Circle* membership. It all happened because she was big enough to choose her own summer activity. Although her summer activity experience had not turned out quite as she expected, Patsy believed this summer was the best by far.

Patamela could not wait to call her Aunt Deidre in the morning and share the good news. She was finally a big kid, big shot! She would even call her old third grade classmates. She would share how she became a big kid way before entering the other Melbourne building and definitely before turning nine. "Told you I'd make huge changes this summer," she said, winking at her reflection in the glass door of her mom's china cabinet. "Told ya!"